MURDER BY THE SEASIDE

JULIE ANNE LINDSEY

WORLDWIDE®

TORONTO • NEW YORK • LONDON
AMSTERDAM • PARIS • SYDNEY • HAMBURG
STOCKHOLM • ATHENS • TOKYO • MILAN
MADRID • WARSAW • BUDAPEST • AUCKLAND

Recycling programs
for this product may
not exist in your area.

Murder by the Seaside

A Worldwide Mystery/November 2014

First published by Carina Press

ISBN-13: 978-0-373-26920-4

Printed in U.S.A.

To Kimberly, my inspiration,
and Janie, my guide.

ONE

"TELL ME THERE weren't any first-floor apartments available on this island." Claire leaned against the gray siding of my new home, her cheeks pink from exertion and the hot summer sun. She reached out to test the weathered wooden stair railing leading to my door. It wiggled, and she inhaled deeply.

"None I could afford." I squinted up the steps to the landing. A stray lock of hair teased my cheek, and I jumped. Islands and bugs went hand in hand. I giggled at the mistake and shrugged. Time to get serious. There was plenty left to do.

"Besides, upstairs apartments are safer," I reminded Claire. "Didn't you pay attention to anything the FBI taught you?"

"Not really. I still can't believe they let you go."

"Hey, I was downsized, not let go."

Claire shifted a box marked Kitchen against her hip, trying to see the steps. Her petite five-foot-two frame was deceptive. She easily maneuvered boxes I struggled with. The fact she did it in four-inch heels said it all. She was small and mighty despite the Southern belle upbringing, of which her smooth Southern drawl served as a reminder. While Virginia was considered a Southern state, Claire was a few borders north of her home state of Georgia. She called it Jawja. I called her cute.

"How will I get through those horrendous meetings without you?" she asked.

"Chincoteague is only a couple hours from you. We can meet on the mainland for lunch." My first trip up the steps and I already wished it was my last. "Or shopping," I huffed. I'd gained a pound a year since I left the island ten years ago. Three of those I didn't mind keeping, if they stayed in the right places. The other seven should be gone by the time I finished carrying everything up these steps.

See? Moving home had bonuses. Never underestimate the power of positive thinking.

Claire puffed air into long, sideswept bangs and waited while I opened the door. She gazed admiringly at the historic two-story next door. Pale blue with cream trim and plenty of detail, it reminded me of a gingerbread house. My new place reminded me of the dough, the kind that had been kneaded thoroughly and hit with a roller. Victorian was a local theme, especially among the homes in the center of the island, away from the pounding waves during storm season. On Main Street, the shops blended easily with the houses. Chincoteague was the picture of peaceful living.

Homes were in demand this time of year. Tourists rented every available space between June and August. I thanked my lucky stars to have been able to get this place—the one house I knew would be available on zero notice. A decade-old rumor labeled the house haunted. On an island rooted in superstition and watered with ghost stories, my new place was the equivalent of swearing in church—i.e., to be avoided. Luckily, I didn't believe in ghosts. I did, however, believe in low-cost rent and proving a point. Moving home was a real kick in the teeth after the big show I made of landing an FBI job on the mainland. Sure, I was working in human resources, but still…making a life for myself on the mainland had been a big deal. While it lasted.

"Wow. This place better come at a discount." Claire's nose scrunched up as she turned in a small circle.

The interior was layered in dust and dead bugs. I sighed in defeat. This was what came with the too-good-to-be-true price they charged me. Linoleum, paneling and shag. But it was nothing some Comet, a few throw rugs and framed pictures couldn't help. I could afford those things, although not much more. My dwindling savings had bigger purposes. Where I slept had to be secondary for a while. Besides, any place could be homey with enough TLC. I hoped.

Wiping a circle onto the window with my fist, I remembered why I loved the island. Water everywhere. I smiled at Claire. "Can you see the ocean from *your* apartment?"

She joined me at the window. Her latte-colored skin lit up with the twinkling of sunlight through very dirty glass. My new porthole-style window boasted a tiny stained-glass schooner in shades of green and blue. Stained glass was a staple on the island, right beside clapboard, shutters and anything in keeping with a marina theme.

"All right. I'll give you that." She blew against the window and a storm of dust kicked up.

I coughed against my forearm and ran for the door. "Lunch."

Claire sneezed her way through the dust cloud behind me.

"Gah!" Sunlight blinded me the moment my eyes were free of the dark wood-paneled walls. I shaded my eyes with one hand and stumbled down the steps toward my car. "Let me grab my purse."

"I think I had lunch upstairs. I ate a pound of dirt getting out of there."

"I'll borrow a hand vac from my mom."

"What about the rest of these?"

I looked at the pile of boxes sitting near the stairs. Carrying them up the steps one by one in the afternoon heat was like asking for a stroke.

A whistle slipped through Claire's glossy red lips, and I followed her gaze. A man made of abs and handsomeness jogged across the street. Hoodie up, he looked our way. I smiled. He didn't. Despite the short distance and a decade between us, I knew him. There would never be another set of eyes that shade of gray. None that made me drop my keys at the sight of them.

"Oops." I dipped down to scoop the keys into my palm. When I stood, he was gone, but the strange look he'd given me seared into my brain. Not how I'd imagined our reunion. In my version, the ten years since high school would melt away and he'd be mine.

If I wasn't still mad. Which I was.

"I'd move here just for that," Claire said. "Do you think he jogs by at this time every day?"

"I hope not. That was Adrian."

Eyes wide, Claire turned her head in the direction where Adrian had jogged away. "Well, he can't go far around here. According to the brochure, this island is smaller than my closet."

"Your closet is ridiculous. It's the second bedroom at your apartment. For your information, Chincoteague is a full seven miles long and three miles wide."

"Excellent."

Across the street, laughter bubbled out of the Tasty Cream. A group of teens stumbled from the crowded ice cream parlor. Smiles on lips. Not a care in the world. Couples moving hand in hand. Nostalgia hit me like a sack of bricks. The giant neon twisty-cone sign transported me back to track meets and prom scandals.

"No one will bother the boxes," I told Claire. "How about I buy you some ice cream for being wonderful?"

"Honey, if that was Adrian, I'm thinking you could use the ice cream more than me." Claire raised an eyebrow. "Show me the way."

Wide brown eyes followed my finger toward the Tasty Cream, their curved lashes nearly brushing her brows. Before we met, Claire had a stint playing a princess at Disneyland. She didn't like to talk about it, but I bet she fooled her share of kids. I enjoyed reminding her she was immortalized in ten thousand family scrapbooks around the world.

"Adrian didn't look happy to see me," I said as we walked. Of course he wouldn't be. "The last time we talked, I smashed a giant twist cone into his face. And shirt. And car." I used to have a temper. Plus Adrian made me crazy.

The fact that he didn't seem glad to see me bothered me and it shouldn't have. My jaw tightened. He shouldn't get under my skin anymore—I'd had a decade to detox.

Claire pushed huge, white sunglasses over her eyes and stepped off the curb. "He deserved—"

The bark of a siren cut her off. She jumped back into me and we toppled, knocking heads and dropping purses. *What on earth?* The sheriff's cruiser tore past, lights blazing, siren screaming. Two dozen locals appeared from thin air before the car was out of sight.

"What the hell?" Claire hoisted herself up, dusting her backside and gawking at the flash mob gathered on the corner. "I thought you said nothing ever happens around here." She collected her shiny yellow clutch and offered me a hand.

"Nothing does. Why do you think everyone's outside staring?" I picked stray hairs out of my lip gloss. The wind blew dust over the pavement. A storm was coming. On an island the size of Chincoteague, even the small storms could be dangerous. I blinked into the sky. Still blue. A few lazy white puffballs lingered overhead, refusing to leave their post.

"I almost got mowed down by a sheriff." Claire examined her manicure. "There's grass under my nails. I'm going to need some fries to go with that ice cream."

"Deal."

We hobbled across the street and pressed our bodies through the crowd on the sidewalk.

The Tasty Cream was empty, but familiar red-and-white checkers smiled back at me from curtains and tablecloths. Black-and-white-speckled flooring led me to the counter, past white iron chairs, their backs twisted into hearts, their tiny red cushions empty. The old soda fountain sparkled behind the glass counter, edged in shiny metal. Abandoned tables carried half-eaten burgers and melting ice cream. Purses lay on the floor under chairs. Everyone had relocated, pacing out front on cell phones, no doubt hoping they'd be first to score the daily scoop. For Claire and me, it was a winning situation.

"Patience Price!" Mrs. Tucker rolled around the glass showcase and caught me in a hug. "Your mother said you were coming home. If she wasn't psychic, I never would've believed it." She stretched my arms out at my sides like an airplane and looked me over. "You're too thin. Let me get you something." Mrs. Tucker had run the Tasty Cream for as long as I could remember, and witnessed things I wish she hadn't—dates, soda sharing, teenage flirting, cone smashing…to name a few.

Claire's brows arched, crowding into her hairline. I ignored them. This was the first she'd heard of my mom's amazing psychic abilities. My parents were a package one had to experience for oneself.

"I'm renting the apartment across the street," I told Mrs. Tucker. "Above the old art studio. You'll be seeing plenty of me."

"Oh, sweetie. You've got your work cut out for you. They haven't rented that place in years."

Claire snorted. "When was the last time anyone lived there?"

"Decades." Mrs. Tucker shook her head. "This is on the house." She pushed a paper basket of fries and two milk shakes our way. "Come by for breakfast. I make a mean cappuccino now." Her round cheeks kicked up in a smile. Sweet as ever, she wiped her hands onto her apron and gave me an approving nod. "Welcome home."

"It's good to be here." Clouds of fresh-baked waffle cones rimmed in chocolate and the scent of greasy burgers loomed over me. The perfect mixture of sweet and salty. A taffy machine twisted and pulled pink strips of heaven nearby. I was ten years younger standing there. All good things came from the Tasty Cream. I took a long pull on the best milk shake ever made. It took effort to get Tasty Cream shakes up the straw, but they never disappointed. "What was Sheriff Murray in such a hurry for?"

"Hard to say. He's been something lately." She leaned across the counter conspiratorially. "Being sheriff isn't easy when your deputy's a doofus."

I snickered. Deputy Doofus. Not long ago, Sheriff Murray owned that title.

Mrs. Tucker lifted a rag onto the countertop and made large wet circles over the glass countertop. Her heavily freckled skin reflected in the glass. The freckles almost made her seem tan, though the woman never made it outside before sunset. She always said she preferred people to nature anyway. "I imagine we'll all know as soon as someone figures it out." She tilted her head toward the knots of patrons outside.

Claire anchored her clutch under one folded arm and hefted the fries into her hand. She never let go of her shake.

I snagged a fry from Claire's basket and groaned. Mrs. Tucker's fries were delicious. The seasoning made my mouth water. I thanked Mrs. Tucker, and then Claire and I moved through the door onto the sidewalk as the crowd shoved its way back inside. From the looks on their faces, no one knew anything. Yet.

"I can't believe I'm home again. Trapped on an island with my parents." I started down Main Street on autopilot. "We should say hi."

"Listen, you got your master's degree for a reason. You've got a plan. Put that plan to work for you. *Patience Price, Family Counselor.* The only counselor on this little piece of heaven. You can't beat that for cornering a market." She shoved a fry into her mouth and moaned. Mrs. Tucker could season a fry with the best of them.

"I made flyers."

"I know. What I don't know is how you're going to make up with that hunky ex of yours. Excuse me, but you never mentioned that Adrian was smoking hot. My high school heartbreak was lanky with braces, some serious acne issues and Bobby Brown hair."

"I have no intention of making up with Adrian. Besides, this island is big enough for the both of us. No need to complicate things. I told you he abandoned me to play football, right? He can't be trusted. Adrian Davis has always looked like that, and he knows it."

By the harbor, we passed the bronze pony statue. A tiny picket fence kept tourists at bay these days. Island kids had hundreds of pictures of the pony, near the pony, on the pony, under the pony. My friends and I spent senior year coming up with the most ridiculous pony possibilities. The varsity volleyball team got a hundred thousand hits on YouTube after an interview with the pony. They dressed it in a digitally added gown and a few of the dimmer lightbulbs performed some raunchy dance moves in the background.

Claire looked at the statue without comment. She was too focused on Adrian. "Mmm-mmm-mmm." She sucked on her milk shake. "At least tell me you left an opening to slide back in with him."

Let's see…what did I remember from the incident? Vanilla ice cream melting against his face and slipping across his lips as a crowd of catty high schoolers laughed and pointed. A combination of humiliation and fire had prompted me to jam the cone into his chest after I pried it from his face. After that, my broken heart caused me to crush it against the new leather seats of his convertible. Not my proudest memory.

"No. No room for sliding."

We continued walking. Tugboats bleated on the shimmery blue water that reflected a perfect sky. Seagulls squawked at fisherman, demanding their share of the day's haul, and a comforting layer of brine tinged the otherwise clean and flower-scented air. All these things spelled h-o-m-e. Houses on the harbor and along the causeway were newer than the rest. The few original homes were weathered to almost black. Along the inner roads, most homes dated back to the eighteen hundreds. Bed-and-breakfasts spilled purple flowers from barrels onto sidewalks. Signs on every corner boasted the home's age and owner's surname. History mattered on Chincoteague.

The town slogan was Relax, You're on Island Time

Now. Growing up we joked the island *was* its own time, stuck somewhere that other places never were. Kids dreamed of leaving home to see the big world. I made it as far as Norfolk. Frankly, Chincoteague was better.

"I can't believe you kept this place from me until now. This island has everything. Hot guys. Good food. What's not to like?" Claire slowed her pace. "Except your apartment. Did the ice cream lady say your apartment hasn't been rented in decades? Ever ask yourself why that is?"

"Islanders think it's haunted." I shook my shake cup, shifting the ultra-thick ice cream inside.

"Haunted." Claire stopped short, looking as if she might not accept any future invitations from me.

"Island stories."

"I'd like to hear that one."

"We have lots of stories here. Small town, long histories, creative minds." I nudged her forward.

"All right then, Miss Secret Pants. Tell me about how your mom's a psychic."

I stopped to wave my arms overhead. "Ta-da." The silhouette of a hand-painted pony stared back from the plate-glass window before us. Wind whipped off the water, swinging the store sign on its hinges above me as I struck my best here-we-are pose.

"The Purple Pony." She pulled her glasses to the tip of her nose, read the sign and looked me over. "What on earth is a purple pony?"

"My parents' shop, of course."

"It sounds a little like a strip club."

"If only." I wrenched the door open and waved Claire inside.

"Holy sh—"

"—ut up." I bumped her with a hip and smiled. A million candles and patchouli scented the air. Flower garlands roped through the wooden rafters. Twinkle lights stretched down to greet us. The little bell over the door brought my mom floating to the counter.

"Patience Peace Price. I thought you'd never arrive."

Claire coughed and choked. I made a point of never mentioning my middle name. This was why.

I gave my mom the stink eye and moved to the counter. "We got a late start. This is my friend Claire." I pulled in a lungful of air. The counter smelled of herbs and incense. The calming twang of Indian sitar music drifted from hidden speakers. Home sweet home.

"Nice to meet you, Claire." Mom bowed in Claire's direction. "We're so proud of our Patience. Embracing a new beginning. Forging her own path." She folded her hands in prayer at her chest and closed her eyes. We looked alike. Sort of. I'd never stand in prayer for no reason, but we shared the same round face, sandy hair and giant brown eyes. The similarities ended there.

"Peepee!" Dad's deep voice sounded nearby.

Claire jumped.

I cringed. As if a name like Patience Peace Price wasn't enough to saddle a girl with. The nickname killed me. Why not Pat?

Dad sat up from a bench not six feet away.

"Daddy." My heart leapt at the sight of him.

"Is that a candle in your ear?" Claire pointed her cup in his direction.

"I'm candling." Dad popped the candle out and dug in his ear with a white cloth. "It removes toxins."

"The Hopi Indians did it," Mom offered.

"Uh-huh." Claire looked at me for help.

I shook my head. They had their own drummer. I'd never heard the tune.

This was why I didn't go into detail about my family. I

might've been born with the only sane genes in the pool. My folks were sweet and harmless but a lot to take in all at once. Mom wore her sun-streaked hair in a long, loose braid. It reached past her waist. Sometimes she put flowers in it, sometimes a pencil. Her long, flowing skirts were handmade. By her. Her peasant tops were older than me.

"We missed you." Mom ran a soft palm over my cheek.

"I missed you too." I dug in my oversized hobo for the envelope I'd stashed there. Thanks to an efficient last day of work, I managed to print a couple dozen flyers for my new counseling business. "Care if I leave these here?" I stacked them on the counter next to Dad's handmade soaps and a henna bracelet display.

"What's this?" She examined the flyer. A small, sympathetic smile appeared on her lips. "Honey, you're never going to get islanders to go to a counseling practice. Everyone would know, and no one wants to be known as the one who needs therapy. Maybe you could work here. You can read cards for us."

"Tourists love that." Dad looped an arm around my waist. "Did you lose weight?"

"No, thank you. I have a master's degree. In counseling. It's my dream job. I refuse to believe no one will come. There aren't any other counselors on the island." I reached up to knock a bead of wax from my dad's jawbone.

"Why do you think that is?" Mom tilted her head.

"I can't read cards for a living. I'd have to sell my organs to pay off my student loans." Images of me in Birkenstocks and handmade dresses flashed through my mind. A line of tourists waiting to know their futures as told by me, a self-proclaimed, type-A personality who didn't believe in Tarot any more than she believed in Santa Claus.

"People do that," Dad confirmed. "On eBay."

"What? Sell their organs?" The possibility he could be right sent a shiver down my spine. "Ew."

"You can leave anything you like on our counter," he said. "Chase your dream, Peepee."

"Thank you." I turned.

Claire seemed to be enjoying the show. Like a spectator at a live performance of an insanity circus. She fingered through a display of Purple Pony T-shirts, but her eyes focused on us.

"All right, guys, I'm going to finish moving in. Then I'll take a walk and look for some office space after dinner."

Claire turned in a slow circle. Crystals reflected rainbows over the shiny hardwood floors. A waterfall of beads separated the retail area of the store from the back room and more private reading rooms. The look on her face was priceless. Her lips parted. Her neatly arched brows pinched. Probably meeting my parents raised as many new questions about my personality as it provided answers.

"Be careful," Dad warned.

Muffled sirens complained in the distance. "There's something going on around here." Mom moved her eyes around the store ceiling slowly.

"Like what?" I looked back and forth between my parents. The sheriff had been in quite a hurry to get somewhere.

"We're not sure. The Pony's been dead today."

Sure enough, the store was empty for the first time that I could recall. People loved The Pony. My parents' shop was a hot spot. Locals came for advice on chakras and star alignment, love and gambling. My desire to help people started at The Pony—I just hoped to help in a different way. No patchouli required.

The front door swung open. We all jumped.

"What are you all doing standing around in here?" Maple Shuster, the local scuttlebutt personified, blocked the doorway, holding the door wide with one hip. "Brady McGee is dead. Someone bashed him on the head and left him at the marina."

"Oh, dear. That's awful." My mother shuffled around the counter. She eased Maple onto a bench where people normally tried on moccasins or shoes made from cork and bamboo. "Can I get you something?"

My father appeared with a glass of water before Maple could answer.

She sipped and came around to a more coherent, less frenzied state. "That's delicious. It's helping already. Thank you."

It was sugar in tap water. Something my dad passed off as mystical and medicinal. I couldn't fault him. I'd seen sugar water cure everything from nerves to nightmares. People were strange.

"What else did you hear?" The words tumbled out of me. I couldn't believe someone had been murdered. Jay-walking was the worst thing I'd ever heard of happening on the island. Once in a while a couple of tourists got into a fight, but nothing like murder. I knew Brady McGee—not well, but well enough. He had a reputation for being hard, sharp-tongued and crude. His family moved to the island my sophomore year of high school. He was a senior and usually in trouble for fighting. Adrian had warned me to steer clear of him, saying Brady wanted to make a place for himself in our little town by showing people he was tough. I'd felt sorry for him after that. Worst logic ever. People crossed the street to avoid him. If he hadn't changed his attitude in the past ten years, the list of locals with an ax to grind was probably lengthy.

Maple's eyes widened with dramatic flair. She leaned

forward on the bench and lowered her voice, as if she was about to tell the best campfire story of her life.

I held my breath in anticipation.

"I heard Adrian Davis killed him. The sheriff questioned him this morning. When he went back to bring him in on charges, Adrian ran."

"Ran?" My folks and I spoke in unison.

"Ran. Adrian is on the lam."

The words twisted and whirled in my mind.

He hadn't been out jogging. He was *on the lam*.

For murder.

TWO

AFTER ANOTHER THIRTY trips up the stairs, my legs gave out and so did Claire. She promised to come back and see me on the weekend. We'd text all week as usual. That wouldn't change, even if the rest of my life was in upheaval.

After she slid out of my new world in her shiny blue Volvo, I puttered around my new place, unable to decide what to do. The sun settled into the harbor beyond my windows, casting lavender and rose shadows over the world. A mountain of boxes rested beneath the window frame. I had no desire to open another box. My fingers were pruny and red from cleaning. I'd set up what mattered hours before. My laptop and printer stood on the kitchen counter, and the bed was made. Tomorrow I'd start again, but right now the rumble in my tummy said it was time to pay another visit to Mrs. Tucker or my parents. Funds were limited. As much as I didn't want to hear about my promising future reading Tarot cards or tea leaves, I equally hated spending six of my fast fading dollars on a burger.

Decisions.

When I shut my eyes, Adrian's face appeared for the ten millionth time. What did that strange look he gave me mean? I flopped into a folding chair at the kitchen counter and tried to label the expression. Not fear. He didn't fear anything that I could recall. Adrian was brave. Overly confident. Obnoxious. And while I, on occasion, itched to shove anther ice cream up his nose, I also knew he wasn't a killer.

I pulled a half-eaten bag of chips off the counter and into my lap. Thinking went easier with something to crunch. In high school, Adrian and I had pledged to see the world together. I'd opened a savings account on the mainland for my eighteenth birthday, into which he and I deposited money every payday senior year. I shoved a fistful of chips between my lips. After we graduated, he left me with no warning. To play football. I ground my teeth together and flung the bag onto the counter. Crumbs dusted out the open end.

My fingernails tapped an aimless rhythm on the Formica. Adrian had trapped spiders in the shower for me and deposited them outside. He carried me two miles on his back when I twisted my ankle on the steps at the lighthouse. He cried during the memorial service on 9/11. I saw him. Those soulful gray eyes melted my heart even in memory.

I grabbed my phone to check my voice mail. Three from work. Any chance they'd changed their minds and needed me back? No. All three were from my co-workers. No one knew where we kept anything in the office. What did they do while I was working? For that matter, if I was the only one working before, how had I ended up as the one downsized?

It was late. They'd clocked out and gone home by now. I tapped a quick set of texts onto the cell screen.

Mr. Fergusen comes for lie detector tests on Thursdays. Remind him on Wednesday how many to expect.
The coffee lady comes first thing Monday morning. She'll need a receipt for the delivery.

IT has a list of all my passwords. You'll need to change them.

I tossed my phone on the counter beside the chips. The apartment smelled dank and unlived in. I'd already pried open all the windows and emptied a bottle of Febreeze. Time was my only hope at remedying the stink. Until then, I'd suffer dirty air coated in a synthetic April Fresh cover-up.

With Claire gone, my mind wandered to the one other person I'd miss on the mainland: Sebastian Clark. Sebastian was a special agent I'd had a crush on since the day he rolled into my office, but guys like him didn't date. They were too busy saving the world, unlike my ex, who was on the lam for murder.

My mind kicked back to Adrian. Could he have gone away to play football and come home a killer? What all had I missed these last ten years? What was he doing back in Chincoteague? So much for seeing the world. Not that I could talk.

I pulled my laptop onto my legs and brought up my new flyers. I had a goal to achieve. Every town needed a counselor. Who better to fill that need in Chincoteague than me? The residents knew me. I understood the island. We were a perfect match. *Counseling with Patience*. Finally my crazy name came in handy for something. Now I needed a few patients. I smiled. Then I thumbed the Print button. My tummy rumbled in warning. The chips didn't cut it. A burger sounded amazing. While I was at the Tasty Cream, I'd ask Mrs. Tucker if I could leave a few flyers on the counter.

Squawking seagulls and bleating tugboats faded into the background, swallowed whole by the enormous rattle and whoosh of my ancient printer. A moment later, instinct tickled my muscles. My ears perked to attention, straining to hear a sound I knew wasn't coming from my printer. I tiptoed across the room and pressed my back to the wall. There was a murderer on the loose. I held my breath. The stairs outside my window creaked again. My purse sat on the coffee table, out of reach. Pepper spray couldn't help me from way over there.

"Patience?" A voice from long ago croaked outside my door.

I righted myself. I needed to get a grip.

"Mrs. Davis?" I shoved the screen door open and motioned Adrian's mother inside.

She made the sign of the cross on her chest and moved to the dusty tweed couch. "Thank God you've come home—and on the day my baby is charged with murder." She whispered the final word and rolled her eyes to my ceiling. "I always knew you'd save him."

Lies. She hated me. I knew it at eighteen as much as I knew it at twenty-nine. She thought my parents were fruit loops and I would lead her baby to a nudist commune out West if she didn't intervene. She'd intervened to the tune of a 2001 Mustang convertible.

"There's always a greater plan at work. You work for the FBI. You can clear his name. You still love him enough for that, don't you?" Her expression challenged me to deny it.

"Hi, Mrs. Davis. It's good to be home. Thank you for asking." I swept my hair into a ponytail to waste time while I cooled my jets. I'd regret using the rubber band on my wrist as soon as I tried to remove it. Adrian was magic. He caused me to pull my hair out without ever speaking to me.

"I *worked* for the FBI," I explained. "Past tense. I'm a

counselor now. Maybe I could offer to talk with you later about how you're handling all this?"

"There's nothing wrong with me. I need you to clear his name. My son is innocent. He needs you, Patience. If you ever loved him at all, how could you let him go to jail for something he didn't do? Adrian isn't a criminal." Tears coated her eyes and my blood pressure dropped a fraction.

"Look, Mrs. Davis. Even if I wanted to help, I can't. I'm not in law enforcement. I worked in human resources. I interviewed new hires and arranged fund-raisers. Sometimes they sent me to colleges to recruit people. I'm no investigator. I'm hardly the one you'd want responsible for Adrian's well-being."

Inch-long black roots sprouted into cherry-red tips on her head. Her hair never stayed the same long. She still stuffed a size fourteen body into size ten shorts though. Years of tanning showed in the wrinkles over her aging face. Owning a tanning salon on an island seemed like a bad idea to me, but Sunny Daze Salon was always busy.

She shifted under my gaze and cleared her throat. "You always did hold a grudge, Patience Price. I know you planned to run away together. You wanted to keep him from being all he could be. Selfish. You wanted a partner to run around with, ignoring civic responsibility, avoiding education, and destroying any hope of a decent future for the both of you. What if he had gone with you? Where would you be? Not working for the FBI. Not holding a master's degree. He wouldn't have played college ball for four years or graduated from a good school—with honors. You'd both be broke and probably divorced after a shotgun wedding somewhere. I'd be raising your kids and you'd be reading cards with your mom."

Blood boiled under my cheeks. "Adrian never talked to me about college. I didn't even know he applied." I kicked myself every day for years over that. Thanks to my parents' obsession with island life, the only thing I thought about back then was leaving town. College seemed like something I could do later when I settled on the West Coast or in Canada. How was I supposed to know Adrian went home at night to fill out applications so he could attend immediately? He deceived me, made me look stupid and feel worse. I should've been the one with college plans. I was the levelheaded one, darn it.

"I was never angry he went to college. I was mad he lied to me. One minute we had plans for a life together, the next minute he's playing ball in Florida. I never saw it coming. He duped me. It won't happen again."

Mrs. Davis jolted upright and snatched up her purse before I could toss her down my steps. *Shotgun wedding.* Jeez. Who said that to someone?

She knocked the screen door open with a loud bang and yelled at me on her way to the sidewalk. "Help my boy. You owe him that!"

If there was anything in my reach, I would have lobbed it at her. I slammed my door shut and locked it. No wonder Adrian was a creep. His mother was the devil. I dragged the folding chair around and grabbed my laptop again. *Raising my kids?* I'd never let her touch my kids. They'd be better off being raised by wolves.

I closed my eyes and took deep, calming breaths. Counting backward from ten, I opened my eyes and resolved to be thankful she didn't wind up as my mother-in-law. Eyes back on the search engine, I typed *Adrian Davis.* He appeared in old articles from his football days. Then in some technology magazine for building the winning fighter robot during grad school. I'd read all those years ago. I sorted the search results, starting with the most recent. His face appeared in various local papers, endorsing everything from the Humane Society to literacy. He donated to St. Jude and his alma mater. He even did a public speaking stint through state high schools about scholarships and dream chasing.

I knew there was a reason I had stopped checking up on him. Adrian Davis was a regular everyday hero.

Bleh.

His eyes pierced right through the screen to mine. Would I have ruined him? His easy smile still ended in one dimple. Heavy brows and lashes still made it seem as if he kept all his secrets in those gorgeous gray eyes. I'd definitely like to turn him in. He owed me an apology. Or at least an explanation. I went to the White Pages and jotted down his address. No harm in walking past his house. I wasn't sure how it would help, but I was curious. How had he ended up an advocate and benefactor while I was broke and living in an apartment haunted by dust bunnies and local legend?

I tapped the address into my phone and threw my purse over one shoulder. I needed to eat something. Keys in one hand and flyers in the other, I headed to the Tasty Cream. The island wasn't that big. If Adrian was here, I'd find him, and then I'd turn him over to Sheriff Murray. Any decent lawyer would get him off. He didn't need me.

I frowned.

Crossing the street to the Tasty Cream, I looked both ways. Music played on outdoor speakers. This time people sat at the booths and tables eating, instead of outside on their phones gossiping. I turned a head or two on my way in. Probably the whole town already knew I was home. I nodded and smiled on my way to the counter. The flyers fit nicely in the corner near the register. Mrs. Tucker winked.

"What can I get you?"

"More fries and a diet soda." I needed to drop off the flyers but I couldn't shell out six bucks for a burger.

"No shake? No burger? Are you sure?"

I hadn't buttoned my jeans since I finished the last shake. "Yeah. Just soda. Did you hear any more about what the sheriff was up to this afternoon?"

She stopped and looked at me. The restaurant seemed quieter behind me. "Surely you know." Mrs. Tucker rested her elbows on the counter between us and settled in for a story. I wished I'd ordered the shake.

"Adrian beat the snot out of Brady McGee in front of a hundred people last night. They had a huge fight over some gambling thing, and Adrian got him good. Then fishermen found Brady dead this morning as they came in from their shifts."

"Where did Adrian and Brady fight?"

"At the football field. One minute they were watching practice, the next thing they were rolling around on the ground."

"Why were so many people at the football field?"

"Scrimmaging. There were buses here from all over the state. Even a couple of vendors. He can't deny what he did to Brady. Too many witnesses." She shoved a fry basket across the space between us. A foam cup followed.

I pushed a fry into my mouth and mulled it over. "Does Adrian always watch football practice?"

"Yeah. Since he came home, he's never missed a practice. Coach Peters thinks he might be after his job. Looks like he won't have to worry about that anymore."

I made a mental note to stop at the school and visit Coach Peters. He'd have details. His keen eye never missed a thing. In the four years I swam for our high school swim team, he never let me get away with giving less than 100 percent. He saw when I cheated, replacing the infinitely easier flutter kick for the dolphin kick or when I stayed underwater an extra second to get away with doing only half the bobs he ordered as a warm-up.

So, Adrian came home to coach high school football? I shook my head. No. Everything I'd read online suggested he'd done well for himself. He was an activist, not a middle-aged overweight man-child who'd been holding on to the good old days for way too long.

"I saw them rolling on the ground." The mailman, Mr. Glazer, stood beside me with his bill in hand. Mrs. Tucker rang him up.

"Brady said Adrian cost him a thousand dollars when he missed a perfect pass his senior year at Miami," Mr. Glazer said. "Adrian told Brady to stow it. Then Brady said he wanted his money back."

This was getting good. "Brady wanted Adrian to give him a thousand dollars because he bet on a game Adrian played in and lost?" That sounded like the Brady I remembered—mean, irrational, ready to fight.

"Well, it wasn't because he played in the game. He missed the pass."

"Who cares?" My voice hitched.

"It was Adrian's fumble that cost Brady the grand."

I dug in my wallet and placed a five on the counter. "Thank you, Mrs. Tucker." I took the paper basket and foam cup and left. I needed to walk. Hopefully Adrian was enjoying his freedom while it lasted. Having a hundred people watch you beat the daylights out of the same guy found bonked on the head twelve hours later seemed pretty incriminating.

My trip down Main Street to the harbor served a dual purpose. I needed to think, and I also had to look for open office space. I plotted my trip in my head so as not to miss any prime real estate. On the way home, I planned to take a walk on Colt Court, Adrian's new street. All the little shops had closed up for the day. Sidewalk displays had been moved inside for the night, signs flipped, blinds pulled. Island Brew and the Wild Horses Saloon, neither of which served any alcohol, despite their names, had lines out their doors. The former kept coffee lovers sated and the latter served couples having a late dinner.

I crossed the street to get a good look at the harbor. A speckle of sailboats skated in the distance. The setting sun made silhouettes out of the farthest vessels. Large fishing boats chugged their way back to dock for the night. On land, four men dressed in waders and ribbed tank tops stood in a huddle under the marina sign. From my vantage on the sidewalk, there was no clue there'd been a murder there that morning. Even the crime-scene tape was gone, or out of sight. No chalk outline of a body anywhere, either. Who could tell? The foursome created a wall.

My soda disappeared long before the fries. I tossed them both into the trash on the closest corner. Decorative iron cases around the cans caused more than one tourist to do a double-take. They were, in fact, trash cans. Pretty ones. I dusted my palms together then anchored them over my expanding waist. Fries for two meals in one day. What would become of me in a year?

Every shop in sight had a window full of cutesy displays. No For Rent signs. My parents paid more per month for The Purple Pony than I dreamed of making. Main Street wasn't the best place for a counseling practice anyway. No parking or privacy.

On Poplar I noticed a space like the art studio downstairs from my apartment. It was a cute cream-colored house with blue shutters and a sign in the window. I dialed. The Realtor's recording advised me to keep walking.

Yeesh. Cute was costly. Message received.

Misty Park looked like it had when I left. Abandoned. The park was named after the famous *Misty of Chincoteague* book and movie. Misty put Chincoteague on the map, though most of the people I spoke with still hadn't heard of it. I walked through the untrimmed grass and slumped onto a squeaky swing.

This was not the plan I'd had for my life. The master's degree was supposed to open doors within the FBI. I wanted to counsel agents who were forced to discharge their firearms. Sometimes women agents had trouble readjusting to full-time careers after maternity leave. The government needed a counselor on staff, and contractors were expensive. I used to acquire them as needed and evaluate the quotes for the contract. Moving me into a counseling position would have saved the government megabucks over the course of my career. Had it been longer.

A black squirrel ran across the wire overhead, through the trees, around a telephone pole and straight to the greatest news I'd had all day. An old boathouse at the edge of the park had a For Rent sign in the window.

"Bingo."

I called the number immediately, listened to the recording and liked what I heard. The place was empty and in my price range, and the landlord meant to help with upkeep. I left a message. I'd take it. My fingers crossed in hopes that it hadn't already been rented. My savings were meager, but I'd put the money away exactly for this purpose. An office.

The smile fell from my lips before I had a chance to relish it. Someone ducked behind the trees in the park. As much as I wanted to run, curiosity took over. I had to know. Was it Adrian? If it was, he was busted. I gripped my phone, ready to call the sheriff.

"I see you. Behind the tree. I see you. You can come

out." When no one jumped out in a hockey mask, my confidence built. They were hiding from me. "Come on." I picked up my pace, heading straight for the tree.

Mrs. Davis stepped out, and I almost had a coronary.

"What are you doing there?" I pressed one palm to my chest. Jeez. Good thing it wasn't a lunatic killer.

"I'm keeping an eye on you." She managed to look angry. At me.

"I'm fine, Mrs. Davis. You don't need to look out for me."

"I'm not looking out for you. I'm making sure you're helping Adrian. From the looks of things, you're on vacation while my son is who knows where. I don't think you're really working this case."

What? My hands flew into the air. My mouth flopped open. "That's because I'm *not* working this case. I'm not an investigator. I'm a counselor. A counselor who needs an office and some clients." I looked back at the little boathouse.

"You're not going to find any patients on this island. Who'd want to be seen getting counseling? No one, that's who. You're from the FBI. You owe Adrian. Help him!" Now her hands were in the air. We stood twenty feet apart yelling and only the squirrels seemed to notice.

"I was in HR." I stamped my foot and turned on one heel. "Stop following me."

On the way home, I thought of the things I should've said to her. I veered past Adrian's giant house on the marsh. I checked the mailbox. Empty. I marched up a couple dozen steps to the front door and tried the knob. Locked. The wide wraparound porch encircled his entire house. As inviting as the rockers and swing looked, it was getting dark.

I bounded down the steps to the road, hoping to avoid any wild ponies. Chincoteague had its pitfalls. One was the island pride: wild ponies. I shivered. The ponies freaked me out. They wandered around loose with their giant teeth and crazy twitchy skin. All the way home I kept an eye out for ponies and stalking mothers of criminals.

Climbing the steps to my place, I sang a victory song. I made it. I'd steered clear of ponies, found some cheap office space, checked on Adrian's house and told his mom to leave me alone. It was a great feeling. A highly successful outing, to be sure.

I took a deep breath and leaned into the door. Safe and sound. I kicked my shoes off and pulled my sweaty T-shirt over my head. The shower called out to me. Humidity was the sworn enemy of unruly hair and out-of-shape human resource workers. I shimmied out of my jeans and checked my e-mail.

Claire would be back Friday night. Excellent.

A creak sounded, and I froze. The window rattled in its old wooden frame. The wind? I slid from the chair and plastered my body to the wall. Of course, my pepper spray was nowhere around. Again. I waited, barely breathing. Listening.

Another creak.

I shut my laptop and grabbed it in both hands. An expensive weapon, but my life was worth it. Moving to the window, I searched for shadows outside and saw nothing. The knob on the door didn't give when I turned it. Locked. I slid the dead bolt and backed away, eyes on the window.

Three Chicken Little steps backward, my life flashed before my eyes. A hand clamped over my mouth. One wide arm wound around my waist, pressing my techy weapon into my ribs. Damn it. I stomped my foot into his and hurt myself. My assailant wore boots. Double damn it. I blanked on everything I learned in the self-defense refresher courses at work. My feet slid against thirty-year-old linoleum as I was dragged into my dark hallway.

THREE

Instead of my pitch-black bedroom, the creep dragged me to the bathroom, where he flipped on the light and eased his grip by a fraction. I wiggled my arms, hoping to elbow him in the gut. No luck. His sweet breath blew over my cheek. He smelled like cherry ChapStick. The cylinders in my brain backfired. No.

"Don't be mad." The whisper heated my cheek.

Fire climbed from my toes to my hair. When his grip loosened further, I connected my bare foot with his shin. He let out a wail and I took full advantage.

He had the good sense to know I wasn't finished and lifted an arm to block my attack. The weight of my laptop knocked against his elbow. I hoped to knock his head off, but I had to settle for his funny bone.

"Yeow!" Adrian stepped back, into the side of my tub, and fell in. I cranked on the water.

My heart hammered, threatening to bust free. I raised the laptop over my head and backed through the bathroom door. Infuriatingly, his dimple caved in. Fully clothed and sitting under my shower, he had the audacity to smile at me.

"What is wrong with you?" The snarl hurt my throat.

His grin hitched further and my near nakedness registered for the first time. I turned tail, ran for the bedroom and yanked on the first thing I saw. Everything was packed and my closet was empty. I'd laid out the ratty cutoff shorts and worn-out T-shirt to clean in later.

Worse? Dad made the shirt with The Purple Pony shirt press during my freshman year in college. A stick figure in glasses declared Counselors Do It On The Couch. Not exactly how I'd hoped to look for my reunion with Adrian. Then again, I didn't expect him to break into my apartment and try to abduct me either. The shower shut off in the bathroom. I headed for my purse. I needed to call the sheriff and also pepper spray Adrian to be sure he got the point.

"Hey." His throaty voice arrived in my doorway before I did. I stopped short. Adrian leaned against the frame. "Don't be mad. I tried not to scare you."

"Oh! Oh, yes, certainly. I often break into people's apartments, slam a hand over their mouth and drag them away. That never frightens them." The heel of my hand bounced off my forehead. "Get out of my way. Why did you take me to the bathroom?"

He stepped aside. I blew past him, toward the living room. "No windows. I hated sneaking in here, but my mom is everywhere. I don't want her in trouble for knowing where I am and not turning me in. What are you doing?"

I pressed my cell to my ear. "I'm calling Sheriff Murray. You're a fugitive."

"I'm not a murderer."

"I didn't say you were. What's the number over there? I don't want to call nine-one-one and spend a bunch of tax dollars."

"You're kidding." He guffawed.

"I can look it up." I moseyed to my bedroom to retrieve the laptop. He followed.

"If you don't think I'm guilty, why would you turn me in?" He studied my face and barked a crazy laugh. "That's just great. Perfect, Patience. You're still mad I went to college. Do you know how ridiculous that is?"

"I am not mad you went to college. You're so self-absorbed." I walked back to the bathroom to grab a brush.

"Really? Because you seem a little irritable."

He squeezed into the tiny apartment bathroom behind me and stripped off his shirt. I gawked as he wrung it out over the sink and slipped the only hand towel I'd hung off its bar. He rubbed it over his wet hair. My body relaxed into the wall behind me. The sharp V of his torso disappeared into low-slung black warm-ups. The waistband showing beneath the warm-ups ruined my concentration. I swallowed.

"You broke into my apartment." I averted my eyes. Adrian could always see through me. "I was mad because you never bothered to mention you were going to college. That's an important nugget of information, don't you think? "'By the way, I changed my mind about seeing the world with you…'"

Breath caught in my throat. I did sound mad. Which I wasn't. "Anyway, I'm not mad anymore. You blindsided me, but that was ages ago."

He didn't look convinced.

"Now, I'm home for five seconds and you want me to help you beat a murder rap."

"I didn't kill Brady. I need you to believe me."

I deflated an inch. I'd squared my shoulders in preparation for his excuses for having left without clueing me in: I was a freak. I had bad breath. He deserved better than an uptight child of hippies. Anything. I'd racked my brain for years trying to make sense of why someone would do that to someone else. But even after I spilled my guts, his only comment was about Brady's murder.

Excellent explanation he had there. *It wasn't me.* Bet that would hold up in court.

"Who cares what I think? I just got here."

"I care." With that, he turned on me. The quarters were tight to begin with, but now we were inches apart and face-to-face. Adrian braced his palms against the wall over my head and leaned down toward me. "I care that someone killed Brady and I want to know who did it. It wasn't me. Help me find out who did this."

His pale gray eyes confused and excited me. His steady gaze skewered me to the wall. My mouth opened and closed without a sound. Heat radiated off him, hit me in the chest and ran south. My mind scrambled. What was I doing again?

"You. You're supposed to be in jail," I said. "You don't get to pick when you go. You just go. It's the law."

"There's something else going on here. Brady was always kind of a douche, but you should've heard him yesterday."

"Before or after you beat him up in front of half the town?" My fingers itched at my sides. I balled them into fists to keep from touching him. "Is it hot in here?"

He straightened and walked into the next room. I followed.

"That's exactly what I'm talking about. Brady and I bantered a lot—we weren't friends, but we weren't enemies. Then yesterday he went berserk, yelling at me about a pass I missed eight years ago. I don't even remember what he was talking about."

"Uh-huh." My fingers waded through the giant purse I brought to haul flyers around the island.

"Now what are you doing?"

"Looking for my pepper spray."

"What? You got tired of hitting me with your computer already?"

"I can't afford a new one. I'm unemployed."

"The way I hear it, you work for the FBI. That's amazing. I'm really proud of you."

I stamped my foot. "First, I was in HR. They downsized me. Second, you don't get to be proud of me. You don't have any claim to me." Ticking off my fingers, I stopped on the second one and waved the finger between us. "Don't you forget it."

He raised his palms in defense. "You're right. I'm sorry, but I'm not turning myself in. So, what do you say? Will you help me find Brady's killer? Clear my name? Think about it—two good deeds in one. You always were a Girl Scout. Can't pass that up, right? Plus, you see through people. I used to think you could see a liar coming a mile away."

"Not all of them." I lifted my chin an inch.

"Please? This island has made up its mind about me. They think they know all they need to, but they don't. I didn't do this." His voice grew soft and pleading. "Patience? Please."

I hated the power he still had over me. Those eyes. That dimple. Too much history. My resolve softened, and curiosity reared its ugly head. I slid a thumbnail between my teeth, a habit I immediately regretted. Adrian knew I was considering his words. "Where are you staying?"

"Nope. Not until you promise me you'll help. You must still have contacts at the FBI. At least talk to people around here. Someone had to have seen something. You'll be able to learn more doing that than Sheriff Murray will doing one of his half-assed investigations."

I appreciated the vote of confidence, but it was my civic duty to turn him in. I wavered. I hated to see an innocent man go to jail. It was unlikely they'd continue to look for the killer if they had Adrian in custody. "I'll ask a few questions."

"Yesss." He lifted two fists in victory. I hated him.

"But you need to leave. I don't want to be guilty of harboring a fugitive."

"Always with the rules. That's why I know I can trust you. You're honest."

I bit my lip to hold back a plethora of rude retorts. Instead, I nodded. When my head cleared slightly, I put down my purse. "Where were you last night?"

"Home. Alone."

Of course. "You should get dressed."

"Do you have a shirt I can wear?"

"If you fit into my clothes, I'll kill myself."

"Right. You look amazing, by the way."

He'd seen me in my underpants. My mind raced to remember if they were my nice ones. "You need to go."

"I'll be back."

"Lucky me." I followed him to my bedroom, where a breeze blew in the darkness.

He straddled the windowsill and swung his legs over the edge. "You need to get a lock on this. Anyone with a little motivation can get in."

He jumped to the porch roof below and then to the ground with a muffled *thump*. Then I locked the window and checked it twice. Adrian disappeared into the darkness.

I took a cold shower.

Adrian Davis might not be a murderer, but he was a menace. As soon as he got the murder charges dropped, I'd consider filing a complaint for breaking and entering.

I tossed under my sheet all night. The warm temperatures didn't comfort me. Every creak and groan of the old house freaked me out. Adrian's words haunted me. Anyone could get in and I'd never know. I vowed to never leave my pepper spray out of reach again.

He'd looked me in the eye and pleaded. As much as I wanted to be indifferent, I couldn't. While I refused to waste my time saving the big jerk, he had piqued my curiosity. When the sun finally peeked over the horizon, I resolved to visit the sheriff. Just to see if Adrian was right. Had the sheriff's office pointed the finger at him and stopped searching for other suspects? What could it hurt to find that out?

An eerie orange glow coated my apartment. The screen door thumped. I ran for my purse and then to check out what had caused the noise. This time Adrian would learn not to break into people's apartments. Pulling back a finger full of curtain, I held my breath, but all I heard was the faint mewing of a cat. No boogey man. No Adrian. Outside my door, a tiny gray fuzzball rubbed his sides against the screen, one after the other. Huh. I went to my kitchen for an empty mug and filled it with water.

"Here you go." I set the mug of water on the little porch outside my door and shook a handful of chips onto the wood plank flooring. "I haven't been to the grocery store."

Back inside I got dressed. No time like the present, as they said. Especially when I had to do something awkward like question the sheriff about things that were none of my business. I flipped through the few things I'd unpacked and settled on jeans and a silk tank top. After yesterday, I opted for Chucks instead of the sandals I'd worn on the mainland.

The little cat sat cleaning its paws. He hadn't touched the chips. "I'm off to be nosey."

THE POLICE STATION had white stucco walls and a pink tile roof. Nothing new there. Sheriff Murray's cruiser sat at the curb. Typical. The deputy's SUV was wedged behind the station. Good thing I brought three of Mrs. Tucker's cappuccinos. Nothing was worse than the stale black coffee in a police station. I'd had my share in high school. It sucked every time.

I slid through a mass of people inside the reception area. Sheriff Murray barked behind closed doors, drawing attention that way. His tenor rattled the blinds in the windows. The deputy fielded a volley of questions nearby. The receptionist's phone rang incessantly. Her mussed hair pointed in every direction. One hand waved off the never-ending stream of visitors, while the other rubbed her forehead.

I'd planned to share the cappuccinos with the sheriff and his deputy and drink mine while I waited, but the receptionist looked like she needed caffeine more than I did. I pushed my cup across her desk and then sat in the last open chair and unwrapped a piece of gum.

Every year the island had a big pony swim and auction. Cowboys rustled up the wild ponies from the marshes, forced them to swim across a section of water between the national park and town, and then sold them at auction. The money went to support our local firemen. The whole shindig lasted a week and culminated with the auction. It was the biggest week of the year for tourists and revenues. People descended on Chincoteague like locusts for the pony swim. Some wanted a glimpse at the wild ponies; others planned to buy them. Most hoped to make some money selling inflatable horses and funnel cakes to other tourists. All those extra people on a seven-by-three-mile island meant lots of police reports filed, vendor permits lost and general chaos. Security gave the sheriff annual fits. Every sheriff. Every year.

From the looks of it, Sheriff Murray had a new deputy and he wasn't prepared. The man looked smart in a Clark Kent way—dark hair parted on the left, combed to the side. Clearly younger than me, and more lanky than any of the field agents I'd gotten used to working with. He was no Sebastian Clark, but who was? The badge on his shirt was covered by the crowd of people waiting for his attention. Thanks to Mrs. Tucker and the Harry Potter glasses he wore, Deputy Doofus would remain his identity for now.

The office door swung wide, and I jumped in my seat. The plaster held surprisingly well when the door bounced off the wall. Sheriff Murray's face looked like a hot tamale. He kicked a trash bin beside an empty desk and stared at the crowd gathered up front with me.

I waved. "Sheriff Murray! Sheriff? A minute?" I swung an arm overhead. He squinted. When his chin went slack, I knew he recognized me.

"Excuse me." I dropped the carrier with my last two cappuccinos on the receptionist's desk and smiled. Then I shoved my way through the vendors arguing over permits. Poor girl was two complaints away from blowing a gasket.

"What can I do for you, Miss Price?" The sheriff moved back into his office and sat at his desk.

"Hi. Well, I wondered if you had any other suspects for the Brady McGee murder?"

He glared at me without speaking. His left eye twitched.

"I picked a rough day to make my homecoming, right?" I sat in a hard plastic chair across from his desk and crossed my legs. "You almost hit my friend and me with your cruiser. Then I heard Adrian Davis is the only suspect in a murder investigation. Wow." I dragged the final word out for three syllables. My foot bounced erratically.

"If you're about finished, Miss Price, I have a lot to deal with out there. I'll be sure to keep you apprised of my investigation."

Sarcasm. Really? "I don't want to be nosey. I—"

"Then don't be." He stood and opened a palm to the door. "If you'll excuse me."

"Sheriff Murray." I stood. "If I can do anything to help...I know how crazy pony week can be."

"You'd be happy to take my job off my hands? The FBI wasn't enough to satisfy you? Not enough things to investigate on the mainland? You thought you'd come home and take over here?" He worked his jaw.

"No, sir. No. I was hoping—"

"To take over? Flash your badge and get anything you want? Not here, young lady. You'll need to take a number, get in that line stretching around the building and flash your badge when you make it to the front again."

"I was in HR." My voice squeaked. What was wrong with everyone? Adrian was right. There were a slew of witnesses to his fight with Brady and gossip traveled faster than a forest fire. Between first—and secondhand accounts, the whole town had enough evidence to convict him. At least in the court of public opinion. I didn't want to think of what a jury of Adrian's peers might decide if the case against him went to trial. Chincoteague was an exercise in groupthink. He needed help. "If I could help—"

"Help who, exactly? Me or your boyfriend?"

"My what?" I bit my lip.

"I haven't forgotten the fact you and the accused have a history together. A long one. Now, you do know if you've seen him and haven't told me where he's hiding out, that makes you a hindrance to my investigation. Perhaps even an accomplice." He raised a puffy gray eyebrow my way. "Miss Price, when was the last time you spoke with Adrian Davis?"

I narrowed my eyes, turned and ran away. With any luck it appeared more like storming out.

"Tell your parents I said hello." He slammed his door behind me, rattling my teeth.

The office quieted long enough to register it was just me before the buzzing of voices resumed.

Adrian had impeccable timing. He picked the worst possible month to be accused of murder. Worse still, the sheriff had no intention of doing anything other than bringing Adrian in. Then what? If Adrian hadn't done it, he'd go to jail unjustly and the guilty party would go free. Could I live with that scenario?

I cast a glance over one shoulder at the pretty stucco station. It couldn't hurt to pay the deceased's wife a quick visit.

FOUR

THE MCGEE HOUSE looked like all the others in the middle-class Chincoteague neighborhood. Little purple flowers curled down from a line of hanging baskets on the porch. A tidy postage-stamp yard was attached to the walk. A pair of gnomes stood sentry beside the front steps. Typical. Quaint. Inviting.

I raised a fist to knock, but hesitated. I had no idea what to say. This poor woman had lost her husband. To murder. Yesterday.

The door sucked open, rattling the screen under my fist. A medley of voices silenced as a group appeared at the door.

"Hello." If only I'd brought some flowers or food. I folded my hands against my hips and tried to look less conspicuous.

Three sets of eyes appraised me. A couple I didn't know strolled out onto the porch beside me, promising to return soon. The blond woman standing inside the door sniffed and straightened her blouse.

"Can I help you?" she asked. Based on my towering five-foot-five-inch frame, she had to be praying for five feet. Maybe if she shopped in the kids' department, she could afford those Seven Jeans on a fisherman's salary. Otherwise, I didn't see how.

"Mrs. McGee? I'm so sorry to hear about your husband. Do you mind if I come in?"

She shrugged and stepped aside, wiping her nose into a white linen handkerchief.

The interior of the home was as simple as the outside. Wooden floors. Walls painted in bright Victorian colors and edged with oversized white woodwork. She led me to a sitting room where every flat surface bowed under the weight of casseroles and pies. A degree hung on the wall above a bookshelf. Mrs. McGee had studied marine biology. That explained how she ended up with a fisherman. Hopeful biologists and future park rangers flooded the island every summer after graduation, hoping to secure an internship. Half the island was protected. The national park and seashore were pristine from the number of graduates still excited to examine scat.

"Are you from the insurance company?"

"No." *Just hoping to get the only suspect in your husband's murder off the hook.* I blew out a long, quiet breath to get my nerve up.

"I worked for the FBI, Mrs. McGee. I moved here yesterday and this situation has my full attention." I straightened my spine, hoping to pull off the mental equivalent of a heist. Taking advantage of a distraught woman was inexplicably low. Adrian owed me big.

"I can't say I'm surprised. After the way that monster attacked him in front of half the town. When Brady got him good, I knew he'd retaliate. Men don't like to look bad. Getting beat up in front of all those people…I knew he'd come back. I never dreamed he'd…" She pulled a wad of tissues from inside her blouse and pressed them to her eyes. The hanky must've been on nose duty.

"Mrs. McGee, is there anyone else who might've wanted to hurt your husband?"

"Macy, please. Call me Macy." She blew her nose. Shifting in her chair, she crossed her legs, exposing the red soles of her bejeweled black peep toes. My mouth pulled open.

"Are those the new Louboutins?" Claire would freak if she knew I was this close to them. The elusive twentieth-anniversary peep toe. We had drooled over them together at Barneys. Recruiting at NYU had its perks. You couldn't get a shoe like that in Virginia. On-line ordering didn't count. Something as marvelous as those had to be acquired through the full department store experience. Men in dress clothes tossing ties over one shoulder had to place it on your foot and tell you how stunning you looked while girls in suits offered you re-freshments. Otherwise, half the thrill was lost.

"Oh." She dabbed her nose and perked up. "You know them?"

I nodded. My mind reeled at warp speed. Those shoes were $3,995. Fishermen probably made thirty grand a year around here. Brady owned the company. That meant he made more, but how much more? Enough to spring for the Louboutins?

"It's nice to meet someone who can appreciate them," Macy said. "My style is lost on this town."

I shook my head to regain my focus. They were *her* shoes. Not mine. Envy was never a pretty look to wear. "Um, did anyone else have a reason to want to hurt your husband? Did he have any enemies or debts?" I let the last word settle before moving on. "Anyone ever cause him any problems?"

"No." She rubbed the pad of her thumb over a mark on her heel. "He fought with Perkins more lately, but that's to be expected." She shrugged.

"Perkins?"

"His partner." She took a long look at me for the first time. "Who did you say you're with? The FBI?"

Lie or no? I sucked at lying. Plus I didn't want to. New plan: avoidance.

"Did he and his partner argue often?" Perhaps Perkins knew something useful in this matter. "Have you spoken to him?"

She blinked, derailed. "Let me get you his card. I think it's best if you talk to him yourself. Do I need a lawyer?"

"No." I stood. "Not at all. I'm sorry. I didn't mean to make this harder on you. I'll talk to Perkins and let you rest."

For a moment, I thought she'd toss me out the front door, or worse, call the sheriff. Instead, she pulled a bright green leather hobo from the coat tree in the hall. Marc Jacobs. Yeesh. Maybe I needed to take up fishing.

"Here."

The business card caught between two perfect red fingernails.

"Thanks." I drifted out the door reading the tiny lead. *MVP Fishing*. McGee and Perkins I understood, but what did the V stand for?

I slid back into my Prius and drove the mile and a half to my parents' house on the water. Dinnertime. Having already splurged on enough meals, I planned to play the I-am-your-child-you-must-feed-me card. I angled my car in beside the Volkswagen bus in the drive. My childhood home looked exactly as I remembered. It towered over the neighboring houses along the harbor. Two tiers of stairs separated me from the front door. The rear decks overlooked the water. The house stood atop massive poles seven feet high, protecting it from a lifetime of East Coast storms. Mom thanked some ginger root or premonition or demigod. I thanked the men who installed the double-sized pillars under their home.

I shut my door and pressed the auto-lock button. A

flock of seagulls protested the sound. From the look and smell of things, I timed my visit just right. The gulls complained but continued to swirl and land on the backside of the house. The air smelled of grilled tilapia and buttered-up veggies. The salty sea air made it all feel like a pair of comfortable shoes.

On my way under the house, I trailed my fingers along the first pole. My initials were carved there above Adrian's. My fingers traced the grooves, but I refused to look.

A few seconds later, Dad came into view. "Hello, Peepee."

"Hey, Dad." I dashed up the first set of steps to the rear deck and stopped short. Something moved in the bamboo beside the house. Waning sunlight hit Mrs. Davis's awful red tips. My shoulders slumped, and I nodded and moved on. Her stalker act was getting old.

"I see you're not alone." Dad waved a spatula overhead.

I looked back into the bamboo. No sign now of Mrs. Davis or her red woodpecker hair.

"You brought your appetite along." A smile formed on Dad's lips.

"Yep. Me and my appetite. What's on the menu?"

He ran a hand over his graying ponytail. "Scallops, tilapia, salad from your mom's garden and mai tais." When he winked, he looked decades younger, the way he had at my track meets and swim competitions.

"We made all your favorites." Mom's tinkling voice arrived with the sliding of the glass patio doors. "The moment we knew you were coming, we visited The Harbor for fresh scallops."

I sighed. Because she knew I was coming before I did. My mom, the psychic.

"Your mom tells me you're going to help Adrian get

back on his feet." Dad pushed veggies around a sea of bubbling sauce on the side burner.

"I haven't made any decisions. I'm curious. Nothing more."

"You remember how curiosity worked out for the cat, don't you, sweetheart." Mom smoothed my frizzing hair.

"Of course." Coming from the most curious woman I knew, the reminder didn't feel weighted.

"How's it going?" Dad flipped fish.

"It's not going. There's nothing to go." I sank into a wooden chair.

The patio table overflowed with Mom's harvest. I rolled an uncut bell pepper between my palms. My parents' backyard was cut short after about fifteen feet by a cement barrier. Low harbor waves lapped against it. Saltwater probably ran through my veins, considering the way I'd lived life surrounded by it. Even in Norfolk, the water was everywhere. Living someplace that didn't smell faintly of brine and fish seemed iffy to me. I couldn't trust a place like that.

My parents exchanged a glance and knowing smiles.

"What?" This again. More about me and Adrian. I placed the pepper on the table so as not to throw it. The island put most people at ease. It raised my blood pressure.

"Relax. Take your time deciding," Mom advised.

"Haste and passion are easily confused." Dad spoke into the air, as if his words of wisdom weren't aimed at my heart.

I rolled my eyes and looked out to sea. A gull made a swoop for the scallops and Dad shrieked. Cooking seafood beside the ocean, surrounded by seagulls, was an at-your-own-risk practice. We'd lost more than one meal on that deck.

HONK! HONK! HONK! HONK!

Mom held an air horn overhead. The birds scattered, swarming and landing on the roof, unwilling to get too far from the feast. She kept an air horn with the grill the way most people kept a small fire extinguisher.

"Let's eat inside." Dad rolled the grill to the sliding doors and moved at lightning speed, pulling his hard work from the grates onto trays. Mom and I followed the food.

Each bite of fresh-grilled seafood saturated my brain with happy hormones. I sipped my frosty mai tai and smiled. Rum overtook my senses, clearing away the buttery seafood goodness and my sinuses in one waft. "Whoa." My eyes popped wide. "What's in this?"

"Light rum, dark rum, triple sec." Mom ticked off her fingers.

I held up a palm and gulped ice water from the glass she'd set before me.

"Lightweight." Dad dug into his salad.

I left the mai tai alone. Then came the questions I knew they'd wanted to ask all along.

"What's your apartment like? Have you noticed anything strange? Maybe an icy breeze or a three-dimensional shadow?"

They looked hopeful. I bit my tongue against the argument that the phrase "three-dimensional shadows" was an oxymoron.

"Nope."

"Do you need any help over there? Rusty hinges, rattling windows, creaky drawers? Your father's still pretty handy."

"Oh, Sheila." Dad waggled his eyebrows at her and sucked on his drink.

"Ew. No, thank you. And please don't gross me out."

"Sorry, sweetie. So, nothing spectral?"

"No. I did find a little kitty."

"Could be a spirit guide." Dad shoveled a forkful of roasted peppers and greens into his mouth.

Oh, boy. Though I could maybe use a spirit guide. I had no idea what to do about Adrian. I couldn't punish him if he was safely behind bars somewhere.

"What do you know about Mrs. McGee?" I forked a scallop and pointed it at my dad. He shifted in his seat. I waited him out. His lips were looser than Mom's. If my parents knew something, he'd talk.

"Your mother knows her better than I do." Clever.

Always a surprise with my parents. I turned to Mom and set my fork down. She had information and I had all night.

"She's a nice lady. Last year she helped me organize a protest against fishermen coming too close to the coastlines. It's practically poaching when they press them into shallow water and net them."

Well, that made zero sense. "But her husband's a fisherman."

They nodded.

"He must have had a problem with her protesting his career. It had to be bad for business." I shoved a scallop in my mouth and let that settle. He had more reason to kill her than the other way around. Maybe he'd tried. An attempted murder gone awry?

"I don't think they were close." Dad looked at Mom for approval.

She rubbed his forearm lying on the table.

My phone buzzed in my purse. I didn't recognize the number. Holding a finger up, I answered.

"Miss Price? This is Jamie with Selvetto Realty. You called about the boathouse?"

"Yes." I held my breath.

"The space requires a deposit equal to one month's

rent, plus this month's rent in advance of occupancy. I shared your counteroffer on the monthly rental fee with the owner. He found the reduced amount acceptable. Does your offer still stand?"

"Yes." The reduced rent was modest, but it was all I could afford, minus a few hundred for paint and cleaning supplies, at least until I found a few clients. From what I saw through the windows, there was plenty of space for a nice waiting room, an office and kitchen area. This was it. Nothing on the island would come at a lower cost than an abandoned boathouse.

He cleared his throat. "The owner accepts."

He told me I could come collect my key anytime. The owner had given permission for immediate occupancy. Never one for squealing, I did a mental victory dance and pushed the phone back into my purse with one finger. Step one: accomplished.

"I have office space."

"Lovely. Where? On Main Street, I hope. You can meet us at The Pony for lunch."

"I rented the old boathouse near the park."

My parents exchanged another sideways glance then filled their mouths with fish.

"I know it needs some work, but it's private. People won't worry about being seen getting therapy. Which—" I raised my fork high "—is silly. Besides, it's all I can afford right now. You'd be proud, Daddy. I negotiated lower rent and won."

"You need to keep an open mind about your idea of counseling, sweetie." Mom lifted her glass. "There's more than one way to reach the moon."

Whatever that meant. Too excited to take another bite, I excused myself. I couldn't wait to admire my new office space. Mom packed a to-go bag and promised to see me soon. I was down the driveway and on the road in ten minutes. This time I vowed to snap a few shots with my phone and e-mail them to Claire. In fact, I considered framing a few before-and-after shots in the reception area one day.

Mine would be the one professional building this side of the mainland without a tropical island or boat theme. Hunter green walls, cherry-stained woodwork. I'd buy black-and-white photographs with one-color detail to add interest. Like a dramatic print of the Eiffel Tower with a distant umbrella in bright yellow, or a black-and-white wedding shot where the bride's lips were romantically red.

The Prius slid against the curb at my new office with a hush. I couldn't wait to get started. When I climbed out onto the street, my dusty Chucks came into view. Not the four-thousand-dollar, twentieth-anniversary Louboutins, but things were changing. No more working HR for the man. I *was* the man.

My shoulders slipped a bit. Seriously, how did she get those Louboutins?

And that bag. The implications of such high-end accessories on a fisherman's wife had my wheels spinning. Could she have been having an affair with a wealthy businessman? If so, would he have wanted to be rid of the husband to have her to himself? Could she have been involved in something illegal? The HBO series *Weeds* came to mind. Selling smack to island folk?

Questions distracted me as I walked the perimeter of the boathouse. I couldn't get inside without a key.

How did she have those shoes?

I held my breath and made a decision while heading back to the car. One phone call. I would make one phone call for Adrian's sake. Scrolling through the contacts on my phone, I dipped back into my driver's seat. There was someone back at the FBI I wouldn't mind talking to. This seemed as good a reason as I would ever have to call him.

"Clark." He answered on the first ring, before I'd thought my plan through. A recurring theme in my week.

Sebastian Clark had been my first new hire as HR manager. I'd based the recommendation on facts, numbers and his healthy two-inch-thick file of achievements. He'd served overseas and led numerous squads and teams on various life-threatening missions. He never lost a man, though he'd been shot twice. He had a degree in psychology, training in military intelligence, and boasted a stint at the White House. On his application he said Secret Service limited him to guarding political figures. He wanted to protect the people, not their representatives. I liked him immediately. The special agent in charge agreed and I took mental credit for discovering Sebastian in a pile of hopefuls.

When he rolled into my office for his first face-to-face interview, I dropped my pen into my coffee. Thirty-five at the time, he looked more like any guy in upper-middle-class America. His suit fit him like it was tailored for the purpose. His shoes were Italian. Not the typical applicant for special agent. His personnel file and his face didn't mesh. He threw me off. No one else ever did that, and I liked it.

His dark hair shined under fluorescent lighting. He wore it disheveled and youthful, not the überpopular military crew cut, or the I'm-trying-too-hard side part. I flipped his file open to the inside cover once more and checked his age again. Thirty-five. I might've given his marital status a quick peek too. Single agents had more time and less distractions. As the woman who hired him, he was off-limits to me. A pipe dream, anyway. Sebastian was fierce. I was a marshmallow.

Now, as back then, air caught in my throat.

"Patience?" I pulled the phone from my ear to examine it then clipped it into the holder on my dash.

"Hey."

"Everything all right?"

"Sure. Hey, can I run something by you? Get your thoughts."

"Absolutely. Do you want to meet for drinks?"

I caught a glimpse of myself in the rearview. My eyes stretched round. My lips opened and shut, looking for words they couldn't find. I looked like a fish out of water.

"I'm sorry. It's okay to ask you that now, right? I heard you're not with the agency anymore."

"Right. Yes. No. They fired me. Downsized. I was downsized. I'm not in town, though."

Idiot. My head hit the steering wheel.

"Oh. Well, go ahead then. What's on your mind?"

If he knew, he'd have me arrested.

I gave him a rundown of the last two days while I drove home.

"So, you're investigating your ex-boyfriend's murder charge?"

I bit my lip. "Kinda."

During the next few beats of silence, I contemplated driving my Prius into the harbor.

"Have you talked to the sheriff?" Sebastian's voice was low and steady. He'd slipped into cop mode while I considered a saltwater death.

I cleared my throat, hoping to sound mature and professional. "Yeah. He hates me, but that's a long story."

"What about the victim's family and friends? What'd they say when you spoke with them?"

"I only spoke with the wife."

"How'd she react? Do you like her for the murder?"

"I don't know. I liked her shoes."

A car door slammed somewhere on Sebastian's end of the line. "I'm on my way to a bust, or I'd stop to see you while I'm on the coast. I've been undercover so long I don't recognize myself."

"I'd recognize you."

He grunted. "It's my last night as Angelo Cordileone, undercover heavy for the Risso crime family. Let me buy you a drink later, and we can talk through this thing with your ex."

"I'd like that."

"You sure he didn't do it?"

"Eighty percent." Hey, if I was too certain, Sebastian might not come visit.

It took a few minutes after we disconnected to text the highlights of our conversation to Claire and head for my front door.

A woman waited on my doorstep.

"Hi, there!" She waved her free arm. The other supported a glass dish. "My name is Mary Franks. I live on Baxter Court. When I heard you were here, I thought I'd drop over and say welcome." She shoved the dish in my direction.

"Thank you." The question in my voice raised her eyebrows. "Would you like to come inside?"

Her head bobbed and she cut in front of me when I opened the door. She took the dish back, set it on the countertop and without any prompting began to tell me about her husband. They'd moved to Chincoteague a few years before to get away from the temptations of the city. She had a jealous streak that threatened their marriage. She knew it.

Lucky for me, she had a chocolate pie under the foil. I grabbed two plates and did my best to cut normal-sized portions. The scent was rich and heavenly. This was the kind of pie a girl curled up with at night and paired with peanut butter straight from the jar. I served us each a modest piece and made plans to live out my fantasy as soon as possible. She accepted the slice with a weak smile and continued her story.

"He's too friendly, if you know what I mean. He gives women the impression he's single and then they can't help themselves. I can hardly blame them. He's gorgeous. And sweet. But he won't listen to me. He doesn't see what I see. Can I get you some more pie?"

My plate was empty. How'd that happen? "That was delicious. Have you thought of selling your pies?"

"No." She put the dish in my sink, the remaining pie in my refrigerator and hefted her handbag onto one shoulder. With a deep sigh, she excused herself. "Thank you so much for everything. It feels good to connect with a neighbor." She offered a small, cunning smile.

"Thank you for the pie." *What just happened?*

Before I could collect myself, she was back on the sidewalk moving away at an amazing speed. I locked the door and transferred the leftovers from Mom onto the shelf above the pie. I needed a nice long bath to relive the conversation with Sebastian. He'd asked me out for drinks. Best. Day. Ever.

On my way to the bathroom, I noticed money on the countertop. Upon inspection it turned out to be a crisp new fifty. The bill was folded in half with one corner tucked under my saltshaker.

I looked at the front door. Mary Franks must have left it. Was the rumor of my destitute condition already making its rounds? Now I had to figure out how to find her and return the cash.

Later. Sebastian Clark had asked me out for drinks.

I slid into my bubble bath with nothing but happy thoughts on my mind.

And those damn Louboutins.

FIVE

I MET THE Realtor, signed my way into a one year lease and pocketed my new office key in record time. He said he had a motivated owner. A three-ring binder of decorating ideas and color schemes lay on the passenger seat beside me. I gathered the binder and climbed out of the car. Suppressing the urge to skip up the sidewalk, I noted a number of weeds shooting up between the cement slates. The small lawn needed mowing. I didn't have a mower.

I leaned against the door with one shoulder, juggling the binder and my purse. Before the key turned in the lock, the door creaked.

"What the—?"

As I pushed harder with my palm, the whole door frame inched inward under my weight. The wood was weathered gray and splintered severely around the door and hinges. Great. With my luck, a client would knock and the door would fall down. Gingerly, I turned the knob and pressed the door wide. The door swung with a mild squeak. The frame stayed intact. Thank goodness. The inside looked like I expected an abandoned boathouse to look. I sighed, squared my shoulders and made a trip to my car and back. I'd nearly wiped out the cleaning supply aisle at Frontier Foods in preparation. My new office had to sparkle. It represented me. If I looked like a mess, no one would trust me to help them with theirs. I shoved the idea that my life *was* a mess from my head and got busy.

Two hours later, the place looked a touch less abandoned and smelled of bleach and Windex. I'd taken my Louboutin frustration out on the place and it showed. How did she afford those shoes? The business card she gave me taunted me from my purse on the countertop. The Mc-Gees were probably up to their eyes in credit card debt like the rest of the country. Sebastian would probably run a credit check on the McGees if I asked him. So would Claire, but where was the fun in that? I picked up the mop and headed for the bathroom. Mr. Perkins, Brady's business partner, probably had the scoop I needed. Partners talked, didn't they? Claire and I always dished about our frustrating dates. Maybe Brady told Perkins something incriminating about his wife.

Something moved nearby. Pressing my back to the wall, I held the mop handle like a weapon. Mrs. Davis had better steer clear or I'd knock her sideways. I'd had enough of being snuck up on for one lifetime.

"Come out. I hear you." I widened my stance, ready for anything.

Silence.

"Come on." I whacked the mop hard against the wall and a herd of rats bounded across the floor at my feet.

"Ahhhhhh!" Not that. I wasn't ready for that. The mop hit the floor. The next thing I knew, my Prius was making its way over the bridge to the mainland.

I dialed an exterminator and told him the door was open and he could bill me.

Half an hour later, I arrived at the Perkins's residence. On the whole, the house didn't impress. A typical Virginia home in an old neighborhood where brick streets from days gone by stood exposed at the bottom of potholes. I slid the Prius in behind a fancy black Mercedes SUV in the driveway. Way to waste money and ruin the ozone. Hairs stood up on my neck and arms. I grew up on an island of fishermen and none of them drove a Mercedes. Perkins and Mrs. McGee had something in common. Both had expensive taste.

The doorbell brought a guy who looked like a Vegas pimp to greet me.

"Yeah?" His gaze ran over my body from chest to toes, never climbing above my collarbone.

I clenched a fist at one side. "Hi. I'm…" *going to hell for lying* "… a friend of Mrs. McGee's."

"Yeah?"

What an ape. Did he say anything else? I considered squatting so we might make eye contact. "I wondered if we could talk about Brady?"

Examining my legs in cutoff shorts, he opened the door to let me pass. He didn't step out of the way. I'd have to burn my clothes when I got home.

"Right this way." He led me to the front room, where he helped himself to a shot of whiskey and offered me one. At eleven-thirty. In the morning.

I shook my head. "I wonder if you know why Brady was at the marina so late the night he was killed."

"They found him in the morning." He rolled the small glass in his fingers.

"The way I hear it, he died several hours earlier."

"What are you, an investigator or something?" He smirked and tossed the amber liquid into his mouth. Clearly, this wasn't his first drink of the day.

True. I had dressed to clean an abandoned boathouse, not visit a stranger's home, but I got the feeling it wasn't my clothes that made him laugh. I saw it all over his smarmy face. A woman couldn't be an investigator. I couldn't possibly have anything above my barely C cups worth offering. I inhaled and counted to ten. "Just curious. Did anyone have a problem with him?"

"How should I know?"

"You're his business partner. He told you things, right?"

A disbelieving puff of air blew through his lips. He poured another shot, ran a hand over his thoroughly greased-back black hair then traced a thumb over each oversized eyebrow. All he needed was a toothpick to roll in his mouth and I'd have laughed.

"He kept secrets, that guy." The scoff on his face said this was a problem between business partners.

"Anyone bothering him? Maybe you saw him with someone? Overheard something you didn't mean to hear?"

Finally, Perkins looked at my face. His glassy brown eyes struggled to focus. This guy had an obvious problem. I hoped it was grief and not guilt. Inviting myself over to a murderer's home seemed stupid on a number of levels.

His mouth opened and shut. He sat on a leather wingback across from me, his knees flopped wide apart. "I don't know nothing." Defeat colored his tone. "He was screaming at some broad that night. We played poker on the boat, and she came yelling at him about breaking promises or some crap like that."

"You saw him the night he was killed?"

He shrugged.

"Was it Mrs. McGee he fought with?"

"I don't know. I never met her."

"Blonde. Tiny."

"Nah. This chick was big." He cupped his hands a foot in front of him. Nothing but class, this guy. "Brunette. Legs for miles." His attention turned to my calves, and I was back on my feet. My hair fell over my shoulders and I wished it were long enough to cover all of me.

"You never met your partner's wife?" I narrowed my eyes.

"Nope." He tossed back the shot in his hand. "We were

partners, not girlfriends. We didn't get manicures and share our deep, dark secrets. We ran a business."

"Thanks, Mr. Perkins. I hope you start feeling better soon. It's hard to lose a friend."

He followed me to the door, keeping a few steps between us. I was on the sidewalk before he spat, "Brady McGee was nobody's friend."

Well, there it was. Perkins was with him the night he died, along with an unknown brunette. Now I had three persons of interest. Not that I believed for a second Brady's little sprite of a wife could lift anything heavy enough to drop him, but goons-for-hire were still a possibility.

Back on the island, I went straight for the shower. Sweat and dust from my rat-infested office space had turned to paste on my skin. I smelled like Lysol. Good thing Perkins had been snockered. I'd hate to think I made such a stinky first impression on a sober person, even one like him.

I toweled off my hair and had dug out my blow-dryer when the doorbell rang. Imagine. Someone using the doorbell.

I leaned my head into the front room, torn between finishing my hair and dealing with Mrs. Davis. "Who is it?"

"Coach Peters."

The current high school football coach, and my old track and swim coach? Perfect. I wanted to talk to him about the fight at the field between Adrian and Brady. Relieved it wasn't Adrian's mom, I pulled my still-damp hair into a loose knot and hustled to the door.

"Wow, how long has it been?" I pulled him into a hug and immediately regretted it. He stepped back and looked around.

"Can I buy you a coffee?"

"Um." Two things came to mind. Why was he so nervous, and should I be? "Sure." I grabbed my purse and slid into my favorite, strappy-heeled sandals. Amazing how some shampoo and a clean outfit could change a girl's day.

"Tasty Cream?" I asked.

"I was thinking Island Brew." He eyeballed the summer crowd outside the Tasty Cream. Lots of teens. Probably he coached a few of them. "You still swimming?"

"Yeah. I don't run as much, but I do swim. There was a nice pool at the apartment complex where I last lived."

"Aw, pools are for girls. Swimming in the ocean, now that takes muscle."

That sounded like the coach who pushed my team to state in track and field. Unfortunately, our swim team had lacked muscle.

A couple of blocks and two right turns later, we arrived. I squinted inside Island Brew. It was dark and almost empty. The opposite of the Tasty Cream. We took seats near the back with our drinks, staying clear of the front windows.

"I have a gambling problem." He exhaled and leaned against the table with his elbows.

I braced myself. This was it. Brady McGee liked to gamble. Coach would put the pieces together for me, and I'd solve the mystery before I ever officially decided to try. Claire would be impressed. So would Sebastian.

"I've bet on high school games since I was in high school. It's half the reason I decided to coach. Figured I'd have the inside scoop on at least one team. Improve my odds." His thumbs twirled. His fingers wrapped around his mug.

"Uh-huh." Talk about starting a story from the beginning. I shifted in my chair, waiting for the punch line. What happened to Brady McGee?

"It's getting harder to mask the losses. My wife's on my case every Friday night. Did I bet on the game? Does she need to have another intervention? She doesn't get it. I can't just stop. Gambling ain't like smoking. You can't just go cold turkey. Her busting my balls ain't the answer, either." He sucked on his coffee and pouted.

"No. Addiction is a serious illness and needs to be treated that way. It's a decision you have to make for yourself. No one else can make it, or you won't stand by it." My mouth spilled details straight from a textbook or any simple Web search, but my brain stuttered. Where was the firsthand information I needed? What about Adrian's fight with Brady?

"Yeah. That's what I thought. That's what I told her." He stood and clapped me on one shoulder. He tossed a fresh one hundred dollar bill on the table and strutted out the front door.

"Hey." I stood, lifting my hand in the direction of his departure. "Coach Peters?"

That was the second person in as many days to feed me and then pay me. Strange, even for island folk. I pocketed the bill. I'd need to stop by practice soon and return his money. He sounded like he could use it, and I didn't accept handouts. As soon as the exterminator moved the current disease-ridden residents from my new office space, I'd be in business. Until then, I had time to think about Adrian's mess.

I swigged my latte and considered the empty chair before me. Mrs. Franks and her pie came to mind. She and the coach were unlikely candidates for giving me a handout.

A slow smile crept over my face. My capacity for missing the obvious astounded me, and frankly didn't bode well for Adrian, but that wasn't the point. Coach Peters needed me. He wanted someone to talk to and he chose me. Mrs. Franks had brought me pie as a cover up. She wanted help too. My mom and Mrs. Davis were wrong. This island needed a counselor.

WAVES CRASHED ALONG the shoreline. The national forest was a part of the island. The seashore stood between the forest and the ocean. There was no place like it on earth. I sat down on the beach and buried my toes in hot white sand. When did life get so confusing? A month ago I accepted my graduate degree and planned to ask for a promotion at the FBI. Now I lived in a bad-luck apartment, owned a dilapidated boathouse and worked for free as a nosey ex-girlfriend to Adrian, the man who had turned my heart to stone. I twirled my ponytail in one hand, contemplating the train wreck.

"Don't hurt yourself." Adrian waltzed across the empty beach in my direction. He had on a pair of low-slung jeans and sandals, looking more like a Hollister ad than a felon. His shirt was untucked and clinging to the planes of his chest from the heat. "You always twirl your hair when you're plotting something. You used to do it so much I wondered if you'd wind up with curly hair."

"Ah, if it isn't the fugitive."

"Don't be mad. You're too cute when you're mad."

"Ha." I spoke the word, unamused.

He helped himself to a seat beside me. Our hips touched. I inched away. He laughed. "Your parents cursed you. You've never had any patience. It's funny, right?"

I squinted into the sun-glistened waves. If I ignored him, he'd go away.

"You went over to the mainland today," he said. "Was that about me?"

"Not everything's about you."

"What were you doing? One minute you're at my boathouse, the next minute you're tearing across the bridge like there's a shoe sale somewhere."

"What do you mean *your* boathouse?"

He bumped his shoulder against mine. "I bought it when I moved back here. I planned to fix it up, turn it into a unique office space. Great minds." He tapped a finger to his temple.

"We don't think alike."

"Then how did I know I'd find you here?"

"Because you're following me." I dug my fingers into the sand. My phone rang.

Adrian got comfortable, leaning back on his elbows beside me.

I rolled my eyes and answered the call.

"Hey," Sebastian's voice cut through the roaring waves. My breath hitched.

"Do you still want to talk? I have time for a trip out there tomorrow."

"That'd be fabulous. Yes, please come." I blushed at my choice of words.

Adrian chuckled beside me.

I shot him the stink eye, and he pretended to button his lips.

"Text me your address."

We disconnected. Adrian rolled onto his stomach and fluttered his eyelids. "Was that your boyfriend?" He bent his feet skyward then crossed and uncrossed his ankles.

"Shut up."

"Boy, everything makes you cranky."

"You make me cranky."

"Yeah?"

"Yeah."

He sat up again and twisted in the sand to face me. "You know I'm innocent."

"Pft." A few pointed accusations came to mind, but he meant of murder. "Yeah. I know you didn't kill Brady." Against my better judgment, I looked into Adrian's eyes. Clouds of blue and gray collided inside them. A summer storm. My lips rolled in over my teeth. I blinked, furious with my idiotic brain.

"Who was on the phone? The friend who helped you move? Do I get to meet her soon?"

"No and no. No one can know I'm talking to you. Plus, it wasn't Claire on the phone." My lips twitched.

Adrian frowned.

"It was an agent. I called him yesterday to run a few things past him. He's going to come over tomorrow so we can talk about your case."

Adrian scowled. "Glad my pending imprisonment is helping your love life."

"We're just friends." Heat crept over my neck and face.

"He's driving two and a half hours from the mainland to talk about my case. You were on the phone. He couldn't have talked about it from there? Or by e-mail? Or text? Video chat?"

I stood up. Obviously I couldn't get any peace anywhere. "Why do you care?"

"I don't." He smiled, wide and ornery. "I just like getting your goat." He stood and shoved his fingers into his pockets.

"I swear, you drive me insane, Adrian Davis." I turned to leave and he reached for me, brushing his fingers against mine.

He pulled me back to him. "Hate is a very passionate emotion. A heartbeat away from love, I think. You know what else I think?"

No. Who could think with those wild eyes looking back at them? Unable to choose words, I shook my head.

"I think you and I are meant to be."

He ruined it. If he'd kissed me, I could've slapped him. Then I would've slept like a baby. Instead, he pronounced the words I'd cried myself to sleep over for years. I stomped my heel into his foot and marched off, back poker-straight.

He chuckled behind me.

I wouldn't look back. Never again.

Again, I tossed in bed until dawn, hating Adrian's effect on my heart and mind. Hating my curiosity and obsession with puzzles even more. I saw Louboutins drinking whiskey all night. Mrs. McGee and Perkins shooting craps in Vegas. The coach betting all his money on them.

I woke with resolve. I would help Adrian. Not because we were meant to be together, but because I believed in our justice system and if I could help it succeed, then it was my civic duty to do so. When I did save his self-absorbed behind, I expected the deed to my new boathouse free and clear. A fair trade, if anyone asked me—a dilapidated office in exchange for his freedom.

SIX

THE PHONE VIBRATED in circles on my nightstand. Claire.

"You're still sleeping?"

"One of the many benefits of unemployment." I looked at the clock by my bed. Nine-fifteen. "I can't sleep here. I tossed and turned all night. Again."

"Well, I hope you got enough beauty sleep to enjoy your day with Mr. Muscles."

I shot upright. Sebastian was coming. "I'm up."

"Call me when he leaves. And, lady, if you call before tomorrow morning, I'll be sorely disappointed."

"The other line's ringing. Who's calling?" I gasped, heart still fluttering at the reminder of Sebastian's impending visit.

"How would I know?"

"I don't know. Maybe because it's coming from your office."

"What can I say, we're lost without you."

I disconnected with Claire and answered the incoming call.

"Patience, thank heavens! Where are the new hire files supposed to go after we complete the interviews? I sent them to Burns and he sent them back." Lucy, my new replacement, who apparently never did a thing until I left, spewed a full-on freak-out into my tired ear. I stumbled to the kitchen for a vat of coffee. I'd have to settle for a pot to get me started.

"Put them in the file marked Completed. It's under the

new hire drawer. Burns will get them when he's ready. If you send them to him, it implies he's moving too slowly and he'll retaliate over the insult."

"Retaliate how?" Her voice quavered.

"Gotta go." Let her sit on that. She could find out the same way I did.

A ton of unopened boxes waited along my walls for attention. I'd unpacked the necessities, but the rest looked daunting. Avoidance was an underestimated survival technique. I checked my voice mails and got online. According to the exterminator, I needed to board up the opening where boats were once parked if I didn't want any rats to find their way back inside my new office. Aside from that, the place was clear. Sebastian had also left a message. He'd see me for dinner.

If I stayed home all day, I'd drive myself crazy.

A trip to the hardware store sounded like a good idea. The problem with turning a boathouse into an office was the lower level. Everything behind the office was open water and a dock for boat parking—also known as a giant rat door. Nothing some plywood and a few nails couldn't fix. I left my name on the hardware store corkboard, seeking a contractor. With any luck I could find one who accepted payments. A hundred bucks later, I loaded my trunk with some gorgeous hunter-green paint and miscellaneous supplies.

It was a perfect summer day. Eighty-five and sunny. The sky reflected its blue onto the water as far as the eye could see. A speckle of wispy white clouds floated above me. I rolled my windows all the way down and let my hand drift outside the window. Air-conditioning might've been cooler, but nothing compared to the scent and feel of the warm, briny air. Summer on the island was sheer paradise.

Unloading the paint from my trunk, I admired my new office space. In a month, no one would remember what a mess it used to be. I propped open the door and windows of the boathouse. The cooped-up scent burned my nose, and breathing in paint fumes with the bleach still lingering in the air would kill more brain cells than I was willing to spare. I brought up my playlist and stuffed ear buds into both ears. One good coat of paint, and I'd head home to shower. Another coat tomorrow. *Voila.* Progress.

The paint went on with ease, transforming water-marked gray into sophisticated green. Rolling beauty over the ugly gave me a thrill. The music made me happy, too. The bass beat in my head as I admired my work. I sang until the very last note. Then I took a step back. A prideful smile split my face. The office looked fabulous. I did that.

I squatted before the paint tray and dropped the roller to dust my palms together. *Look at me getting things done.* My head bobbed with satisfaction as I pulled my purse across the floor and settled back on the linoleum. The moment needed to be memorialized. Stage one of the boathouse resurrection: complete.

While my arm was elbow deep in my purse, a resounding crash sent me facedown on the floor. Glass shattered everywhere, spilling and skidding across the floor around me. A series of loud pops followed and then the screech of tires. For a moment, I imagined the place was hit by an airplane. I dragged myself over the floor to peek out the open door. No flames or crashed cars. No fuselage. My car sat at a tilt.

On my knees, I dusted myself off, while outside a horde of people appeared out of nowhere. Most kept a safe distance for optimal gawking. A kid carrying a skateboard lifted his phone my way and took a picture before moseying away as if the spectacle wasn't worth more of his time.

A few brave souls crunched through the broken glass to my side and rubbed my arms. They looked into my face, mumbling. Their words bounced off me. I wriggled free, pulling my purse behind me, and zombie-walked to my car. I opened the door to my Prius, which almost scraped the ground since it sat on one completely flattened tire. From a distance I took in the scene around my office. People yammered into cell phones. A splatter of black spots covered the walls. Shattered glass sparkled in the sunlight.

I blinked.

Someone had shot my car! And my office! It had to be the first drive-by shooting in the history of the island. The local media would love this. My brain revved so far into overdrive I couldn't deal with it. Fight-or-flight kicked in—I needed to get away from there.

My skin tingled as I shuffled along the sidewalk through a shimmering mirage of heat. My heart rammed against my ribs, making it hard to catch a full breath. Every tiny sip of oxygen took effort. Hyperventilation. I was experiencing my first panic attack. Well, there was no time for that. Sheer stubbornness forced my feet forward. I shuffled, half breathing, half dazed, around the corner to Main Street and kept going until shops came into view.

A family wearing sun visors and fanny packs snapped my picture with a giant camera. A kid wearing swim trunks and swim fins over his flip-flops stuck out his tongue. My ears rang. A duo riding a two-seated bicycle waved. My wrist lifted and fell to my side. Three doors to go. Past the artisan jeweler. Two more. Past the photography studio. Bells tinkled overhead as I shoved my way inside the cool glass door. I collapsed inside The Purple Pony. Resting my head on the bench where my father liked to nap, I curled my legs behind me on the floor.

"Patience!" My parents materialized. "What happened?" Some psychic. If Mom didn't see that coming, I didn't think she'd fool anyone anymore.

"Help me move her," Mom commanded.

Dad scooped me up and carried me through the bead curtain to the back room, wobbling slightly under my weight. I regretted all the French fries when he heaved me onto the window seat with a groan. I used to nap in the back room after school. Mom kept the window seat covered in the fluffiest pillows on earth.

My heart rate settled by a fraction. "There was a drive-by shooting." The words were stupid. Where was I? Compton? Who did that? "At the boathouse."

"Patience, you could've been killed." Dad handed me his magic sugar water.

I waved it away and shifted into a sitting position. "They shot out one of my tires, too."

"Honey, lie down a minute." Mom hovered mere inches away, looking as serene as ever, despite the tension in her voice. "Did you call the sheriff?"

"No."

She worked over my face and arms with a warm wash-cloth, checking for injuries. "You're all scratched up. Does anything hurt when you move it?"

"No. Just cuts. There was a lot of glass." I really needed a handyman now. How much did windows cost?

"Here." She handed me a Purple Pony T-shirt and took Dad into the next room.

I carefully ran the washcloth over each eye, and the cloth came back black. The boathouse must not have been as clean as I thought. I needed to go by the hardware store again, this time for a few dozen dead bolts, chains and sliding locks. People didn't do drive-by shootings on Chincoteague. That honor was a special treat for me. Who had I pissed off? Cute little Mrs. McGee with her fancy shoes? Perkins, the sleazy, drunken partner? Maybe someone with a grudge against counselors? Or someone else who thought I was sticking my nose where it didn't belong? The last option scared me the most. Hiding or defending myself from the unknown would be more difficult.

"Your chakras are a mess." Mom approached me on my way to the door. "Stay for tea. At least let me call Nurse Higgins to give you a once-over."

I grabbed my purse from the bench and wandered out onto the sidewalk. "No, I'm okay. I need locks."

"Your dad and I will get your car to the mechanic for you."

"Thank you." I shut the door behind me and shuffled toward the hardware store on autopilot.

AFTER SCREWING THE last of my new dead bolts in place at my apartment, I face-planted into the couch. What next? Bars on the windows? Bulletproof glass?

A shadow crossed over the window above the couch. *My life.* I held my breath and waited. No sounds. I pulled the pepper spray from my pocket. If I was going to die, someone was getting a blind eye for it.

My phone vibrated, and I picked up.

The muffled voice coming through the wall sounded crisp in my ear. "Miss Price, you have a delivery."

I leapt from the couch to the door in a ninja move and whipped it open. Sebastian stood blocking out the sun. A bouquet in one hand, his phone in the other.

"Hi."

"Hi." My word was a whisper. I cleared my throat. "Come in." I accepted the flowers.

He took in the boxes stacked against the walls. "Still unpacking?"

"It's been an unbelievable three days." The air gushed from my lungs.

"You look pale. Are those cuts on your arms?"

"I was in a drive-by."

"Sit." Sebastian pushed me in the direction of the couch and headed for the kitchen. He pulled open the refrigerator door and grabbed a bottle of water. "Is that a chocolate pie? You want a piece of pie?"

I started my story there, with the pies, and while I recounted my short history of counseling in Chincoteague, Sebastian shoved the flowers into a glass of water and returned with two slices of chocolate pie.

"So, one guy paid you a hundred bucks for having coffee with him and some lady brought you a pie and a fifty?" He bobbed his head. "It's good pie." His fork disappeared between his lips.

"Yeah." Blinking away the image, I went on to tell him about Adrian, his mother, my bad chakras and the details of my drive-by shooting.

"You're in over your head, boss."

"Tell me about it."

"Bad chakras are nothing to shake a stick at," he deadpanned.

I tossed a pillow his way, missing by a mile. "What do you think?"

"I think you should let this alone. Tell the sheriff what you know and let him handle it." He anchored an elbow over the back of his chair and stretched his legs out before him.

"I can't." I fell sideways onto the couch. "I literally can't. I'm incapable of letting things half this interesting go. I'll never be able to stay away."

"Why haven't you made an official report?" Sebastian's expression was unreadable, but I had a feeling he was gauging me.

"It happened fast. Getting shot at is disorienting. I left. I'll go to the station later. Not that it will matter. The local sheriff isn't exactly a case cracker."

"I want a look at the crime scene. You'll show me later?"

"Yeah." *Later.* How late was he staying?

"Which door is your bedroom?"

"Excuse me?"

"Is this a one-bedroom or two?"

"One."

He ducked his head. "How's the couch?"

I crinkled my nose at him.

"I'm staying. Don't argue. I know it's rude, but I'll take rude over dead any day. I leave you here alone and you're a goner."

"You're staying the night?" Claire would be so proud. I'd leave the couch part out.

"No."

Oh.

"I have the week off. Mandatory. They're looking into some…details surrounding the bust. After what you told me on the phone, I planned on spending a couple evenings on the island helping you figure things out, but someone made an attempt on your life this afternoon." His voice lowered an octave on the last statement. "I'm staying."

"Okay." A week? I didn't know if I wanted to celebrate or run away. A week of him seeing me without makeup in the morning, and dirty from cleaning the boathouse. Also, how would I keep Adrian away? I had no way to tell him I wasn't alone.

"I'll get a room at one of the inns I passed," he said, seeing my hesitation.

I shook my head. "No way. Every room on the island's booked by now. Pony Week's upon us."

He raised a serious eyebrow, but didn't ask. "I keep a few of my things in the truck. I'll be back in a minute. Tomorrow I'll make a trip home for more."

When he returned, I'd already texted Claire the entire situation.

Sebastian stopped inside my door and braced his palms against the doorjamb overhead. I shivered. Sebastian didn't look like a special agent. He looked like trouble. Dark eyes, messy black hair, olive complexion. His skin glistened with a thin sheen of sweat from the summer heat. His biceps bulged against the sleeves of a fitted T-shirt. He slung a duffel bag onto the floor. "I hear you're one hell of a swimmer."

"Says who?"

"Claire."

A million dollars said Claire wanted me to get Sebastian into his swim trunks and take secret phone pics for her. "I don't suck." A blush burned its way across my face.

"Let's go."

"Swimming? Now?"

"Sure. We can think this thing through while we enjoy a little sun, sand and surf." He rummaged through his bag. He came back with a pair of black board shorts. If he also found a volleyball in there, I'd lose my mind. Volleyball guys were mad sexy.

"Give me a minute."

Fifteen minutes later I had on the first suit I tried. Never mind the six others I tried before reverting to the first. I pulled on a pair of jogging shorts and a T-shirt to cover the bikini.

Sebastian sat on my couch smiling out the window.

"You know there's a lady with woodpecker hair watching your place from across the street?"

"It's Adrian's mom. She says she's making sure I'm working on his case." I climbed on the couch beside him and looked. "Where is she?"

"Behind the white bread truck." Sure enough, her red-sprouted hair popped into view. She was on the sidewalk staring at my window through the windows of a bread truck across the street.

"She's in serious stealth mode. Even brought her own binoculars."

Now that I had Sebastian in tow, I could almost guarantee she'd stay close. Her and every other woman in town.

"How'd you spot her?" I threw a beach bag on my shoulder and headed for the door.

"It's my job."

Sebastian ran into me when I stopped short at the top of the stairs. Sheriff Murray's cruiser angled in at the curb in front of Sebastian's silver Range Rover. Men and their SUVs. Freud would have a field day. The sheriff tore out of his car and stormed toward the steps. He slowed at the sight of Sebastian.

"Are you aware your new rental was shot up today? There's a crowd over there with conflicting stories, there's extensive property damage and your car has a flat." He crossed his arms over his chest and stared at my arms and face.

"I know. I was there." The words caught in my throat. A long arm looped over my shoulders. Sebastian tugged me closer, leaning my weight into him protectively. His cologne fought Sheriff Murray's rant for my attention. The perfect mix of sweet and spicy. Like Sebastian.

"I know you were there," the sheriff snarled, bringing me back into focus. "It's like you attract trouble. Were you planning to inform local law enforcement of the crime?" He scrubbed his face with both hands. "This is a lot of paperwork. Your parents are a wreck." He was losing steam. "Are you all right?"

"Yeah. I planned to call, but I wanted to install some added door locks at the apartment first." I tossed a thumb over my shoulder at the house behind me. "Then I crashed."

"Then I showed up. Hi." Sebastian extended his free hand to Sheriff Murray. "I'm Special Agent Sebastian Clark."

The two of them couldn't have appeared more different. Sheriff Murray looked exactly like the sheriff of a tiny, zero-crime town, which was to say more like a Boy Scout than anyone who'd ever dealt with real criminals.

The sheriff took his hand without enthusiasm. I could almost hear the wheels turning inside his head. I called in the FBI to do his job when I hadn't bothered to so much as report it to him.

"I have no choice but to assume that hit was meant for you. You're going to need to be careful. Maybe stay at your folks' house for a few days."

"I've got it covered, sir. I'm staying with her."

"How long?" He raised a graying brow at Sebastian. "Awhile."

The men exchanged silent appraisals.

I prayed the whole town wasn't hiding behind the bread truck.

When the cruiser's taillights disappeared, Sebastian slid his arm off my shoulders. "He's intense."

"It's not his fault. Next week is the pony swim. Tourists are pouring in and they're short-staffed with everything going on. Deputy Doofus isn't any help. Everyone's gear-ing up for the added headcount and now there's a murder. No one gets murdered here."

"Don't forget the drive-by." He opened his door for me to climb inside. "Point the way. And what is a pony swim?"

"Believe it or not, it's exactly what it sounds like."

We drove three blocks before we caught the only red light on the island. Sebastian turned the radio down while we waited. His eyes ran over my face and neck.

I pretended not to notice. Probably, he was judging my injuries from the drive-by. "Does it always smell like buttered seafood and fresh waffle cones on this island?"

"Only between noon and nine, then everything closes. During pony week it smells like fair food twenty-four/seven."

He pulled in a deep breath and exhaled. "Nice."

I chuckled. "Nice? This place is addictive."

"In more ways than one."

I turned my face away and smiled. A commotion inside the Dress Barn ruined my moment. The island wasn't exactly putting its best foot forward to welcome my friends these days. First the sheriff nearly flattens Claire, now people were shouting like heathens for no apparent reason with Sebastian in earshot.

"Stay the hell off this island!" A woman's livid voice shot through an open shop front.

Sebastian frowned and reached for his phone.

I stared wide-eyed as a big-busted brunette barreled out the door and climbed into a pickup truck. She sobbed loudly, all dressed in black. An arm reached into the sunlight and pulled the door to the shop closed. The Dress Barn was having a day like mine, from the looks of it.

Honk!

Sebastian put his phone in his lap and rolled through

the newly green light. "Something in the seawater or is this just your homecoming?"

"I'm starting to wonder about both."

We rode in silence to the guard gate at the national park. I showed my lifetime pass and the candy-cane-striped barrier rose, allowing us to pass. When the ocean came into view at the end of the tree-lined road, it hit me.

"Perkins told me Brady argued with a brunette the night he was killed. That lady was dressed in black. What if she was in mourning?" My palms itched to slap the dash. I missed a golden opportunity. Was it Mrs. McGee in the dress shop? "Shoot. I should've gotten her name."

Sebastian pulled his Range Rover into a space near the sand. He held up his phone to show a clear picture of her license plate. A sneaky grin curled up one side of his face. "I got you one better."

Nice.

SEVEN

I WOKE BEFORE sunrise. The sound of my shower set me into a panic. Through the width of one wall, Sebastian was wet and naked. In my bed, I was sweaty and gross. My bedroom window had stayed shut tight since Adrian's last visit. His parting words after his last visit weren't forgotten. Anyone with the smallest amount of motivation could get me. Until this mess was sorted out, I needed to invest in an air conditioner or at least an oscillating fan because that window was staying shut and locked.

Hair stuck to my face and neck, and my mouth tasted like an armpit. I slipped out of my pajamas and yanked a cotton sundress over my head. Thankful for the stash of travel toothbrushes with paste included, I jammed my finger through the foil and shoved one into my mouth for a good scrub. All those HR recruiting trips left me prepared for life without a bathroom.

Tiptoeing past the bathroom door, I stopped to listen. Puffs of shampoo and men's body-wash-scented air crept under the door, enticing me. Whatever he put on his body did things to mine. His cologne could be sold for hundreds an ounce. I'd pay.

The water shut off. I bolted out the door and down the steps, resisting the urge to twirl for joy. Sebastian was staying with me for a week. Un-freaking-believable. The tiny gray kitty ran after me. He weaved between my feet, mewing and purring. Early morning traffic dotted the empty streets. Fishermen, teachers and forest rangers made their way toward coffee. I joined them.

The cat followed me to the Tasty Cream door.

"I'll be right back." He tilted his head and crooned.

I floated inside, Fred Flintstone-style, on a tendril of cappuccino-scented air. Pure heaven. Standing at the counter, I couldn't work up hunger. My tummy bubbled over with butterflies. When a woman walked out of the restroom, I ducked in. Raking a brush through my hair, I jammed a clip in place and called it done. A little lip gloss and mascara later, I grabbed a bucket-sized cup of coffee instead and headed off to check out the damage at my office. New day, new problem. I'd get a good inventory of the damage to take back to Sebastian. He stayed to keep an eye on me, but I didn't love the reasoning. His time on the island shouldn't be more work for him. I'd only intended to pick his brain and see what we came up with for Adrian's defense. If I wasn't careful, the whole invitation would seem like a ploy to get Sebastian out here. Needy wasn't sexy. I could handle reconnaissance, and if Sebastian insisted on working, I'd suggest he drive me to the hardware store. I needed supplies too heavy for me to carry. I sent him a text to avoid a lecture about new island safety protocols. I was independent, tough and mostly fearless. He was on vacation, not assignment.

During my walk, the day bumped into full swing. Traffic picked up. Shop owners flipped signs in their windows. Breakfast scented the air. I tossed my emptied coffee container into a pretty iron trash bin and jogged across the street.

Sunlight filtered through the trees around the park beside the boathouse. A sprinkle of glass lay around the perimeter of my office. I lingered at the door, unsure if it was legal to cross the crime-scene tape. Sheriff Murray had already marked me as trouble. Ducking under the flimsy yellow barrier felt like a solid compromise. Behind me there was a steady beeping. A bomb? My poor office wouldn't survive a bomb. With imprisoned breath, I struggled to clear my head. A truck groaned and rattled outside.

Not a bomb.

"Mrs. Davis?" A man with a clipboard approached quickly.

"Nope." I peeked out the empty holes where windows once stood. I didn't see Adrian's mom for a change. She probably decided to stake out the hunk at my apartment.

"Mrs. Patience Davis?" The man in navy Dickies and a work shirt kept up his brisk pace.

When I didn't respond, he shoved his clipboard through the giant window hole. "Sign at the X. We'll be out of your hair in no time."

Unable to get past the fact someone had tacked Adrian's last name onto mine, I turned to the paperwork. New windows. I scratched my fake name on the line and smiled at the man. He waved an arm at the truck, and it settled into the spot where my car had come under fire. Having the Prius towed to the shop for a new two-hundred-dollar tire killed me. My dwindling savings account couldn't handle many more accidents.

"Who ordered the windows?" I stepped aside as two men hauled a giant pane of glass covered in blue tape through my door. Clipboard guy snapped the caution tape with an X-Acto knife faster than I could protest.

The clipboard guy glanced at his record. "Your husband." Then he gave me a look. I guess I was supposed to know what my husband was up to. He produced a whisk broom from his back pocket and cleared the frame of loose glass. The men carrying the new window grunted and shifted the glass into position.

How a fugitive could go about normal business like ordering windows and renting boathouses was beyond me.

The voice of reason told me to run far away from Adrian's case, but someone had tried to kill me. I couldn't let that go. I shuffled through debris from the shooting. Behind the office portion of the building, a fiberglass door provided access to the docks and boat parking. Or, as the exterminator called it, the rat invitation.

"Miss Price?"

I jumped, clutching my chest and wheezing. "Are you trying to kill me?" I scolded.

"No." The middle-aged man in coveralls and a tool belt looked as frightened as I felt.

"Can I help you?"

"I heard about what happened. I'm a handyman."

"Right." I took a few quiet breaths. "I left my name at the hardware store."

He frowned and then turned back toward the front door. "This is a good door. The frame's loose, though." He squatted to evaluate the frame. He looked like a handyman. I had witnesses if he tried anything funny…although the glass guys bantered and worked as if we weren't sharing the room with them.

"My name's Henry Franks." He pulled a hammer and a few long nails from his belt. "You can call me Hank. I like working on things I can fix." He whacked the nail once and it shot into place. Hank lined up another. I leaned on the wall near him.

"You don't have to do that." Normally workmen offered a quote or bid or something, didn't they?

"I don't mind. Like I said, it's nice to know how to fix things." Another whack. Another perfectly placed nail. He stood and lined up another. "Not like a marriage. People are harder to figure out."

"Don't I know it."

"Ever been married, Miss Price?"

"Please, call me Patience. No, never married."

He sighed and drove another nail home. "I've been married fifteen years to a woman who floats my boat. You know what I mean?"

"Sure."

"She's jealous, though. Worries every time I leave the house. I know she's been hurt before, but there comes a time you have to move on, right? It's hard loving someone like that. I'm too old to have a babysitter. Women are half the population. How can I avoid them all?"

"You can't."

"But I can't live without her. What can I do?"

"Broken hearts and grudges are my specialty." I didn't mean to say it. No, bitterness solved nothing. I still planned to pepper-spray the snot out of Adrian, new office windows or not.

Hank looked at me and nodded.

"Be patient, I guess. You can't force her to come around. She'll have to do that on her own."

He finished with the door frame and gave it a sturdy shake. Then he opened and shut the door a few times. He looked around the room. I grabbed a broom and dustpan, embarrassed he fixed the door to such a disaster. I had plenty of cleanup ahead of me.

Hank pulled a toolbox off the floor near the window. "Excuse me." The glass guys all bobbed their heads and kept working. I could barely smell the cleansers or paint over the gallon of Old Spice these men wore between them. My nose twitched in protest.

Hank stopped at the closed door and tightened the

screws on the locks and doorknob. "I know you're right, but it's hard. I want her to trust me. I thought moving would help. Maybe getting away from the city to someplace like this would put her mind at ease. It didn't. She yells or gives me the silent treatment all the time. She's an extremist, that one. Thinks every woman I meet wants to run off with me."

I stopped my broom and stared. He and the pie lady should get together. Then she could keep herself busy instead of worrying about her husband.

A few pushes of my broom and I sucked air. All the hoopla with the murder and Adrian and Sebastian moving in. I was losing my touch. Hank was Henry Franks, Mary's husband. Oh, jeez.

"You know, I think your wife loves you so much she can't imagine life without you. I know what she's doing is rough on you, but maybe remembering it comes from fear and love will help. I bet she's not mean and controlling, just a little insecure. If I was you, I'd ditch this mess—" I motioned around us "—head home and woo your wife. Make her believe there's no one else in the world but her."

Hank stood and looked me over. A proud smile improved his weary face. He shook my hand rapidly. "Thank you. Thank you so much. I'm going home right now." He pulled a phone and business card from his pocket.

He put the card on the counter, collected his toolbox and tipped his hat to me. On his way out the door he pressed the phone to his cheek. "Honey, are you free for lunch?"

Why wasn't I that good with my relationships? I'd run away from Sebastian this morning, and every time I thought of Adrian, I made plans to hurt him.

"All right, Mrs. Davis. You can pull off the tape and give them a good scrub tomorrow." Clipboard saluted me.

"Thanks."

The truck rumbled to life at the curb. Time to clean up. Again. Behind me, James Bond theme music played in my purse. Sebastian. I dug through the giant bag, promising myself to downsize to a purse I could find things in.

"Hey." I leaned on the counter to catch my breath. I'd nearly missed his call.

"Hey. You feel like shopping? I thought we might take a trip to the mall."

He didn't strike me as a mall person. Also, my funds were nonexistent. "We don't have a mall."

"On the mainland. I could use some new sunglasses. What if I buy you coffee?"

"Coffee?" I liked coffee. I lifted Hank's card with my fingertips. It was nice he went home to make up with his wife, but I needed massive amounts of help here. I hated that he left in such a hurry. What about the rat door? We hadn't even talked about my to-do list. "Oh, my word."

"You don't want coffee?"

"What? No." Under the business card was a neatly folded set of twenties. Four, to be exact. Hank had answered my request for a handyman, fixed my door frame and given me eighty dollars. "This guy came to work on my frame and paid me eighty bucks."

"I'd pay a hundred."

I laughed. "Shut up and come get me."

"Boathouse?"

"My office." I let the words envelop me. Tragedies aside, hope lifted in my chest.

"Come on." A horn beeped out front. I tossed my phone in my purse and locked up on my way out. He was already here. I could get used to that.

He looked past me to the windows when I got to the truck. "You've been busy today."

"Busy, busy, busy."

The Range Rover pulled a U-turn and headed over the bridge. An hour later Sebastian pulled across three parking spaces at the rear of the mall parking lot. He stepped out and rounded the hood of his truck while I watched shamelessly. Watching Sebastian was a guilty pleasure I'd taken full advantage of whenever he was in the office. I had to make up for lost time before he was gone again. He tugged my door open and reached for me. I looked him over. He wore giant mirrored aviators, a Hollister T-shirt, and jeans with flip-flops.

"What?" He towed me from the seat and beeped the doors locked.

"You look like my kid brother."

"I thought you were an only child."

It bothered me he didn't argue the brother part. "I am. I meant you look young."

"That's supposed to be a good thing." He peeked at me over the top of his glasses.

"But you're older than I am."

He wrenched the glass door to the mall open and stepped aside. "I blend. How do you think I got my nickname?"

His file called him a chameleon, but I assumed it was more about sneak attacks or sniper shooting than wardrobe. Disappointing.

Seeing Sebastian outside the office gave me all sorts of concentration problems. At least back at the FBI I had some idea of my purpose. In a mall with a grown man wearing flip-flops, my role blurred. One friend helping another? Two buddies buying new sunglasses?

"Which way to Starbucks?" Sebastian anchored his glasses in his shirt collar.

I lifted a finger in the general direction. "What do you

order? I have a theory about how our coffee order gives an implication of personality. The fact we drink coffee is factor one. Tea drinkers would frown at the entire concept of Starbucks. They drink tea to relax and unwind. I drink it to soothe a sore throat."

His pace slowed as I rambled. A crooked smile climbed up one cheek. "Sounds like you have a doctorate thesis going."

"Dr. Price. Never say never, I guess."

We got onto the escalator and I nodded toward the coffee shop. The mall brimmed with kids out of school for the summer and tourists catching a movie or getting in a little shopping. The aroma of Cinnabon rose up to meet us. The food court was my territory. I caught a spot in line for coffee and waited. I scoped out the level above us. If he wasn't with me, I'd make a trip to my favorite lingerie store, Sugar and Spice. Mom put an emphasis on nice underwear. One never knew when one might wind up in an emergency room. No one wanted to be there wearing tatty underpants.

"What can I get started for you today?" A perky blonde tipped her head from side to side. Her ponytail swung over her shoulders.

Sebastian bumped me with his elbow.

"I'd like a grande, non-fat, no whip, five pump, upside-down, soy, caramel macchiato."

She scribbled on the side of a green-and-white cup.

"For you?" the girl prompted Sebastian. He let his eyes run to the tiny blackboard propped on the countertop. She beamed, awaiting the masterpiece she could create for him.

"Small black coffee."

Disappointed, she turned away and got busy.

"Care if I join you?" Sebastian nodded in the direction of the lingerie store. My heart stuttered.

"You in the market for women's unmentionables?"

"You have to ask?"

"Grande, non-fat, no whip, five pump, upside-down, soy, caramel macchiato, and a tall bold." The barrista's enthusiasm waned at the end.

"She thinks I'm boring." We headed back to the escalator. "Is that what your coffee thesis would say about me?"

Yes. "No. I'd say you weren't complicated."

"Wonder what your order says about you, then?" He sipped his plain bold coffee. His eyebrows lifted, teasing me.

"I'd say my order tells people I know what I like."

"Or that you're a control freak."

I shoved my free hand in my pocket and bit back a line of retorts. We reached the store and stopped. "I can handle this myself. You can wait here." I looked pointedly at a nearby bench. No way was I buying anything beyond the pretty pink-and-white door with him beside me.

"No can do." He stepped past me into the brightly lit store. "I don't want to miss this."

A throaty noise escaped my lips. "Excuse me."

"I didn't really come for sunglasses." His arm snaked out to pull me inside. Coffee sloshed inside my cup. "I'm here for your protection."

The inside of Sugar and Spice looked like a cloud. Pale blue walls, white fixtures. Pink angel wings and teddy bears on display. A group of teens sprayed one another with perfume samples from the fragrance wall. The shop smelled of powder and flowers, all as light and inviting as the decor, which was not remotely ominous. Unless you feared clerks in white T-shirts and nylon wings.

"Can I help you find anything?" A brunette with silver wings approached me.

I turned to make a joke about security, but he was gone.

"Do you have any specials on your boy shorts?" My cheeks heated with the words. Sebastian's women probably wore black lacy things from the high-end store on the other side of the mall. The one where the clerks brought customers bottled water while they tried on strips of lace and ribbon. I turned in a circle, looking for my partner. He flipped through hangers near the window, flirting with a little redheaded angel. When we made eye contact, he narrowed his eyes at the lady piling boy shorts on one arm for me.

"Small, right?" She offered a stack of panties in varied colors and fabric. High on one biceps was a black band. The kind sports figures wore when they lost a player. I looked more closely at her. Brunette. Check. Big boobs. Check. Without the tears and screaming, it was hard to know for sure, but I had a hunch Sebastian had found our mystery woman. I turned to give him a thumbs-up, but I didn't see him.

"You look familiar. I think you knew my friend Brady."

The woman made an audible intake of air. Her mouth dropped open, and tears glossed her eyes. She threw the stack of underpants in my face and ran.

EIGHT

ANOTHER ANGEL WORKER dashed over to help me. Her ice-blue feathers rammed up my nose as we both fell to the floor collecting panties.

"I am so sorry. She hasn't been herself lately. I hope you won't hold this against Sugar and Spice. We can offer you a discount on your next visit here." A little silver name badge identified Blue Wings as the store manager.

"It's fine, really." I scooped a handful of super-cute underpants into my free hand. Trying not to spill my lidded coffee made the process tricky. "Here." I stacked my pile of floor panties in her hands. "I need to go check on her."

"Patience."

I jumped to my feet and ran in the direction of Sebastian's voice. My mind reeled. Why would she run? The manager called out apologies behind me. I waved a hand overhead. "No worries." Six elderly women in purple hats stood outside the store watching as I slid out around the corner into the mall. Masses of shoppers crowded the corridors. Business had picked up. Through the skylight there was the telltale flash of lightning. A storm was on its way.

"Patience." I jumped. The group of purple hats pointed across the hall to where Sebastian stood outside the ladies' room. If I didn't know it was his voice, I wouldn't have connected the voice calling me with the man leaning easily against the wall. He'd tucked ear buds in and tapped a rhythm on his thigh.

Before I reached him, the ladies' room door swung

open. An infinitesimal nod told me I needed to go inside. I grabbed the swinging door and slipped in. Stopping at the mirror, I set my coffee on the counter and dug in my purse for lip gloss. Face fixed, I washed my hands and fluffed my hair. When nothing happened, I bent down to look under the stalls. No feet.

Sebastian raised an eyebrow when I walked back out. "No one's in there."

He lifted his chin. "Wait."

I sipped the lukewarm coffee and looked at Sebastian a hundred times. Why did he think she went in the bathroom? Why had she run? What was going on?

I opened my breath to tell Sebastian I'd had enough shopping when the bathroom door sucked open. A woman with a silk scarf tied over her hair and around her chin swept out. Oversized white sunglasses hid her face, but her red nose said she'd been crying. Sebastian pushed off the wall in a saunter and maneuvered through the crowd with ease. It took a minute for me to catch up. I glanced over a shoulder at the bathroom door. She must've been standing on a toilet.

"How'd you find her?" I edged up beside Sebastian.

He smiled. "You're like my bumbling sidekick. Ever thought of being an agent?"

"Oh, sure. I kept an eye out for bumbling agents when I was recruiting. Can't find enough of those."

"You did good. You really never considered being an agent?" He nudged me with an elbow.

"No. Now, are you going to tell me how you found her selling women's underwear?" I was curious, not crazy. Agents wore Kevlar for a reason. And that didn't sound like fun to me.

"I had a buddy run her plate. I used that to get her address. She lives in an apartment, so I contacted the landlord. He told me where she works. I called the store. Got her schedule. Her name's Tara Wilkins, by the way. You should ask her about the fight she had with your victim the night he died."

"Wow. All I did this morning was watch windows get installed and listen to Hank complain about his wife."

"At least you got paid."

"Yeah. I made eighty bucks getting my door fixed."

Sebastian slowed his pace and I followed suit.

"Why didn't you tell me what we were up to?" I asked. "I have a feeling that exchange could have gone a little smoother with some warning on my part." I planted my feet and waited for an answer.

"I'm just seeing what you're made of, boss."

What was the proper response to that? Whatever he thought about me, if it involved me becoming an agent or chasing bad guys into darkened warehouses, he was out of his mind.

"Why do you think she ran?" I returned my focus to the woman ahead of us.

"Why does anyone run? She's scared."

"Of what?" Was she guilty? Did she know the killer? Think he sent me?

"That's a good question. Looks like it's time you find out."

The woman took a side exit into a small parking lot and broke into a run. I recognized her truck from the island and sprinted for it, overtaking her in the last ten yards. She stopped. I spun in victory, blocking her driver's-side door.

"What do you want?" she asked. "I don't have anything. I didn't do anything. I don't know anything."

"Tara, my name is Patience Price. I'm a counselor from Chincoteague. I saw you the other day and wondered how you're doing."

Her expression softened. Confusion set in. "You want to give me counseling?"

"No. I mean, I will, if you want, but I'm trying to figure out what really happened to Brady. I don't believe Adrian Davis killed him."

"Why not?" She scanned the parking lot, wringing her hands.

"Why did you run when I mentioned Brady?"

"I don't know. I mean, he was murdered and you show up at my work asking about him…that can't be good, right?"

I shook my head and mashed my lips together. How had she gotten to the point in her life where a simple question led to fleeing work in the middle of her shift?

"Who were you fighting with at the Dress Barn?"

Her eyes went saucer wide. "You saw that?"

"It's a small island."

Tara shifted her weight from foot to foot, looking at the truck behind me. "I wanted to go to his funeral, but she said no."

"Who?" She looked paranoid. Maybe I misread her anxiety.

"His wife." Tara looked at her feet. "It was stupid of me to ask. I didn't think she knew about me, so I approached her to ask for the details on calling hours. She went nuts."

"His wife knew he was having an affair?" She hadn't said *affair,* but I put it out there. She nodded.

Intriguing. Maybe little Mrs. McGee was mad enough to cause some damage after all.

"Do you know Brady's business partner, Perkins?"

"No."

"He says he saw you fighting with Brady the night Brady died. What were you fighting about?"

"He told me he'd leave his wife. He said it all the time,

and I wanted to know when. Soon is not a date. I'm not getting any younger. A woman's only got so many good eggs."

"Eggs?"

She tilted her hips at me and tugged her purse high on one shoulder.

"Oh." Good grief. "So you gave him an ultimatum?"

"Yeah." Her jaw worked back and forth.

"That's got to be frustrating." I looked around for Sebastian. "Were you mad enough to want him dead?"

"What? No. I loved him." Tears sprung up and rolled over her cheeks. "We had plans. Talk to his crazy wife. She threw me out of the store, nailed me with a high heel." Her hand stroked one elbow and I thought of the scuff on Mrs. McGee's heel. She'd need something bigger than that to kill him, plus a step stool.

"Did Brady ever mention anyone else who might've wanted to hurt him?"

"Brady wasn't what you'd call a people person. You know?"

I knew.

"Hey, what about his partner?" Tara said. "That guy's a certifiable slimeball. He was always trying to get more money out of Brady. He tried to cheat and scheme every penny he could out of him. Between that Perkins guy and his wife, Brady never had a penny to spare. I had to get a job here to help save up. We were going to get a place somewhere far away from here." She wiped her nose on her wrist.

"I thought you didn't know Perkins."

A shoulder lifted and fell. "I didn't know him *personally.*"

I stepped aside, biting my tongue. Tara was a flip-flopper. If selling women's panties fell through, she might have a future in politics. She didn't know Perkins when I asked, but she knew *about* him when it suited her. She ran when I mentioned her murdered ex-boyfriend. I couldn't help wondering how much of what she said was true. One hundred percent true anyway. "If you ever want to talk." I handed her a business card from my purse. "We can meet here. You don't need to come to the island if it's too painful."

She climbed into the truck, keeping an eye on me. "Sure."

"If you think of anything else that might help us find out who really killed Brady…"

She nodded.

"That went well." Sebastian appeared at my side and I whacked him in the stomach. An eight-pack met my hand like a brick wall, ruining the effect I'd hoped for.

"How do you do that? Where did you go?"

"I was around. So now we know Brady's partner was a sleaze working him over for money. Plus his wife knew he was cheating. I'd say we found solid motive for both of them and we know both had access to him on the night of his death. Of course, so did Tara."

"What about the means? He took a blow to the head. What was the murder weapon?"

"Let's go find out." Sebastian clapped me on the back and directed me toward Neiman Marcus, where he bought new Ray-Bans on his way through men's accessories.

"You did want new glasses."

My phone buzzed and I grabbed it. I scrolled through a slew of texts and messages while Sebastian steered me to his Range Rover. "My car's ready. Damage to my new office, thousands. One new Prius tire, two hundred dollars. Life on Adventure Island, priceless."

He wrenched the door open and shook his head at me. "You're cute when you're being weird."

"How about when I'm chasing down suspects and questioning them about murder?" I climbed in and waited.

"That—" he braced his palms against the roof over my head "—was very sexy."

When he folded his body behind the steering wheel, I filled him in on the rest of my texts. "My parents are worried about my safety. The sheriff says I still need to fill out some kind of paperwork about the shooting. The insurance company wants to come take pictures. My car is done. That's two hundred bucks."

"You mentioned that."

"Lucy, the girl doing my old job, needs to know where to find the number for the company who provides coffee to the break room."

"Wow. I had no idea your work was so important." He grinned and pulled onto the road. "What do you think about Miss Sugar and Spice as a suspect?"

"I think she's grieving and afraid of something. She threw a stack of underpants at me."

He chuckled. "I saw that. You think she'll call you?"

"I don't know, but I can't believe Mrs. McGee knew Brady had a mistress. No wonder she didn't look as distraught as I expected her to."

"You like the wife as the killer?"

"No." I hated to admit it, but I didn't see her having killed him. Mistress or no mistress, if he was providing that level of shopping, he was a keeper. In fact, maybe the fancy shoes and bag were apology gifts for sleeping around.

"What are you thinking about?" Sebastian looked at me. One wrist lay over the top of the steering wheel. He could've been lazing on a couch instead of zooming down the highway.

"Louboutin and Marc Jacobs."

"Friends of yours?"

"I wish. Can you please drop me off to get my car?"

He slid his new Ray-Bans over pretty brown eyes and turned up the radio. I sent a text to my replacement about coffee and to the insurance adjuster agreeing to meet him in the morning at the boathouse. We crossed the bridge back to the island and a weight lifted. Whatever was happening, it was on my turf.

"Don't sneak off again tomorrow morning. I want to come with you to meet the adjuster." He threw a palm up between us. "I want to make sure he is the adjuster, not someone up to no good."

My brain declared I was a full-grown, fully capable woman. My internal coward refused to argue. I shut my mouth and nodded.

Sebastian decided to do some digging on his own for a while. He wanted to see what kind of record Perkins had. We agreed to meet later. I'd go home. Clean up. Rest. Ponder.

"Here you go, 007." He shifted into Park.

The island mechanic worked from a pole barn in his backyard. Mills Westley had gone to high school with me. He was the kind of guy who picked his nose and stuck the findings under his desk. From the looks of things, it was in the genes.

A kid with bushy red hair and a finger up one nostril walked onto the porch when I slid out of the Range Rover.

"You drive the white car?" He twisted his finger knuckle-deep.

"Yep." I squeezed a dollop of hand sanitizer onto my palm in preparation for entering the facility. Who knew what this child had already touched. "I got a text saying my tire was on."

"We never had a car come here that was shot before." He examined his finger and then wiped it on his overalls.

"Hey there, Patience." A bigger version of the kid ambled over the gravel driveway toward us. He tugged the kid against his side. "This here is my oldest, Mills Jr. Shake her hand, son."

Yikes. I shoved my fingers into my back pockets. "I've had a cold." I turned my head and coughed against my shoulder. "Wouldn't want to get you sick."

Mills Jr. shrugged.

"Sorry I had to charge you so much," Mike said. "We made a trip over to the mainland last night to pick up the tire. It would've cost more to have it delivered. Taken longer, too."

"Oh, you didn't have to go out of your way for me. I didn't realize."

He rubbed his grease-black hands onto a rag. "It's no problem. Not too often I get vehicles in here involved in crimes. You sure do have the town talking."

"Right. I'm back for five minutes and things fall apart. I was hoping to be useful when I got here."

He turned for the office area inside the pole barn, and I followed. Everything smelled of WD-40 and motor oil. A card table with a metal money box sat beside a receipt book. My car shined beside the table.

"I hear you're helping people around here already."

"If you count buying the boathouse and keeping the hardware store in business." I handed him the rest of the cash in my wallet.

Mills followed my gaze to the Prius. "I hope you don't mind I washed it. The kids were playing in the water and I thought, *What the heck*."

"Thanks."

I rubbed a ready wipe around my steering wheel before pulling away. Without making a conscious decision, I drove to the boathouse and pulled the Prius into the spot out front. There was no one on the street, no unusual sounds, no traffic. My thumbs drummed against the wheel

Something big was going on. Sebastian knew it. I knew it. I needed to find a way to convince Sheriff Murray to look into the case further. Only one problem, I didn't have any evidence yet. I had a sleazy partner who saw Brady fighting with his girlfriend and a girlfriend who said his partner was pinching him for more money. Also, I couldn't forget the wife with high-class taste who knew about the girlfriend. It was all very dramatic, but none of what I found so far equated to a smoking gun. The sheriff already hated me. I couldn't approach him until I had proof for my theories.

The facts whirled inside my head, trying and failing to fit together. Maybe a walk through the office would shake something loose. I looked around again and weighed the odds someone would be back so soon after a drive-by. No one had bothered the place earlier when I stopped in. Sure, the glass guys and Hank arrived right after I did, but a bad guy wouldn't have known they were coming. I shook my head. I'd only be a minute.

I unlocked the office door and checked for rats. The door frame didn't budge when I walked in. A nice improvement. I shut the door so no one would walk in on me. At the sink, I wet some paper towels for the windows. I'd clean and think. The blue tape peeled easily off the new glass. It was nice of Adrian to send windows. He didn't have to.

I smiled as I worked. Seeing Mills Jr. was kind of fun.

He was his father's son. If I had kids, I imagined they'd be more like my mom than me. She never worried, never stressed, didn't make lists and plan everything until she wanted to scream. I hoped my kids would be like her.

The island did things to my brain. Thinking about children when I hadn't had a date in two years was ridiculous.

I took a step back to admire my work. Not a single sign of the tape. Gorgeous. I almost hated to hang curtains. The view through the park and up Park Street was magnificent. Bright green leaves on two-hundred-year-old trees lined the park's edge, and a circle of sunflowers taller than me stood near the old slide. I used to play inside a circle just like it, weaving flowers into head wreaths for my mother. A punch of color from wildflowers accented the lawn where the wind had planted them. The park air was sweet with fresh blossoms and tangy with the briny harbor so near. A red convertible crawled past. The woman in the passenger seat snapped a picture of the man in the driver's seat. They both smiled, mouths open, heads thrown back. Their bumper had a Virginia Is For Lovers sticker on it.

I turned away from the disappearing car and caught sight of a white van headed my way. This vehicle pulled up beside my car and stopped.

Panic rushed through my chest, saturating me in endorphins. Abductors drove vans like that. Raper vans. I grabbed my keys and hunkered down. Stupid. Stupid. Stupid. What was I thinking? I touched the phone in my pocket. Who to call? Sebastian? My mom? On instinct, I dropped to the floor and army-crawled around the piles of my old windows. If someone came here to hurt me, I'd slip out the rat door for a quick escape. Maybe it was a good thing I hadn't boarded it up.

I held still and listened. No car doors. No squealing

tires. Were they waiting for me to leave? My car was sitting out front. Maybe keeping the dock was a good idea. I could walk to the beach every morning and paddle a raft to work every day. Good exercise, and I'd live longer.

I waited a few more minutes for footsteps that didn't come. Feigning brave, I scooted on my knees toward the window and lifted my head. No van, and no gunslingers in sight.

Then, a shock of red hair across the park caught my attention. I rolled my eyes in relief. Mrs. Davis's lurking might have scared the van away. Excitement rolled over me. Maybe she'd gotten a license plate number. Sebastian could run it for me, just to be sure it didn't belong to a convicted manic. I dusted off my knees and walked to the door. With one strong tug, I got a good look at the wild expression on her face.

Fear.

She looked as if she'd seen a ghost. I took a step toward her, watching my back, scanning the area. She waved her hands in front of her, and made the sign of the cross over her chest. Something awful was happening, but I didn't see what it was. I took off at a sprint down the cement walk toward her.

"No!" she wailed.

My heart spiked. What was happening? My feet pounded the ground beneath me, closing the space, needing to make sure she was all right. I yanked my cell free from my shorts. I knew who I needed to call. Whatever was happening on this island was bigger than a mistaken murder charge. I needed Sebastian—fast. Hopefully his brush with the Mob had nothing to do with my office in the crosshairs, but one way or the other, I'd landed myself in the middle of something huge. I doubted the island sheriff could help me.

KABOOM!

Pain shot through my ears. Air forced me back a few steps and heat washed over my skin. My car exploded at the end of the path, thirty feet away. The new windows behind me shook and burst. Shards of glass filled the air and sliced through my skin. Flames shot out of my car windows, and acrid smells of burnt upholstery assaulted my nose. I choked on black billows of smoke rolling in the air. Melted rubber brought tears to my eyes. Every breath I pulled in seared my throat and lungs. I couldn't see Mrs. Davis anymore.

"Help." I coughed until my chest ached. My head swam. "Help." I pressed my cheek to the cold cement sidewalk. Tears blurred my vision. It hurt to shut my eyes, but it hurt more to keep them open. My ears popped. It was as if someone threw a blanket over the world.

"She's cut up. A few burns, I think. No. She wasn't in the car. She wasn't far…" Mrs. Davis's voice filled the hollow space around my clogged-up head.

"What happened?" I choked the words through burning lungs.

"The white van." Mrs. Davis's face was six shades paler than I'd ever seen it. If she looked in a mirror, she'd climb back in her tanning booth for a year. "They shoved something under your car and took off. I was afraid to get too close, so I stayed to warn you, but you went running toward the road. Why would you do that?"

"Ugh." Blood whooshed between my ears. Everything I had hurt, and it smelled like my flatiron when I forgot to clean the loose hairs away.

Sirens approached. I hated that I was going to die and hadn't even had a shower. Who knew what sort of underwear I had on. My poor psychic mother would be devastated she didn't see this coming. Red flashed over my eyelids, and fatigue swept through me. Adrian would go to jail for murder.

I hated leaving things the way they were, but darkness stronger than any determination I had left overtook me.

NINE

A STEADY RHYTHM lulled me. I could make out a few voices nearby, but I couldn't understand the words. My body felt both light enough to float and also made of sand. Drugs. I hated the woozy tingle over my body and the muddled thoughts pain relievers delivered. I took a mental inventory of my faculties and appendages. Everything seemed to be where it belonged, but my face burned despite the goose bumps on my arms.

Whoosh. Whoosh. Beep. Whoosh. Whoosh. Beep.

The scent of rubbing alcohol hung in the air with a sidekick of iodine and Band-Aids.

Whoosh. Whoosh. Beep.

Crap.

Memories of Mrs. Davis's face popped into my mind. I felt around with a heavy hand. Metal guardrails. Stiff sheets. My eyelids peeled open, and I sighed as relief and frustration beat me back against the pillow. Good news. I was safe in a hospital. Bad news. Someone had tried to kill me—again.

"Honey." Mom's face hovered over mine. She swept hair from my forehead.

I grimaced.

"Oh, Patience." Her voice croaked. "You were so lucky. Your burns are minor."

Burns. I swallowed. My throat felt like knives scraping across hot ash. "What happened?"

"Someone blew up your car." Mom pushed her bottom

lip out. "Your father's helping clean things up over there. We assume that's what you were doing. You never could leave a mess alone."

"Mrs. Davis?" I rasped.

"We hear she called nine-one-one, but she wasn't at the scene when the sheriff arrived. He's been looking everywhere for her. You don't think something happened to her?"

Tears blurred my vision. She'd seen everything. She would've told the sheriff if she could have. "She saw." I tugged Mom down to me. "What if…"

"Shhh." She placed a finger to her lips. "We'll talk about this in two minutes. Save your voice for the doctor."

"Miss Price?" A chipper voice arrived on the *clickety-clack* of heels. "I'm Dr. Marshall." She extended a hand to me.

Mom excused herself from my side. "I'll be right outside."

"You are one lucky lady." Dr. Marshall worked methodically, checking my pulse and bandages. Her fingers traced the line of my scalp beneath my hair. She looked into my eyes with a penlight. Touching beneath my chin, she began to make small talk.

"I admire you moving here to start over. It takes real tenacity to start a new business on a small island." She gave me a warm smile. Probably she wanted to take my mind off the fact that I could've been killed, but I couldn't stop wondering where Mrs. Davis ran off to or what she saw.

"I'm a workaholic," she continued. "I understand the drive it takes. The way it pushes you to stay longer, work harder, accomplish more. There's never a point where it's enough, is there?"

She sighed and set the stethoscope to her ears. Listening to my chest, she pressed on with her soliloquy. I wasn't even certain she was talking to me any longer, but we were alone in the room. "I had a husband in medical school. He gave me an ultimatum. What could I do? Choose a man over a future? I had a life to live. Who wants to be so-and-so's wife? Or Jr's mom? I mean, I want those things, but why can't *I* be something and so-and-so is my husband. Why couldn't my kid be Dr. Marshall's son?"

I scooted up in bed, willing the cotton in my head to dissolve. "We have to find someone who gets us, I think."

"Exactly." She moved the IV stand away from the bed and unplugged the drip from my hand. "When I find the right guy, he should understand my work is important to me."

"He should. Wouldn't you?" I rubbed the mark left by the needle.

"Of course. I'd never expect anyone to stop doing something they love for me. Our careers are part of who we are. It's like saying, "I only like the left side of you. Please remove the rest.""

I laughed and it hurt. My hand went to my throat on instinct.

"Here." Dr. Marshall handed me a Dixie cup of lukewarm water and a prescription. "These are for pain. Your burns are minor but they'll hurt, and so will your head and throat from the smoke. I don't see a reason to admit you, so I suggest you head home and get some rest. You were really lucky today. Apply cool compresses to the burns on your arms and face if they bother you and stay out of the sun for a few days while the burns heal. Drink plenty of fluids."

I swung my legs over the edge and braced my hands beside my hips. No dizziness. With my feet firmly on the ground, she led me by an elbow to my parents outside the door. Dad had a sports bottle with him. Dr. Marshall motored to the front desk without a formal good-bye. Just when I thought I might make a girlfriend on Chincoteague, she ducked out.

"Good bedside manner," I told my mom.

She petted my head and took me to the desk to pay. My heart spiked. I'd never had a medical bill without insurance before. According to research, medical bills, not credit card debt, were the number-one reason for bankruptcy in the United States.

"You're all set, Miss Price." The girl behind the counter pushed a piece of paper my way. "Sign here for discharge."

I scribbled my name. "You'll bill me?" I hadn't given my address. Sure, it was a small island, but that was no way to do business.

"No charge."

I narrowed my eyes at the girl, prepared for a fight. If she handed me money, I'd lose it. "No charge?"

"Pro bono."

I frowned. "I can pay my own medical bills." Maybe. Hopefully. Pro bono was for people without insurance or a steady income. People…exactly like me. My eyes slid shut a moment in frustration. I used to have a dull, predictable life complete with paycheck, and government health care benefits were exceptional. I had no idea what an emergency room visit cost without insurance. Further protest dissolved on my tongue. My head hurt.

"Sorry." The receptionist gave me a wide, toothy smile. "Doctor's orders."

"Come on, honey. You need to rest." Mom steered me out the door while I fumed. I used to have a steady and predictable life. Last week. I rubbed my forehead. Somewhere across the bridge life made sense.

DAD SLID INTO the backseat of the VW bus. Mom buckled me in like an infant and drove me home.

"Guess that new tire was a wasted two hundred bucks," Dad joked.

Mom glanced at me.

My tire. I let my head fall back against the headrest. "My car."

"Yep. Those brand-new windows were a bust, too." Dad snickered.

"Marvin," Mom scolded.

"Too soon?"

"Yes." We groaned in unison.

"Can we talk about something else right now?" I asked. "I need time to process."

"Well, I could use some more flyers at the Pony," Mom said as she pulled up to my apartment and shifted into Park.

"You want me to make flyers for the store? For pony week?"

"No. I need more of *your* flyers. They're all gone. Went like hotcakes." She tipped her head back and forth. "I was wrong. It happens."

"They literally disappeared." Dad leaned forward, resting his elbows against our seats. "The stack kept getting smaller—then, *poof.*"

"Gone." Mom nodded.

"Poof?" It might've been the smoke inhalation, but I didn't know what they meant by *poof.*

"Word around town is you're the best thing going since Dr. Phil." Pride erased the worry on Mom's face.

"What?"

"You're all the rave. Having a flexible meeting place so islanders can be at ease was smart, Patience. You're finally thinking outside the box. The anonymity is priceless."

"People stop me at random, tell me things and leave money behind." I barked a laugh and grabbed my throat.

"They were paying you for your time. We're really impressed with your ingenuity. Way to take what you love and fit it to your circumstances. Very well done, honey."

My phone buzzed with a text. I didn't recognize the number.

You shouldn't have sent the FBI guy away.

Dad pulled my door open and leant me a hand. "Everything okay?"

"I'm not sure."

My knees wobbled a bit. I moved toward the stairs. Kitty waited outside the door at the top of the steps. Whispers floated around from behind the house.

"Who's there?" My gravelly voice cracked as though I'd smoked a pack a day since kindergarten. Dad jumped beside me. The pepper spray was locked and loaded in my grip.

"No one." A foursome of teens rolled into view. Two boys and two girls shuffled from the backyard to face us. The girls looked sheepish, arms wrapped around their tummies. One smirk-faced boy raised his palms as if I might arrest him. The other shoved his hands into his back pockets and avoided eye contact.

"What are you doing lurking around this building?" I asked.

"We heard the place was haunted." The blondest girl shot me a pleading look.

"Ah." I nodded. Motioning between the two boys, I added, "And you were showing the girls how brave you are? Perhaps scaring them silly?" I looked at the girls for confirmation.

They nodded.

"Well, I hate to ruin your moves, fellas, but the place isn't haunted. I live here."

They looked up the steps. I remembered daring my friends to climb the same steps. Whoever got the highest won. The loser had to do the winner's bidding.

"Nothing to see here," I told them.

"Well, it looks haunted. Things move in there."

They pointed at the darkened windows of the empty art studio downstairs. I shook my head. Dejected, they moved on.

"It could use a new coat of paint." Dad's eyes were bright with ideas. If he had it his way, the old gray clapboard would be purple by morning, trimmed in green or gold, covered in latticework and petunias.

"We're going home to get you some dinner. When will your friend be back?" Mom asked.

"Later." I shoved the door open and Kitty ran inside. "No, Kitty. You guard the porch." I scooped him up and put him back on his roost.

Dad made the circuit through my place, tugging on windows and checking behind doors. Assured all was empty as it should be, he joined Mom at the car.

"Give us half an hour. Maybe less." He waved from the passenger seat.

Well, if anyone was watching for me to be alone, that was their cue. My phone buzzed and I squealed. I needed to meditate.

"Hello?"

"Miss Price," Sheriff Murray growled. "Once again you're the center of a crime and yet there's no report. You didn't stop here after your date last night as promised. Now you owe me two reports."

"I'm so sorry. I completely forgot yesterday and then today…" *I was out looking into your case.*

"You're trouble, Miss Price. This kind of thing isn't new for you. I'm not the same deputy you drove bananas ten years ago. I'm the sheriff now and I expect things done properly. You will be at this station first thing tomorrow, and you will complete these reports. No excuses."

"Yes, sir."

"I'm sorry this is happening to you, Miss Price." His voice softened. "I cannot keep you or anyone else safe if I don't have the facts, though. I need to know what you know. Fill out the reports."

"I'll be there in the morning."

I disconnected and scrolled through my phone for Sebastian's number. In true chicken fashion, I texted him.

Car bombed today. I'm okay. Car is kablooey. Dinner with my parents?

Good grief. Dinner with Sebastian and my parents.

I sent one more text to my insurance agent. He'd really want to get those pictures now.

My head fell forward. I dragged myself to the bathroom and started the water for a hot bath. Every muscle in my body ached. I hadn't unpacked any bubble bath, so I squeezed some Pantene into the running water. Before peeling off my disgusting clothes, I checked the front window. The VW bus wasn't back yet. Neither was Sebastian's silver Range Rover. I had time to scrub the fear off me. With any luck, my teeth would stop chattering by dinner. If not, my dad would be on standby with the sugar water.

The bath was hot. Steam clouded the mirror. I slipped into my bedroom for something cotton, clean and comfortable to take with me to the bathroom. My fingers slid over the wall toward the switch and stopped cold. A breeze tickled my skin and stopped my heart mid-beat. The window. Sheer curtains ruffled in the wind, reaching into my room.

My throat swelled. I backed up, banging my heels into the baseboard. I crept in reverse to the bathroom and shut myself inside. With the water running, I could make some noise without being heard, but so could whoever lurked outside the door. The window over the tub was too high and too narrow to slip through. Not to mention the two-story drop beyond it. If only I'd unpacked. Somewhere in the living room sat a box with bath candles, a lighter and all my aerosol products.

My mind was sliding on ice. Weapons. Aside from Sephora and feminine hygiene, I had nothing. I twisted the tiny doorknob lock between my thumb and first finger, careful not to make any noise.

Footfalls came to a stop outside the door. I scooted into the corner. A tap came against the door. Someone needed to show up. Anyone. My apartment was like Grand Central Station all week. Where was everyone when I needed them?

Tap. Tap. Louder this time.

A whispered, "Patience." The doorknob turned. They had a key? I didn't even know the bathroom door had a key. I grabbed my flatiron with both hands and held it overhead. Sliding into place behind the door, I waited. If I was going down, someone was getting an injury.

The door creaked open. The whisper came again. "Patience." A tall, murky reflection showed through the clouded mirror. I screamed and brought the flat iron around to connect with the intruder. In a flash, the iron landed on the floor beside me. My hands twisted behind my back. A wide arm held me fast. He moved in and kicked the bathroom door closed behind him.

I screamed and thrashed against his grip.

He released me and jumped away. I spun around ready to fight.

Adrian's eyes bugged out. He had one long finger pressed to his puckered lips.

TEN

"Jerk!" I turned off the water and held back tears. One heart could only take so much. Mine heaved and flopped in my chest.

He turned on the water in the sink and ran a cloth under the water, then held it in my direction.

I swatted it from his hand and shoved my head into the bowl instead, splashing cool water over my face.

The water ran over my cheeks, masking a few escaped tears. I never had emotional outbursts in Norfolk. With as little attitude as I could muster, I patted my face dry. It hurt. A few patches on my face matched a ripe tomato.

"I didn't mean to scare you. I called your name."

"You whispered my name like a serial killer. What are you doing here? My parents will be back soon."

"Yeah. In half an hour. I heard."

Exasperated, I twisted the towel in my grip. "You didn't answer my question. Why do you keep attacking me?"

Adrian lazed against the wall, crossing his arms over his chest. "I'm not attacking you. I'm hiding from my mother. I don't want her in trouble for knowing where I am. Plus, I'm watching you until your parents come back."

My eye twitched. Yes. He wouldn't want to get his mother in trouble. I pressed a fingertip to the corner of my eye. "I don't need a babysitter."

A tuft of dark hair fell over his forehead. He shoved it aside. His hideout lacked hair products. "You kind of do."

I kind of did.

"No. I don't." I matched his body language, crossing my arms and staring across the narrow room at him. "My parents will be back any minute. Sebastian will be here all week. You can go."

"Where's your secret agent man, anyway? He picked a fine time to leave you, Lucille."

"Listen. Don't quote stupid song titles at me. We aren't doing that." I hated the history we shared. Eighteen years on an island with a limited number of kids made the friend pool pretty small and the dating pool exclusive. We grew up on *Scooby Doo* together, guessing who those meddling kids would foil each day after elementary school. Adrian was as much a part of me as the island, or my parents, or myself. "He went to look into something. Obviously, there's something bigger going on here than an ex-college football star killing a fisherman. Even if he was stewing over the humiliation of being beat up in public."

"I wouldn't say I was a star." His smirk melted before the last word concluded. "He didn't beat me up. I had him. Someone has to have it on video."

"His wife told me everything. Don't worry about it—you're older now, probably out of shape."

His jaw worked, and his lips rolled in over his teeth.

I moved on. "Everyone I talk to seems guilty. They all have motive, and means is easy enough at the harbor. Although I keep forgetting to ask the sheriff what the murder weapon was." I settled back against the sink. "He's always yelling at me."

Lightning flashed outside the small bathroom window. Heat lightning. I wished the storm would arrive already. The air grew thicker every day, and winds and temperatures climbed, too. Mother Nature had a show of her own brewing. I could use the release. She probably could, too.

"What's your deal with that guy, anyway?" Adrian's

shoulder flinched. Not much, but I noticed. "He's all glares and attitude. Doesn't seem like much fun."

I lifted my chin in Sebastian's defense. "Well, we can't all be wanted for murder. Besides, he can be fun. Sometimes." Maybe.

"Yeah. He looks like a real down-to-earth guy."

"We're trying to help y-o-u."

"Thank you for that." He squirmed a little, readjusting his nonchalant stance. "Are you guys...?" He let the inference hang between us.

"That's none of your business."

He smiled. His ridiculous dimple mocked me. "You're not. I see it in your eyes. You're not, but you don't want me to know that. Why? You want to make me jealous?" He rubbed his chin and guessed again. "No—you want to be with him, but you haven't told him."

"If you're so intuitive, I don't see what you need me for."

"We used to be good together."

I guffawed. All the wrong things came to mind.

My screen shuttered lightly against the front door. Adrian tensed to spring.

"Settle down, hero. It's Freud."

"How many men do you have guarding you?" His voice hitched and fell.

"Not as many as are trying to kill me. Freud's a kitten. He wants in." I nodded toward the window over my shower. "Storm's coming."

"Not yet. He'll be dry another night." Adrian relaxed and looked me over. "So, who's doing all this? What are they afraid of? What do you know?"

I slid my backside up onto the counter beside the sink. "I don't know anything, but I guess I'm looking in the right places. Someone's worried enough to try to kill me twice in broad daylight. On Chincoteague."

"I bet they aren't from the island. Islanders know this place has eyes."

Adrian straightened and anchored his palms to the back of his head. "What do we do now?"

For the first time, I felt bad for him. He was at the center of something he couldn't get involved in. Hiding out when there was so much to do sounded like torture.

"You do nothing. Keep hiding out wherever you've been. Where have you been?"

"Downstairs."

I mulled that over. "Fine. It's good to know my neighbors. Now, get out. I want to take a bath. If I don't get in soon, my parents will show up before I have a chance to get out of the tub."

"I'll watch."

The towel I kneaded between my fingers landed in his face. "Get out!"

"I meant I'll watch the door for your parents. Not you in the tub." He snickered and slid out into the hall.

I yanked the door wide. "Where did you get a key to this door? I locked the door and you waltzed right in."

"No key. The lock's broken. I could fix it for you."

"Gah." I shut the door. "Don't fix it. Don't touch it. Don't touch anything. Call me when you spot my parents."

I waited to see if he'd open the door again. He didn't. After a few minutes, whistling began. I worked up the courage to wrap up in a bath towel, undress beneath it, climb into the tub, pull the curtain and toss out the towel. The skin on my forearms screamed at the touch of the water. I laid my arms on the tub's edges and blew cool air over them.

With much trepidation, I risked a dunk ear-deep to wet

my hair. When I came up, the Pantene-scented air reeked of ash. One little car bombing and a lifetime spent using products seemed a waste. My blow-dryer had nothing on a good car bomb for drying and damaging hair. I peeked through the space between the shower curtain and wall. Still alone. Door secure.

No whistling.

"Hello?" I cleared my sore throat. This couldn't be happening. My protection was abducted while I had a soak. "Hello?" The second time I tried, my throat wimped out.

Why didn't I have a bay window over my tub instead of a tiny rectangle six feet up?

Whoever blew up my Prius could've hurt Adrian and planned to take me, too.

The crazy person who failed to kill me twice might believe the third time was the charm.

Fear launched me from the tub. I yanked my terry-cloth robe from the wall hook and crept to the door. The lock was broken. Was there no justice in the world? Tiny windows. Busted locks. Men. Fail. Fail. Fail.

Smoke drifted up from under the door. Anger boiled in my blood. Why was this happening? I imagined physically attacking the person out there trying to burn my apartment down. I couldn't run. Couldn't hide. No weapons in the bathroom.

But I did have the element of surprise.

Tying the belts on my robe in a knot at my waist, I swallowed my pride and closed my eyes. I only had to make it to the front door. Thirty feet, tops. A finger of smoke curled up from beneath the door. Flat on my tummy, I pressed my cheek to the linoleum. There were no feet or shadows on the other side of the door. Pulling in a deep breath, I gave myself a tiny pep talk. If I made it out the front door, the entire island population would materialize and save me. Thirty feet. I stood up and swallowed. Then I prayed for my aching throat. I needed to scream like a banshee in 5…4…3…2…

The door ripped open in my grasp. I ninja-jumped into the hallway, feet wide, chin up. "Ahhh!" I screamed and ran until two other screams answered me. Halfway across the living room, my parents clutched one another around a tiny bowl. Mom held a candle under a miniature roll of hay.

For a long awkward beat we all stared at one another.

"It's PTSD," Dad whispered to Mom. She nodded infinitesimally and waved the hay around over the bowl.

"I do not have post-traumatic stress disorder. I thought someone was trying to burn down my house."

They exchanged a glance.

"It's sage, sweetie. You know."

"Oof." I slumped onto my couch, tucking the robe ends over my knees. "Sage. Yes, of course." Mom burned sage to rid rooms of negative energy. My room reeked of it for three years in high school. What she called hostility, I called puberty.

"How'd you get in?"

Dad's brows climbed his forehead. "You left the door unlocked."

"Right." I let my gaze drag over the room, half-expecting to see Adrian pressed inside a cabinet, holding a finger to his lips.

"Are you hungry?"

"No." My face hurt. So did my pride. I didn't appreciate needing to be looked after like a child. "My head's still kind of woozy."

"The doctor gave you a little something in the IV for pain. She said you needed to rest." Mom looked more concerned than I knew what to do with. "Why don't you finish your bath? We'll set up for dinner. Maybe you'll feel more like eating then." She circled the room, waving her smoking sage.

A little added smoke wasn't what I needed.

"Has your FBI friend called? Where'd he go?"

I went for my phone and checked the messages. Two from my old office. An insurance adjuster rescheduling his visit in light of my new claim. One from Sebastian. On my way. Sit tight, boss.—S

"He's coming," I said.

Mom smiled.

I FELL ASLEEP on the couch after my second bath and woke in my bed to the smell of coffee. My head felt like someone had wrapped it in a blanket. Sunlight streamed in through my locked window and a little fan in the corner blew strands of hair over my cheeks. Someone had bought me a fan. I squinted at my nightstand. Seven o'clock. I hadn't slept ten straight hours since infancy. The sweaty glass of water on my nightstand looked like heaven. I levered my tongue off the roof of my mouth and sipped with care.

"Hey." Sebastian leaned against the door frame, mug in hand. His faded U.S. Navy tee clung in all the right places. So did his dark-washed jeans. What a way to wake up.

"I've been checking on you."

I discreetly checked my face for drool or eye gunk and shoved a finger full of hair behind one ear.

"Thanks." I scooted up and took the coffee. Securing the sheet over my torso, I winced.

"It's the smoke inhalation. You need rest and hydration. Does your head hurt?"

I nodded. The motion made my eyes bulge.

Sebastian disappeared. He returned with a pair of

extra-strength Tylenol. "I don't suppose you intend to rest today."

"Nope." I tossed back the Tylenol and chased them with coffee. In fact, the more alert I became, the more I wanted answers.

"I looked into our suspects yesterday. The girlfriend's had a rough life. Looks like she's trying to straighten out but struggling. Tara's had her share of misdemeanors, including a drunk-and-disorderly last year. I don't see the motivation for her to kill him. She didn't stand to gain any money from it. Jealousy, maybe, because he hadn't left his wife? I don't know. She feels like a long shot. The wife has enough credit card debt to surpass as a third world country. She's in the red on a dozen cards. Her joint bank accounts with the victim don't reflect the debt. They have nice nest eggs growing. Makes me wonder if Brady knew about her debt."

"How about life insurance?"

"Couple hundred grand on each of them."

I let out a low whistle. "There's her motive. If she doesn't care about the girlfriend, I know she cares about the money."

Sebastian narrowed his eyes. "I looked up those shoes."

"The Louboutins?"

"Yeah. A couple hundred grand wouldn't last her long. Like putting a Band-Aid on a leaky dam."

"Would it last long enough for her to find a new honey pot?"

"Maybe. You rest. I'll keep digging." He took my empty cup and left the room.

I slid out of bed and into my favorite white terry-cloth robe. Heading for the bathroom, I called over one shoulder, "Want to come with me to talk to her?"

"The little missus?" he answered through paper-thin walls.

"Yeah, I don't like her. You know she's a marine biologist? She has a degree, and my mom said she's been protesting local fishermen getting too close to shore."

A few minutes later I looked as good as a tomato could. I eased into the living room. Sebastian sat in front of my laptop eating cereal. He spoke before he saw me. "I sent her address to my phone," he said. "Sea-life lover married to a fisherman sounds like a problem to me. Let's go. We can be there and back in time for lunch."

"She lives on the island. No GPS necessary. How'd you know I was in the room? I tried to be quiet." I stuffed my bare feet into old Chucks and searched for my purse.

"You always smell like peaches."

My already red cheeks burned hotter. "It's my conditioner. Whoa." I glanced at my phone. "Claire texted about seven hundred times."

He sent me a sheepish look. "I might have called her after you called me."

"Uh-huh." I began deleting her messages without reading them. Then I sent her a text, took a picture of my face and sent that, too. "Wherever she is, she'll like the last one. I look like I forgot to wear sunscreen for a year."

"She's coming for lunch."

"When? Today? No. She shouldn't make the trip again already. She just left here. She does too much for me." Emotion crushed my chest. She was the best friend I'd ever had. My heart tugged.

Sebastian watched me. "I think she's just coming for the fries."

"Shut up." I smiled and my lips cracked. "Crap. Let's go. Wait till Mrs. McGee gets a look at me." I dabbed gloss onto my lips as I walked.

"What do you mean?" He beat me to the door and held it wide. I passed under his arm.

Freud lay sunning his tummy on the stoop with a tea-cup of milk and what looked like oatmeal. Poor kitty.

SEBASTIAN INSISTED ON driving the quarter mile to see Mrs. McGee. Something about hydration and heat and exertion. All I heard was I was a baby who needed a sitter. Hard to get a man's attention when he thought I had one foot in the grave all the time and looked like a tomato.

When we pulled up to the curb, Mrs. McGee was climbing out of her pearly white Lexus. She hauled a rainbow of crisp new shopping bags out of the trunk.

"Mrs. McGee?" I caught up with her as she was struggling up the walk under the weight of the packages. "Can I help you with those?"

She startled, then stopped. "What on earth happened to you? Chemical peel?" Her bottom lip pressed out.

"Car bomb."

She shrugged and continued up the walkway. "What do you want today? Did you see Perkins?"

"I did. I also met Tara Wilkins."

Mrs. McGee unlocked her door and nodded me inside. I kept a close eye on her. I wished Sebastian had joined me, but he said he wanted to keep watch on the perimeter. Entering a place that needed him to watch the perimeter put me on edge. "How long did you know Brady was seeing Tara?"

"Who are you?" She leveled a hard look at me. "Did you tell me you were FBI last time you came? Why is the FBI so interested in my husband's death?"

Classic deflection. I'd hit a nerve. She didn't plan to answer my question.

I glanced out the window. Sebastian leaned against

the side of his Range Rover, looking like he was the most dangerous thing on my island. No sign of the easygoing guy who wore flip-flops to the mall. His fitted black tee emphasized his muscles. The new dark glasses looked more like a warning than an accessory. He nodded as if he saw me looking, though I was on the other side of a now-closed door, peering through a lacy curtain.

That nod gave me a boost. I could do deflection, too.

"Tara said Perkins was dirty. She also said Brady and Perkins fought about money. I got the impression Perkins might've been pinching your husband."

Color drained from Mrs. McGee's face.

"I grew up here. I've known my share of fishermen. None of their wives shop at Burberry." I stared at the bags at her feet.

Mrs. McGee shifted from foot to foot, and her eyes swept the room. I inched closer to the door. She dipped her head low. "Perkins is shady. I don't know what those two were up to. I don't care. Brady and me got along fine. He let me shop and I let him run around with that trailer trash. I pretended I didn't know what he was up to. Brady returned the favor."

"Do you think Perkins had anything to do with Brady's death?"

She tugged on the hem of her shirt and rubbed the back of her neck.

"Mrs. McGee, if you know something about your husband's death, you have to tell someone. Otherwise, Adrian Davis is going to be put away for a murder he didn't commit. The murderer, whoever it is, is going to go free. If you know something…" As much as I wanted to threaten her, and to point out how someone tried to kill me twice since starting my investigation, I didn't want to scare her. Maybe she was safe.

She flitted past me to the door, tripping over her bags on the way. She couldn't get rid of me fast enough. "You need to go now. I've told you what I know. You need to talk to Perkins about Perkins." Swinging open the door, she stood off to the side against the wall. Her voice cracked. "Don't come back without the sheriff. I don't know what you're up to. Go."

I stepped onto the porch, catching sight of Sebastian. Mrs. McGee didn't miss him, either.

"I want to help." I worried the sight of Sebastian might give her the wrong idea.

"Go." The door whipped shut and locked with an audible *snap*.

Sebastian dropped me at the Tasty Cream three minutes later. Claire's car was outside my place. She stood at the counter talking to Mrs. Tucker.

"I'll be back in ten." Sebastian leaned across my seat and pushed the door open.

"Where are you going?"

"I saw someone outside the McGee place. I want to go back and check on her. If they're watching the house, she could be in trouble."

I slid onto the pavement and said a prayer it was only Mrs. Davis lurking outside the McGee house.

My fingers gripped the door to the Tasty Cream and released. Right beside Claire stood my high school nemesis. Karen Holsten, choosing a flavored soda water. A rock the size of my head twinkled and glistened on her ring finger under the fluorescent lighting. She hadn't gained a single pound. Somehow she was more beautiful. No acne. Tailored sundress. Peep-toe pumps. One look at my worn-out Chucks sent me across the street to my place in a hurry. I planned to grab a pint of ice cream from the freezer and eat in front of my window until she left. How long could it take to buy water?

Hustling across the street it occurred to me she might walk out and see me running away. I picked up the pace. Freud wasn't on the stoop. I wrenched open the screen and fell into the safety of my apartment.

Before the door clapped shut behind me, an arm wrapped around my waist. A hand clamped over my face, pinning my lips and crushing my nose. The urgency in the movement sent ice through my veins. This wasn't Adrian. This man was mad. His body was fuller. His breath stank. The air around me vibrated with tension. Before I could get a look at his hands for some clue to identify him, a cloth bag was yanked over my head. The man dragged me through the room and mashed me down into a chair. He tied my arms behind my back and whispered low against my ear. "You're getting in my way."

ELEVEN

THE SPACE INSIDE what I came to believe was a pillowcase moved slow and hot like lava over my brain. Every second seemed like forever. My muscles were rigid and aching with fear. If my current abductor was the culprit who shot up the boathouse and bombed my car, what would he try next? I mashed my lids tighter, erasing that thought. This situation had hope. Sebastian would soon return and discover me missing from the Tasty Cream. Then he and Claire would find me here.

Heavy footfalls circled my chair like a shark waiting to attack. Both wrists burned with my effort to free them. The inside of the pillowcase smelled like fish. I suppressed a gag crawling up my throat. Leaning my head to the side shifted the stinky fabric, which afforded me a measure of fresh air. As the folds of material moved away from my shoulder, cooler air rose up from the ground into my shroud. Through the small space, a pair of black work boots came into view and stopped.

The awful whisper began again. He leaned into me, bracing one palm on each side of my head. His hot breath scalded my face through the fabric. "You need to go back to where you came from. This is island business, my business, and I want you out of it."

Silence.

Half of my brain wanted to bawl out, "I promise! I'm leaving right now. Tonight. As soon as I get this fish bag off my head. I'm out!" The rest of my infuriating, inquisitive mind wondered who he was. As if it mattered. As if staying was an option. That same idiotic part of me wanted to stamp my foot and declare, "This is *my* island, buddy. Not yours. You owe me major money for shooting up my office, and you owe me a new car and a new bonus tire."

Tears streamed over my cheeks in frustration. Anger and fear coiled inside me, and a growl wedged in my throat. Images of busting free like the Hulk ran through my mind, but I wasn't the Hulk. I was a wimpy twenty-nine-year-old whose arms still ached from carrying boxes up my steps four days before. If I had my pepper spray or my laptop, I'd give him something to remember me by. His island. Ha.

"You're all out of warnings, Miss Price." The *s* and soft *c* in the words slithered on his tongue. Misssss Priccccccce.

"I don't know what you're talking about." I held my breath, waiting for a blow that never came.

"You know what you did. What you're doing." A finger poked hard against my chest, grinding into my sternum until I whimpered. "Leave this alone."

"I haven't done anything." My mouth didn't know when to quit. "You're the one who needs to stop. You're the one who should leave *my* island. We don't put up with murderers here."

He ran. I waited. His feet disappeared first. Light jogging steps coursed over the shag, down the short hall and ended in my room. What did he have in there? The windows rattled. Something was happening. Did I scare him off?

CRASH!

My lamp? The window? I imagined his boots busting out the window. A series of small thuds and muffled grunts came from the direction of my room. Not good.

I tugged against my restraints with full force. Nothing but pain.

He hadn't tied my legs. I stood as far as I could before I lost my balance and fell on my face. The carpet stank like fifty years of mildew. I inched forward so that the chair was eventually left behind. I sat on my knees and put my head on the floor until the pillowcase fell onto the carpet. I shook it free and sat back on my haunches.

Somewhere in my apartment, a man screamed and so did I. Before I could orient my harried thoughts, Adrian slid headfirst down the hall from my bedroom and into the living room on his back. I crawled against the wall and pressed my back to the front door. Was he the one who tied me up? Was that why he whispered? My legs were too limp to stand. We locked eyes. What if the town was right all along and Adrian had duped me again? He rolled onto his stomach and pushed up to his knees. I scrambled to stand, failing miserably but refusing to give up. He wouldn't hurt me. Would he? One hand on the doorknob behind me, I froze. Adrian fell facedown. My grip eased on the knob. What happened to him while I escaped the chair? I looked out the window to the street below. No Claire. No Range Rover. On the floor, Adrian groaned.

One side of my bindings gave an inch. I wriggled and tugged hard against the twine until I worked it loose. Then I painstakingly looped the material over the doorknob and pulled. With a great tear, the ties gave way. I pried a replica boat oar off the wall in the kitchen and walked toward Adrian. I hated those oars when I was younger. Every house on the island had one somewhere. In case the homeowners forgot they lived in a marina town, I guessed. Mom had a set of blue-and-white oars in her kitchen, a wedding present from her mother. Who knew someday a little oar would come in handy?

"Get up. Now, Adrian. I mean it." I inched closer, keeping my right leg back in case I needed to kick him in the head or nether regions.

"He got away. I'm so sorry." He spoke against the shag, not bothering to roll away from the stink. Something was wrong.

"Are you hurt?" Sounds from the scuffle made their way into my cyclonic thought stream.

"He zapped me." Adrian rolled onto his back and his arms fell wide.

"Zapped?" Aliens came to mind. That's how messed up I was.

"Tasered. Call the sheriff." Adrian cringed and rubbed his chest. "Don't tell him I'm here."

"Sheriff Murray?"

"Yes." He rolled his face toward me. A cut along his cheek was smeared with blood. "Tell him someone broke in and tried to hurt you. He got in and out through your bedroom window."

I went for ice and a dishtowel. "Here." I handed the ice to Adrian and looked for a first-aid kit. Seated on the floor beside him, I dialed the sheriff and let it ring on speaker while I went to work on Adrian. As a full-grown tomboy, I knew a little something about first aid.

The call went to voice mail. I redialed.

"Did you get a look at the guy?" I dabbed ointment on Adrian's cut.

"Not a good one. He had a ski mask. Can you believe that? It's friggin hot in here. So, clearly he's crazy. I tried to sneak up on him, but he zapped me. How about you? Did you see him?"

I shook my head. "Just his shoes."

He snorted. "Well, he was my height, a little heavier than me, and he had a stun gun. When he raised it, I

almost wet my pants. In the dark, it looked a lot like a
gun gun."

I pushed his hair off his forehead and laid my hands
in my lap to keep from touching him more. "I'm glad he
didn't have a *gun* gun."

"Are you okay?" He rolled onto his side and touched
my wrists with featherlight fingers. "My turn." He took
the first-aid kit and hit Redial on my phone.

"This island has gone to crap since I left."

"Most things do." He blew softly over the cuts, working the remaining twine away from my skin without hurt-
ing me more. "I'm sorry." His deep gray eyes searched
mine. They looked like a vortex of heartache I wanted to
fall into, but I'd never do that again.

"It's not your fault. You saved me." My lips tried to
smile and failed. A million suppressed emotions marched
on my heart. Adrenaline still coursed through my veins
from the fear.

In true moronic, muddled-brain-from-recent-trauma
fashion, I leaned. He leaned. We leaned.

"Hello?" Sheriff Murray huffed through my phone
speaker. I snapped back to reality, snatched up the phone
and hopped to my feet.

"Sheriff Murray, this is Patience Price. I need to report a break-in."

When I disconnected a few minutes later, my limbs
began to tremble. I slid down the wall to the floor and
wrapped my arms around my knees. "He's on his way."

Recovered from the zapping, Adrian came to me. He
rubbed his palms over my arms and massaged my hands
in his, careful to avoid my aching wrists. His voice was
low and steady. "You're okay. I'm here and I won't leave
you alone. I promise."

A tear crept over the edge of one eye and rolled out,

betraying me. Being seen so shaken unnerved me. Never mind that someone kept trying to kill me.

"I left because I was afraid." His quiet, uncertain voice startled me.

I pulled my hands from his and dared a look at his face. "When?" Fear wasn't an emotion I thought him capable of. With his jaunty gait and easy smile, Adrian didn't know a stranger. He never walked away from a dare, or a challenge. As far as I could remember, the only thing he ever walked away from was me.

"After high school." For the first time, his eyes left mine first. "My mom begged me to go to college. When I got the full ride to Miami to play ball, I tried to work out a way you could come, too. The more I ran through the scenarios, the more it didn't work. You wanted to take off with the few hundred bucks we saved and leave. Your goal was to skip town any way you could. My goal was to marry you. I couldn't do that on a high school education and seven hundred dollars."

My breath caught in my throat. Adrian had wanted to marry me?

"I couldn't take care of you. At the time, I thought the answer was a good job, as if I already had everything else we needed." He laughed softly.

I stood and walked to the door. I'd wait for the sheriff at the curb. I flicked the dead bolt open and reached for the knob. Maybe I'd walk to his station. What was taking so long anyway? Why hadn't Claire or Sebastian come yet?

"You should leave before the sheriff gets here." I didn't look back. Emotions pooled in my tummy and chest. There were too many feelings to sort out and no time.

First, I had to fill out a police report and relive the most recent horrors of my life.

"Stop running away." A huge hand landed on my shoulder.

I spun on him. "Me? Me! I'm not the one who runs away."

"You were."

His stable, reasonable voice made me want to kick him. Why did he do this to me?

"You wanted away from your parents so bad you'd take off with seven hundred dollars to see how far you could get. I don't know how you remember it, but I remember you crying. A lot. You wanted your parents to understand you and they didn't. You wanted them to have regular jobs and buy clothes at stores. That's not who they are."

My cheeks burned. Humiliation set my chest on fire. I'd forgotten. Or rather, I hadn't thought of it in years. Adrian was right. I had been embarrassed by them. Worse, I had guilt to go with it. Guilt for feeling embarrassed because I loved them so much. I hated that I cared about what they wore or what they did for a living. I wanted them to push me and they never did. I needed structure and rules and security, but they gave me endless freedom and cared more about my horoscope than my GPA. Adrian knew that. He knew everything.

"Why didn't you tell me you applied to colleges? I could've done that, too. I have felt so completely naive and stupid for a decade. How did I not think of going to college? I had the second-best GPA in our graduating class."

I hated missing the obvious, and I'd missed that one by a mile. Not that my parents talked about college. The entire concept of college eluded me until I realized Adrian had a real plan and I was more like my parents than I could accept. Running away was a child's plan, but I didn't see it as that. All I saw when I was with Adrian were roses and sunshine and love. Hey, all you need is love, right? And a boyfriend, but mine bowed out.

"How did I not know you planned to leave me for something better? I was supposed to be the smart one. The logical one. I made the plans. I wanted to be normal, but I was so far from that I couldn't see it." A decade of emotion ripped through me, unleashing more tears than seemed humanly possible. Adrian's pretty blue eyes went dark and stormy. His expression became guarded.

"I wanted normal, too—I just didn't want to run away. I wanted to be something you'd be proud of. The night I told you about Miami, you creamed me before I could ask you to come with me. In hindsight, it would have failed horribly, but at the time, I had tunnel vision."

I ran a fist under my nose and blinked. Could I have been the problem? Imagine that. Humbled and deflated, I stepped toward him. Without looking into those eyes, I laid my head against his chest.

"I waited for you to call so I could tell you I left the money in our account. I hoped you'd buy a ticket and come see me." He pressed one huge palm against my back, bringing me closer still.

"It's still there. I couldn't bring myself to use it." A laugh slipped out. I'd thought of a million ways to punish him with the money. Sending him seven hundred dollars of manure was my favorite, but shipping and delivery costs in Miami were crazy.

"I was all in," I said. "You had a backup plan."

"In hindsight, I should've told you I applied to schools, and I should've encouraged you to do the same, but back then it felt like betrayal. You were happy with your plan, and I wanted you to be happy."

I wiped my eyes, letting his perspective settle in. He was right. If he'd told me, I probably would've felt betrayed and I'd have made sure he knew it. I had a temper back then.

Curiosity reared its ugly head, ruining a nice moment. I turned to look at him.

The look on his face shook me. A crease ran between his brows. His lips were tight. The corners of his eyes crinkled with worry.

"Why'd you come home? You were out and doing pretty well—at least according to Google—but you came home."

The familiar cocky grin emerged. "You did an Internet search on me?"

"Answer."

"I like it here. Who wouldn't?"

"And?"

"I planned to run for mayor. Past tense."

"What? You don't think this town will elect a murderer for mayor? Mayor murderer has a certain ring to it. I can head your campaign."

"No, thank you. That would be suicide."

I pushed him away, smiling. Red flashing lights lit and dimmed outside my window.

"Patience!" Claire's hysterical voice screeched from the distance. Boots thumped up the outside steps. A car door slammed.

"Go," I whispered, flashing Adrian a warning look.

He hesitated, looking between my face and the window.

"Go. It's the sheriff. I'm okay. Claire's here."

His mouth tipped down on the corners. "I won't be far."

One quick nod and he disappeared. The door burst

open and Sebastian stared past me to where Adrian had vanished.

Sebastian brushed past me to my bedroom. I followed him with my heart in my throat. I didn't want him to find Adrian.

"Were you alone a minute ago?"

"Why? Did you see someone?" I pretended to look around the room. When I glanced back to see if he bought it, his steady brown eyes leveled on me. Uh-oh.

"Miss Price?" Sheriff Murray called my name and I hurried into the living room to report a break-in.

THREE HOURS PASSED before everyone left. My parents closed up shop and came running when they heard. Mom fixed lunch out of what little I had in my kitchen. Mrs. Tucker hauled milk shakes and fries over from the Tasty Cream for everyone. Dad ran for anything Mom needed to make proper sandwiches and sides. The sheriff took his time asking five thousand and twelve questions. Twice. His hands held a tremor I hadn't noticed before. He was grayer than the other sheriffs we'd had. With all the excitement this week, maybe he should consider retirement before he had a stroke. Turned out Deputy Doofus was known as Deputy Fargas, though the former fit better than the latter in my opinion. After he examined the crime scene, he suggested I get an alarm system and better window locks. A regular Einstein.

Sebastian hovered, listened and roamed. He was trained to see things I missed, so I kept one eye on him. He made nice with my folks and mingled with the sheriff and deputy, asking questions and gauging their responses. The sheriff made it clear in severe attitude alone that he didn't need any help closing the case. I smelled a spitting contest on the horizon.

Now that someone other than Adrian had broken in, I planned to nail every window shut. I'd call a locksmith and a security system sales rep. Annoying ex-boyfriends were one thing. Being tied to a chair and threatened by a guy with bad breath and a stun gun was something else entirely.

The moment I shut the door behind my parents, the last of my guests to leave besides Claire and Sebastian, Claire exploded. "What the hell is wrong with this place? You made it out to be a fairy-tale land of sunshine and pretty ponies. This island is a nightmare. That creepy sheriff nearly ran me over an hour after we got here, and how many times has your life been threatened since then? Patience, that was only five days ago. You need to come home. Stay with me while you look for work. You can use my closet for an office. I'll rent the apartment next door for a closet."

"I'm fine." I wished I had counted every time I said that and didn't mean it. "Wow. Only five days?"

"Yeah." She looked heartbroken. "Please, come home."

"It's not like this all the time. Whatever is going on right now isn't normal. Something big is going on. Aren't you even curious what it is?"

Her expressionless face turned left and right.

"Why do you think the sheriff's creepy?"

"He's got beady little eyes under those big caterpillar brows, and he's jumpy. Shouldn't sheriffs be calm? You know—more like Sebastian."

"The sheriff's old. His hands kind of shake. Plus he hates me."

"I noticed you didn't tell him about your chats with Perkins or Mrs. McGee and her gorgeous accessories."

"I didn't want him to tell me to stop snooping. I need to talk to her some more. I don't like her. She knew about the girlfriend and looked the other way so she could keep shopping. That's weird."

"I don't know. I'm thinking those shoes smelled better than a fisherman after his shift."

"Oh, hey, listen to this. Adrian came back here to run for mayor." I twisted the lid off a peanut butter jar and climbed onto the couch beside her. I hadn't been able to eat with everyone crowded around staring at me. She looked at the jar and I dug a finger in. "Politics get people pretty riled up. I wonder if Brady was involved in local politics?"

"Honey, you're grasping at straws. I don't know if Adrian killed that guy or not, but I do know you aren't safe here. You need to leave with me today."

"He didn't do it. He's trying to figure out what's going on here, too. He knows this place, and he loves the people, even the crazy ones. Running for mayor proves it. Why would he mess up a dream like that?"

"Are you in contact with Adrian Davis?" Sebastian's voice boomed from the other side of my paper-thin walls. He'd been nailing my window shut.

"What? No. No. No. Of course not. No."

Claire's eyes popped. I shoved a quiet finger to my lips and smudged my face with peanut butter. She dug into my jar and wiped a fingerful on my nose.

"Bad." She mouthed the word.

"It's very quiet out there." Sebastian stuck his head around the corner. "Something I said?"

"Hmm?" I wiped peanut butter off my nose and jammed some in my mouth.

"What do you think, Sebastian?" Claire asked. "Do you think this could have to do with politics?"

"Doubtful. Big political scams are usually centered around money. From the research I've done, it looks like this island's broke. Most businesses in Chincoteague rely on tourist season to get through the year and the draw of the wild pony swim every July makes up a good portion of that. Quite a few residents are transient, spending only half the year here. I don't see a political scandal at the core of this."

"Brady McGee wasn't," I pointed out. "How's the window coming?"

He appraised the two of us. "I'd prefer it if you let me sleep in the bedroom tonight."

Claire elbowed me in my ribs.

"You could take the couch," he finished.

"What about the front door?" The couch sat under my front window, two feet away from the door.

"Too visible. If I wanted to get in here, I wouldn't climb the steps sitting on Main Street. The bedroom window is in a shaded part of your rear yard, with tree coverage, a porch roof to climb on and it can't be seen from the street. I'd prefer the intruder meet with me if he tries this again."

"Me, too." I shivered and sucked another hunk of peanut butter off my finger.

"Can you stop doing that?" He eyeballed my finger.

"Why?"

"It's disgusting."

Claire laughed into my new pillow, her gift to me. The shiny gold fabric was just what my sad little apartment needed. She said she saw the pillow and thought of me. When I saw it, I thought of her, too.

Sebastian went back to my room.

"Come with me to talk to the mayor," I asked Claire.

"Uh-uh. No way, Nancy Drew. You need to stop this now."

"Please?" I pleaded. "Pretty please? I have to know. Sebastian says this isn't a political scheme because political schemes are about money. What if it's a political

scheme about keeping Adrian out of office? Maybe Adrian
was set up? What if whatever's going on here is related to
our elected officials and they don't want anyone new in
office poking around their shady dealings? It's not like
the mayor's going to do anything to us at his office. Let's
see if the mayor's hiding something."

"Sebastian? How long will you be?" I called.

"Half an hour. Why?"

"Claire and I are going for a walk to talk a little. Girl
stuff."

"Drive."

I'd forgotten he didn't like the idea of me walking
around in broad daylight these days.

I stuck my tongue out at the wall. "My car was bombed.
Want me to take the Range Rover?"

"Right." He chuckled.

"He has a nice laugh," I whispered.

"Thank you," he called after us.

Man, these walls were thin.

Claire grabbed her pillow tighter and cracked up.

"Your mom left you some wheels out front. Take
those," Sebastian said.

I yanked the curtain open, praying my mom didn't
expect me to drive the hippie bus. She didn't. "She left
her golf cart?"

"Ah!" Claire popped her head up beside mine and burst
into hysterics. "That is so fabulous. Please, I beg you, let
me take your picture in it at the stoplight? For my desk,
please?"

I grabbed my bag and headed for the door, fresh out of
words. The lavender cart with Purple Pony personalized
plates and deep plum seats mocked me. I closed my eyes
and pretended it was an open-sided Jeep instead.

"If you're not back in thirty minutes, I'm coming after you," Sebastian warned.

I hurried out the door, refusing to acknowledge the way his words shuddered through me. Weirdest week-long first date ever.

Not that it was a date.

Like most everything on the island, the town hall and mayor's digs were packaged inside an enormous turn-of-the-century home. I drove the cart into a tiny lot behind the elaborate brick number at the center of the island. White pillars twenty feet high stood out front of the large wooden door. Inside we walked an ornate green-and-cream floral carpet runner over heavily lacquered plank flooring.

I tapped the bell on a desk older than the house. The town librarian shuffled out to meet us. Her tightly curled white hair and signature horn-rimmed glasses on a silver chain made me smile.

"Miss Alice! What's my favorite librarian doing at the mayor's office?"

"Staying busy. I only volunteer now. Had a heart attack in oh-five."

"Oh." How much more had I missed? "I'm sorry to hear that, but I'm really glad to see you. This is my friend Claire. She's visiting from Norfolk. We wondered if the mayor's available?"

Alice smiled. Her skin was more translucent than I remembered. When she hugged me to her, her body felt like little more than bones beneath her simple brown dress. Claire shook her hand and we moved together toward Mayor Hayes's study.

"Mayor Hayes, you have visitors." Alice bowed out, leaving us to talk.

The mayor leaned his golf club against the wall and

walked from the tiny green to his desk to have a seat. "What can I do for you two lovely ladies today?" His round face and sharp features announced his American Indian ancestry, even if his name didn't.

"We wondered if you could tell us who is running against you in the election this fall."

He looked between us. One hand stroked his shiny mahogany desktop. "I'm afraid I've done my terms. This election is an open book. So far as I know, Adrian Davis is in the running, as well as Beau Thompson. There could be others, but those two were the most vocal about it. Of course, now I suppose Beau's a shoo-in." He took a deep breath but said no more. His gaze wandered over Claire, lingering on her hands, folded primly in her lap.

"Do you think Adrian killed Brady McGee?" I asked, jumping in feetfirst. What I did best.

"I don't know what to think. It's hard to understand why an innocent person would run. If he'd come to me, I would've represented him."

His walls were covered in degrees from Stanford and Brown, surrounded by certificates and photos of him with President Reagan and a lot of others I didn't recognize.

"I'm glad to know that," I said. "I don't think he's guilty. I think he loves Chincoteague and wants to know what's going on before anyone else gets hurt."

"I hope you're right. I'd be honored to see Davis take over my seat in office."

My knee bounced a mile a minute. Small talk escaped me. The only thing on my mind now was Beau Thompson. "Thank you for seeing us. I know you're busy." It took effort not to look at the tiny golf green. "It was nice to meet you."

"Anytime, ladies. Claire?"

We stopped moving.

"Yes, sir?"

"If you're ever in need of a tour guide. I'd love to show you around our fair island."

My jaw dropped. Her lashes fluttered. "Thank you kindly."

He cleared his throat and smiled. "If you need anything, Patience, I'd be happy to oblige."

I shot past Miss Alice on my way to the cart.

"Who lit a fire in your pants?" Claire ran on tiptoes behind me. Her strappy, silver stiletto sandals were much cuter than they were practical.

"What time is it?" Excitement coursed through me, raising goose bumps down both arms.

"Four-ten. Why?"

"Good. We've got time." I jammed my foot on the accelerator. We buzzed through town at twenty miles per hour. Outside Beau's office, I rammed the cart into Park. If Beau Thompson planned to run against Adrian for mayor, that gave Beau motive to frame Adrian and get him out of the race. I didn't know Beau well enough to decide if he'd kill for the position, but I planned to find out.

Claire was still in the cart when I blew through the door to Thompson's Insurance. Eep! Karen Holsten stood sipping from a coffee mug ten feet away. Her back was to me, and the line of her simple blue sundress showed off the glow of her skin and infant-sized waist. The way she stood, head back, laughing, proud, I knew where that giant ring came from. She'd set her sight on becoming Mrs. Mayor. Poor Beau Thompson—no one deserved a lifetime chained to Karen.

"Be with you in a—" Beau called from the back office.

His voice was cut short by the door closing at my back. I'd stop by later. When my high school nemesis wasn't around. Karen monopolized every conversation, and I was interested in what Beau had to say.

Claire met me on the sidewalk. "Have you lost your mind? What are you doing?"

"Leaving." I pushed her toward the cart and gunned the engine to life.

Deputy Fargas's SUV flew past us before Claire drew her legs inside the cart. No lights. No siren. No warning.

"For crying out loud!" she screamed, annoyed by another close shave with a police vehicle. A black town car pulled up beside us five seconds later and powered down the window. Mayor Hayes leaned out.

"What's he doing, chasing you down for that tour?" I muttered softly.

She shushed me.

"Hi, Mayor Hayes." I waved, eager to leave before Karen noticed me out front of Beau's office.

The mayor's expression was grim. "Ladies, they think Brady McGee's wife committed suicide."

TWELVE

I SPUN ONTO the road with a bark of the tires. My little golf cart rocked into a full U-turn down the center of Main Street. Claire's eyes widened, but she kept them on the road. A good thing. There was no time to argue traffic laws or my inability to be ticketed if local law enforcement was already at a crime scene.

With one hand braced on the tiny dashboard before her, Claire dared a glance my way. "Where are we going? The deputy went the other way."

"Shortcut. We can cut through the old ball field."

"You don't think Mrs. McGee killed herself."

"Not a chance. She just got paid. Didn't care he had a mistress." I shook my head. "Nope. No way." I cut down the closest alleyway and then jumped a curb onto the sidewalk. The cement broke into gravel ten yards farther and launched us onto the grass of a ball field.

"Look out!" Claire covered her eyes.

I banged my hand against the steering wheel, praying the cart had a horn.

Arroooga! Figured.

I caught a glimpse of horror on Claire's face as I bounced the cart over a row of aluminum baseball bats. The field I remembered as perpetually empty was speckled with tiny ball players clad in red-and-white uniforms. A spattering of moms in lawn chairs turned in our direction, their mouths hanging open. I gawked back a second too long. Our cart nicked the side of a card table, sending Gatorade and fruit snacks splashing down the front of us before sailing over the back of the cart and rolling in the field.

"Can this thing go any faster?" Covered in kiddie snacks, Claire pointed at the maternal mob forming behind us. Half ran onto the field to comfort screaming ballplayers; the other half glared, red-faced.

I gunned it around second base and a man wearing polyester shorts with tube socks. He puffed his whistle and waved his arms. The angry moms gave chase, fussing and screaming about snacks and respect. As I ran out of field and into a bordering yard, I cornered the cart on two wheels, deftly avoiding a pristine flower bed. We were losing the moms until lawn sprinklers doused us in ice water, setting the cart on a hydroplane path of destruction.

"Hold on." I turned the wheel into the slide. We banked a tiny hill and turned on water-slicked grass until we faced the women. "Uh-oh."

Weighing the options, I did the only thing I could and headed right for them, steering one-handed while shading my face with the other. With any luck, I could pretend later it wasn't me scaring children and destroying property. Wisely the crowd parted, and I escaped a vehicular homicide charge.

Crossing another backyard, the cart shot between two houses at the edge of the field. We picked up speed on the asphalt driveway. Thirty seconds later I parked the cart behind a shiny silver Range Rover.

"You're in trouble," Claire teased, enunciating each syllable.

"Shoot."

"Mm-hmm."

Across the street, Sebastian stood tight-lipped in a group of EMTs and rubberneckers. His arms crossed over

his chest and he nodded at the sight of me. Mirrored aviators hid his full expression. I hoped it was amused and not
agitated. If he was agitated, he needed to take a number
and get in line. In the distance behind me, muffled complaints erupted and at least one child cried. We hadn't hit
anyone, so the snack situation must've been the problem.

"What happened with Sebastian's bust?" I asked. "He
said he has mandatory time off. The FBI never gave him
time off for anything before. In fact, they called him first
most of the time."

Claire looked conflicted. "The bust didn't go as
planned."

"I gathered. Would you like to expound on that?"

She looked at Sebastian for several seconds. "A lot of
people got dead."

"Oh. Oh, no. I had no idea. He didn't say." How much
did he hide behind those glasses?

"No one from our team, but Sebastian's under investigation for allegations of excessive force. Five members of
the Risso family were killed. Sebastian played the role of
Angelo for a long time. They never knew what hit them."

"Wow." All those wives and children who lost their
dads and fathers…crime family or not, they were loved
and needed at home. "Did they get enough evidence to
put Jimmy away?"

"No."

"No?" I guffawed.

"Jimmy the Judge got away."

Terror ripped through me. "Jimmy knows Sebastian
was undercover FBI."

"Yeah." The sadness in her voice wrenched my heart.

Sebastian had time off work and probably instructions
to lie low. When Jimmy the Judge put a mark on someone's head, it rolled. No wonder Sebastian was so eager

to come to the island and help me out. It was perfect timing, and no one would look here.

I was a hideout for him. My heart sank a little further in my chest.

When I started toward him, he met me halfway. Claire tugged and swiped at her once-white tank top. She kept pace, not speaking. Despite two dozen onlookers, you could hear a pin drop on the street. The occasional bleating tugboat punctuated the tension in the air. Expressions on the crowd of somber faces confirmed my suspicions. No one believed this alleged suicide to be true.

Someone had killed Mrs. McGee. Just like they killed her husband.

"What do you think?" Sebastian approached, coming so near to my side that his hip brushed mine. "I liked her for Brady's murder. Well, her and the partner. This…" Words escaped me. "I didn't see coming." She'd been nervous the last time we spoke, but I assumed it was the telltale sign of a guilty conscience. Now I had to wonder, what did she know?

I took a long look at the crowd. Often killers lurked in plain sight, listening, basking and whatever else crazy people liked to do.

Sheriff Murray stepped onto the porch, one hand in his hair, the other carrying his hat. He looked beleaguered. The deputy mingled in the crowd, taking statements. He scratched against a little black notepad, engrossed in his work. If only I read lips.

"This is bad, Patience. You know that, right?" Claire tugged at my hand. "You were with her before your car was bombed. Now she's dead. You're driving a golf cart. Living alone in a haunted apartment. None of this is good." Wide brown eyes pleaded with me to turn tail and go back to Norfolk with her immediately.

I squeezed her hand and gave my best please-love-me-anyway smile. "Don't worry. The apartment's not really haunted." I crossed the McGee lawn to see the sheriff. He narrowed his eyes when he saw me coming. His mouth turned down at the corners. The midday sun had drawn a line of sweat across his brow and upper lip. He replaced his hat and forced a hard smile. "Miss Price."

"Hi. Hello. Hi." I swallowed the brick of fear in my throat with one big gulp. Time to woman-up. He might be the sheriff, but this was my case. He'd all but signed Adrian's guilty verdict without considering any other possibility. "Has the coroner had a chance to take a look?"

He raised a puffy gray brow in warning.

I rolled my shoulders back. "I don't think Mrs. McGee committed suicide. I spoke with her the same day my car was bombed. She wouldn't talk about what happened to Brady. I think she knew something."

"Knew what?" His beady eyes edged in close behind a long, straight nose. He'd thought I wanted his job when we first spoke. I needed to proceed with care.

"I don't know. She didn't say, but she made it clear she didn't want to talk to me."

His cheeks dropped into a droll expression. I guessed it wasn't hard for him to imagine. Not wanting to talk to me likely topped his list of dreaded activities, right above having a colonoscopy or adult circumcision. He widened his stance. "Is there something you aren't telling me? I can't do my job without all the information. Is there something you want me to know?"

If he wanted the information I had, he could have easily gotten it. He didn't bother looking any further than Adrian from the start. No one besides me had considered other possibilities, and now a woman was dead. The sheriff's question felt like a threat. Threats made me defiant. "No."

"No?"

We stared into one another's eyes until my equilibrium strained.

"I've spoken with everyone, sir." The new deputy cast a shadow over me.

"If you'll excuse us." The sheriff made a show of walking away with the deputy. Several paces into the yard, he turned back to me. "If you think of anything you'd like to add to this investigation, you know where to find me."

So it was an investigation. Even the sheriff knew this wasn't a suicide.

"That went well." Claire had dried off, tied the bottom of her bespeckled tank into a side knot and pulled her hair away from her face in an easy chignon. She looked stunning even in Gatorade.

I picked strands of crusty hair from my face where it had dried. "Ouch."

Sebastian lifted a brow in amusement as he admired my parent's golf cart. Grass and mud covered the tires and headlights. Fruit snacks peppered the floor and backseat. Sticky puddles of orange liquid scarred the soft leather interior. With any luck, a swarm of bees or hummingbirds wouldn't follow us home.

"We should talk about this. She didn't kill herself." I looked at my partners, who nodded.

"Agreed," Claire said. She studied the cart.

"Here." Sebastian squeezed a sports bottle of water over the seats and grimaced. He popped the hatch to his Range Rover and tossed a gym towel our way. "I'd offer you a ride, but…"

"We're fine." I folded my body in behind the wheel.

"Ew." Claire shut her eyes and climbed aboard.

We rode back to my apartment in silence. I followed the Range Rover, taking real roads and stopping at the lights. A swarm of Little Leaguers buzzed outside the Tasty Cream. I cringed, parked and ran up the steps to unlock my door.

Doink.

A baseball beaned Sebastian's Range Rover and rolled into the street. I motored inside and peeked out the curtain. Clueless, Sebastian retrieved the ball and lobbed it back across the street, where no one attempted to catch it. He rubbed his neck. Pausing to examine the Range Rover for damage, he looked up at me through the window. I dropped the curtain.

Claire was already in the shower. Before I got my key out of the lock, she'd raided my closet and ducked into the bathroom. Water ran full blast behind the closed door. The whole place smelled like Lysol and mildew, but I didn't risk cracking a window anymore. Summer heat filled every inch of space between my ugly paneled walls and choked me. If the thermostat had worked, it would've read *TILT.*

"Why don't you change and I'll make us something to drink." Sebastian walked into the kitchen and opened my freezer. He unloaded a tray of ice before I headed to my room. "Don't plan on going anywhere soon, either. We need to talk."

I checked the closet and under my bed before I undressed in my room. Lying on the bed were a pair of cotton shorts along with three T-shirts Claire must've considered and passed on. They looked cute to me. Content in a well-worn FBI cotton tee and my black shorts, I dragged a brush through my hair. My hair had survived the Gatorade better than my shirt. I plucked a fruit snack from my cleavage and headed back to the living room, bringing the little oscillating fan with me.

Sebastian worked at the counter, lining up glasses and plugging in my blender.

I stopped at the sink for a wad of paper towels and soap. I washed up surgeon-style to my elbows, then my face and neck. "You want pizza? It's dinnertime, and I'm too tired to worry about what it costs."

"It's well after dinnertime, and it's my treat."

I gave him a crazy face. "You're my guest."

"I invited myself to stay for a week. You only agreed to a drink, which we never had. The least I can do is cover one meal."

What could I say? "I'll call." I leaned across the counter to grab a pile of takeout menus Mom left.

"You smell good." Sebastian filled a blender with ice and tossed strawberries in by the handful. "What were you two covered in earlier? Smells like oranges."

"Gatorade."

"Why?" A muscle twitched in his cheek.

"We won the Super Bowl."

The blender whirred to life. Gnawing and crunching flowed into a steady whoosh. Sebastian removed the lid and spooned out a taste.

"Milk shakes?"

"Daiquiris."

"Daiquiris?"

"I told you. I owe you a drink."

The water shut off in the bathroom. Sebastian poured three tall glasses of pink froth and wedged a strawberry on the rim of each. I plugged the fan into an outlet near the couch. Sebastian sat on the floor facing the fan and me. My muscles tingled as I sank into the cushions and tucked my feet under me.

"I figured you for a beer guy."

"I'm flexible." Good to know.

"What happened with your bust the other night? You were on your way when we spoke on the phone. You never told me how it went."

"It didn't go well." He had the cop face again—no expression or body language to clue me in to his mental state. Was he as worried about his safety as I was? Did he have a plan for catching Jimmy the Judge?

"You want to talk about it?" My mind raced for words in this scenario. *When you deceive a crime boss and he gets away* wasn't in any of my counseling course books.

"Nope."

"I'm a good listener."

He shook his head and pressed the glass to his lips. "I'm fine."

"You're hiding."

A flash of heat lit his eyes and faded. "I'm not hiding. I'm helping a friend save her ex-boyfriend's ass."

"Drinks?" Claire floated into the room looking refreshed. She dug around in the kitchen for a straw and came to sit with me. "What are we doing?"

"I'm hoping we muscle information out of your BFF here," Sebastian said. "She's tight-lipped."

I snorted, suppressed a comment about kettles and pots and sucked on my straw to keep my mouth busy.

"On another day I'd appreciate discretion in a woman. Today I need to know what she's gotten herself into."

Claire pressed the straw to her lips and smiled widely. "Go on." She nudged me and got comfortable.

"I don't think Adrian killed Brady," I said. "I think there's something else going on here. Something huge. At first I thought Sheriff Murray was lazy or preoccupied with Pony Week coming, but now I'm certain this is all part of something bigger. Brady's murder wasn't personal like I thought. I bet whoever killed him was hiding something else and they got rid of Brady's wife to cover the trail. Just in case he confided in her. In fact, I think that's the same guy who's after me. He knows I talked to Mrs. McGee. Probably thinks she told me his secret, which explains the car bomb and drive-by. I think those were warnings. I can't figure out why the sheriff's not looking into this more. He can't think Adrian's on the run, but making time to kill and terrorize women. Maybe the sheriff's being blackmailed to keep quiet."

"Or he's in on it," Claire interjected.

"I'm not sure. I don't think so." Sheriff Murray was rude and a number of other unpleasant things, but not a killer. I sipped my drink to buy some time. Icy strawberries masked the rum. I had another sip. "I think the man who broke in here and tied me up is the murderer."

"You don't sound positive." Sebastian leaned forward and looked me over.

I emptied my drink.

"What aren't you saying?"

I lifted a finger and dialed the Pie Corner. Nothing on the island was what it seemed. "Hi, I'd like two pony pies, please. One veggie. One…" I looked at Sebastian. "Pepperoni?" The kid on the other end asked my name. "Patience Price."

Claire handed me her drink.

After I was done ordering, I tossed my phone onto the couch between us. "Twenty minutes."

"Are you picking it up?" she asked. "You didn't give your address."

"Everyone on this island knows where to find Patience." Sebastian turned to me.

"You've been checking up on me?"

He nodded, unruffled by my screechy voice. Digging

into Adrian's life made sense. I, on the other hand, wasn't sure I liked being investigated.

"Who have you talked to? What did they say?"

"I'm more interested in what you aren't saying."

I counted to ten and waited. Sebastian gave no indication of answering my questions. "Fine. If the man who broke in here was the killer, why didn't he kill me?"

Maybe he would have killed me if Adrian hadn't interfered, but then why did he take the trouble to tell me to stay out of it if he planned to kill me five minutes later? The whole ordeal bothered me on multiple levels.

"What does the sheriff say?" Claire scooted to the edge of the couch and pushed up onto her feet. She looked cute in my yellow sundress.

"I didn't mention it. It's just a hunch, and the sheriff doesn't want to hear from me."

"He really doesn't like you. What's that about?" Claire asked. She returned with two more drinks and set them on the coffee table in front of us.

Memories raced through my mind. "I wasn't always what you'd call a law-abiding citizen." I sucked on the straw in the glass Claire had given me. "I had a couple of tough years."

"How many?"

"Five."

Sebastian snorted. Claire drew out a long, "Mmmm-mmm."

"Once I figured out I liked order and structure and facts, I had a problem with my parents' lifestyle. I rebelled a bit. Sheriff Murray was a deputy back then, so he had to deal with me. Aside from wasting his time for five years straight, chasing me off the water tower and bringing me in for skinny-dipping, he had my parents to answer to."

"They were mad?" Disbelief colored Claire's voice.

"No. They were disappointed the sheriff would send him out to stifle my creativity and self-expression. He hauled me in and they called his boss to complain."

"Do you still express yourself with public nudity?" Sebastian wondered.

I rolled my eyes.

Claire cackled and grabbed one of the drinks from the table. Her laughter set off mine and vice versa. Like tumbling dominoes, the giggles built and carried on until I was spent.

Ding-dong.

Holding my side with one hand, I put the second empty glass on the table. Sebastian handed me some cash and helped me haul in the pizzas.

"Your adolescent misadventures explain his attitude." Sebastian folded a piece of pizza in half and carried it on a napkin back to where he'd been sitting on the floor.

"Senior year I tried everything I could think of to get my parents to crack down on me. They never did. Eventually I gave up, but not before I broke into the deputy's cruiser, put it in Neutral and rolled it to the station. The next morning he woke up in a tizzy and reported it stolen. The whole island heard about it. He had to walk to the police station since he'd driven the cruiser home. His car was there. The old sheriff was embarrassed. Murray knew I did it but couldn't prove it. We were careful to wear all black and never look up in case of cameras. There weren't any, of course, but I'd watched enough crime shows to know looking up was dumb."

"We?" Sebastian locked eyes with me and waited.

"Adrian and I."

He shifted on the floor without speaking.

Claire patted my knee. "Eat. This pizza is delicious. I swear food tastes better here."

"Yeah."

An hour later we had circled back to the matter of figuring out who was killing people before he killed again.

"Well, I'm here until Monday." Sebastian's voice held a new tenor. "We need to get to the bottom of this before then."

"What if we don't?" Considering the stellar job I'd done so far, faith in my investigation skills was lacking.

"Then you'll need to stay with your parents or with Claire for a while. You aren't safe here. That's been proven again and again."

"I'm not leaving the island, and I'm not endangering my parents, either."

"You're welcome at my place anytime for as long as you'd like. You know that." Claire rolled onto her side and tucked the little gold pillow under her head. "Right now, I am full and tired and probably going to dream about that golf cart."

I tossed an afghan over her and shuffled toward my room. Sebastian followed.

"Where are you going?" I leaned against the wall and looked up at him.

"You're not going anywhere alone for the next two days. While I'm here, I'm keeping an eye on you. I'll be gone soon. Until then, consider yourself under my watch."

I didn't hate it.

"So you're sleeping in my room?"

"On the floor, but yes. And not yet. You've had a rough couple of days. Mine weren't so exciting. Care if I use your laptop?"

"No."

I pulled spare blankets and pillows from the closet and handed them over. He made up a bed under the infamous window and stripped off his shirt. Then he put the gun under his pillow and lowered himself onto the makeshift bed beside mine.

I crawled into bed and worried I might snore. After flipping off the light on my nightstand, I curled up under the sheet. Yes, I could sleep well with Sebastian at my side. Everything inside me unwound.

"How serious were you and the suspect?" Sebastian's voice punctured the dark.

"Adrian?" When he didn't correct me, I assumed I won the prize. "Serious."

"You're sure he's innocent? Because you're right, something bigger is at work here. What if he's part of it? Could you handle that?"

"He's not. He wants to know what's going on just as much as I do."

Silence.

I bit my lip. I'd practically admitted to talking with Adrian.

"Do you still have feelings for him?" Curiosity leaked through his words. He'd let his guard down. Only a little. But his perfected stoic tone was gone. Not an accident. He let me know he *wanted* to know.

"He was my first love."

Sebastian grunted.

"I was a different person then. It was a long time ago. I grew up. Settled down. I'm all right with my parents being themselves, and I'm all right with who I am, too. It took me a while to figure out who I was, but I like this girl."

"Me, too."

"Thanks."

"I know you saw a lot of things in my personnel file I don't like to talk about. I want you to know, I'm glad you know those things, and I like that you've never asked me about them."

All his secrets were in a personnel file, and I'd read it. Interesting. I didn't have a file. The only person who knew all my secrets was Adrian.

The only man to capture my attention in the last ten years was lying on the floor in my bedroom, and he wanted me to know his secrets.

"I also know Claire told you more than she should about the bust and my new situation. I appreciate you not pushing for details on that, either."

"You can stay here as long as you need to. Chincoteague's a little loopy, but it's normally a nice refuge."

"I'm fine. I need to get back in a couple of days and sort out my loose ends. You know this island loves you? I've been here less than a week and everywhere I go, people ask about you. They tell me stories about you. They missed you while you were gone. Whatever trouble you got into all those years ago, everyone but the sheriff has gotten past it. And your parents…" He paused. "I can't figure them out."

"If you ever do, let me know."

"They look at me like I'm about to steal something."

"You did show up out of the blue and move in with their only daughter."

He grunted. "You've got a great family. All twelve hundred or so members. You're like an island princess here."

"Shut up."

"I'm serious."

For the first time I realized how much I didn't know about Sebastian. What was his life like *before* the file?

THIRTEEN

"YOU DON'T NEED to follow me everywhere." I picked up large pieces of glass and stacked them inside an empty box. "I feel horrible. You finally have time off work and end up looking after someone anyway." Hiding out from a Mob family was stressful enough.

"It doesn't feel like work. I like it here." Sebastian dumped a dustpan full of glass in the trash and strode through the rat door to the dock out back.

He never took time off. Ever. And it worried me that he was hiding out with me instead of figuring out his next move with Jimmy the Judge out there. I grabbed the broom, and surveyed our cleanup efforts. Aside from the broken glass and the myriad creatures who'd taken a lap through my office after the windows broke, things looked good. The paint was rich and warm. Hope lifted in my heart. My office had potential. The lunatic who shot it up would be caught soon. Sebastian would see to it.

As long as we figured out who he was in the next twenty-four hours.

"This is beautiful." Sebastian's voice carried through the open door.

"It's rotting." I assumed he was talking about the deck. "Watch where you step."

"I meant the view."

Unable to contain my curiosity, I walked through the door to his side. Weathered boards groaned under my added weight. Cattails clustered at the corner of the dock, tall grasses swayed in the midday breeze, and still waters reflected a mirror image of geese flying in V-formation overhead. Their steady *honk, honk, honk,* settled my pulse. I hadn't realized I was anxious until the stress rippled off me at the sound of the geese. The briny air assured me I was home. I could get used to the view. A small unused portion of the harbor ended at my dock. The water brimmed with cattails and duckweed. From the looks of it, no boat had been here in years. Land was taking over the water, planting flora around the dock and into the shallow water. A gorgeous metallic green-and-purple dragonfly buzzed past my head.

"I'm trying to imagine what it must've been like growing up here. Tightknit community, island life, fishermen, fresh seafood, quiet…" He gave me his trademark guarded look, searching me silently. "It suits you."

"Thanks."

"Your parents are fun, yeah?" His expression softened and so did my heart.

"For sure. They're a blast." I bumped my shoulder into him and laughed.

"They answer some questions I had about you, that's for sure."

I squinted into the sun, trying to read his face, embracing the new easiness between us. "What questions?"

He stalled long enough to make me wonder if he'd answer. "The way you pack seeds and sprouts in your lunch, for one. Or your obsession with recycling *everything.* You keep your desk pens in an empty soup can."

"Recycling will save the earth." I stalled my lecture at the sight of his smile.

"You bring your seed lunch in a cloth bag and lidded glass containers. You have a tiny herb garden near the picnic tables outside the office. You drink wheatgrass juice."

"Wheatgrass provides lots of health benefits," I teased. Maybe I was more like my parents than I knew.

Sebastian froze and his smile disappeared. He made a signal I didn't recognize with his fist and moved toward the door.

I backed up against the wall and stayed put while he crept through the door, gun drawn. I checked the water for a clear spot to jump overboard.

"Company." Sebastian jerked his head. Beyond the rat door, Hank meandered outside the wide-open window holes.

"Hi, Hank." I walked back through the boathouse and shoved the front door wide in invitation.

Sebastian stayed behind.

"You've got a mess going here, but the door's looking good." He pulled on and shoved the doorknob in one hand, admiring his work.

I remembered what my mother said about my counseling services and tried out the new possibility. "You do fine work." I bent to empty the trash and replace the bag. "What brings you by?"

"I figured you needed help." He ran a handkerchief over his forehead then stuffed it in his pocket.

"I do. It's very kind to offer, thank you."

He bobbed his head.

"Where should we start?" I grabbed the broom and looked around. The inside looked pretty good, considering. I swept a few shards of glass into my dustpan.

"I guess I'll clean up a bit out front so they can work." He looked over one shoulder and closed the door behind him.

Outside the giant delivery truck had returned. *Beep. Beep. Beep.* It backed up to the curb, and the same man from a few days before slid out onto the sidewalk. He looked at his clipboard, at the boathouse then back at the clipboard and shook his head.

"Mrs. Davis?" He rubbed his neck with his free hand.

"Yes?" I spoke through the missing window hole. The fact I answered so easily to "Mrs. Davis" was something worth thinking about later. Or never. Never ever.

"You got some new windows coming." His brows crowded together. Behind him a pair of guys in coveralls carried the first plane of glass toward us.

I signed my fake name and went back to sweeping.

"Peepee!"

Dad's voice scared the air out of me.

"Let me do that. You're going to get cut." He took the broom and dustpan from me without further warning. As a child, I always thought my parents materialized rather than arrived anywhere. Maybe there was something to that theory.

Mom sashayed through the door with an oversized pic nic basket swinging in the crook of her arm. I kissed her cheek and went outside to check on Hank, who was picking up pieces of glass and my Prius. Counseling without counseling wasn't something I could get my mind around, but I knew I had to at least be *with* the patient to be useful.

"I appreciate the help, Hank. I'm not off to a great start with the boathouse."

"You're doing fine."

I tried to make eye contact without success. Instead, I turned to pull weeds. We worked in companionable silence for several minutes.

"How are you doing?" I was careful to keep my voice level.

"Good. I'm good." His head bobbed and he moved a few feet away from me. "My wife was pretty upset last time I came home from here. I took your advice and tried to show her she was the only woman for me, since she never believes it when I say it."

"She wasn't happy?" I remembered how excited he'd been to go home and woo her into understanding his love.

"Nope." He rested on his knees in the grass, lifting half of my rearview mirror and a spattering of rubber shreds into a trash bag. "She accused me of feeling guilty for something. I told her what I was doing, but she accused me of cheating and said I was trying to cover it up." The timbre of his voice broke my heart.

"Hang in there. Relationships aren't easy."

"Hank, Patience, come on in. I made lunch." Mom waved wildly from the boathouse door ten feet away.

How could I be taken seriously with my mom calling me to lunch?

Hank headed inside first. I dawdled. It wasn't easy to go inside. I worried for the safety of the accumulating vehicles out front, but my resolve melted when scents of Mom's cobbler wafted out to meet me.

Clipboard guy and the glass carriers sat on empty five-gallon paint buckets eating salmon and asparagus. Mom had lined the contents of her basket up on my counter and dished several plates out like a buffet. Sebastian grabbed two and met me at the door.

The floor was clear of glass and my new windows looked great. The strange lunch gathering tugged at my chest. My parents fawned over one another and served lunch to Hank and the complete strangers from the glass company. Sebastian hung back a little. No one else seemed to notice, but I did. The chatter turned to laughter as the group enjoyed the impromptu lunch break. I didn't even know half the people present, but they were all there to help me. I was humbled.

"This place cleaned up nice." Clipboard guy shoveled

his second helping of salmon into an already full mouth. "I used to come here to buy a fishing license every summer."

"Really? I don't remember that." I had few memories of the boathouse. The park outside the boathouse, yes, but the not the boathouse.

"That's because we don't believe in fishing." Mom looked proud of her stand on animal protection. Never mind the salmon.

"What is it you're going to do here?" Hank asked.

I stopped mid-chew to look between him and my mother. Was I not counseling him?

"Um…"

"The windows look great. When did you have time to order them?" Sebastian leaned into the wall with one hip, apparently enjoying Mom's cobbler.

"Err…"

BANG! BANG! BANG! BANG!

At the sound, I dropped to the floor, landing on top of my plate. My pulse beat in my head. Fear constricted my chest until it burned. No one else moved for a few long beats.

"Honey?" Mom's feet came into view. I lifted my head and shoulders, drowning in humiliation. She smiled warmly, concern crinkled the corners of her eyes.

Hank jumped to his feet and strode to the door. "See what I mean about her?" he asked before ripping the front door open. "What is wrong with you?" he yelled through the open door.

I dared a look in the direction of my new friend and handyman. Eggs were smashed over my new window. Inside, six pairs of eye were trained on me.

"No-good cheater!" a woman screamed outside. Hank's wife, I presumed. Reality slid into place through the haze of my fear. Hank's jealous wife had found him here with me and egged my office.

An engine roared to life outside. Tires barked and screeched into the distance.

Shiny black boots came into view, stopping beside my Mom. Sebastian squatted before me, hands hanging loosely between his knees. "You okay, boss?"

"Of course." I jerked upright. Mom's salmon clung to my shirt. Asparagus spears left butter sauce on my cheek. "I slipped."

Logically, I recognized the mess on my windows was only eggs. Irrationally, I saw little grenades glaring through the thin layer of glass separating me from whoever wanted to hurt me. I didn't believe in coincidence. I could no longer avoid facts. My life was in danger. Someone had threatened me not-too-subtly by shooting my car and later bombing it. Someone had broken into my apartment and held me hostage. Likely the same one who murdered Brady McGee and his wife. It was only a matter of time before this monster tired of threats and eliminated his problem. Me.

"I need a little air. I'm going to take a walk." I managed a calm voice despite the hurricane brewing in my chest.

Chin high, I stood, marched into the sun, jogged across the street and kept going. For the first time in my life, I understood the scene in *Forrest Gump* where he just kept running.

Within moments, blinding rays of light glinted off the shiny silver Range Rover trailing me down Front Street. I turned onto Main at the light and caught a glimpse of myself in a storefront window. Disaster didn't begin to cover it.

My phone sang in my pocket "'…been through the desert on a horse with no name…'" A tear rolled down my cheek. I assigned Dad the ring tone the moment assigning ring tones was possible. I loved him for wanting to protect me. That thought added guilt to my tapestry of problems. My curiosity affected more than me and Adrian. It worried my folks and Claire, kept Sebastian working when he should be planning a new life in witness protection, aggravated the killer and plain old-fashioned pissed off the sheriff.

"Hello." I kept moving, ignoring Sebastian's Range Rover crawling at a snail's pace beside me in the street.

"You all right, Peepee?"

"I will be. Sorry I left. Lunch was delicious and very thoughtful. Thank you."

"Anything for you, baby girl. You go on and take care of yourself. Me and your mom and Hank will get things righted here."

"Thanks." My throat swelled.

"We love you."

"You, too."

I disconnected with Dad and gave Sebastian a wave good-bye. He sat stock-still in the driver's seat of his Range Rover, expression hidden behind those damnable glasses. I appreciated him seeing me home safely, but it was time for me to be alone. I dragged my feet up the stairs to my place. Freud ran to me, winding around my ankles as I climbed. Tripping down the stairs would be the perfect end to my week. I scooped him into my arm, hoping he didn't have fleas.

"Mew." Freud licked my shirt with abandon. Not every day did a homeless cat get grilled salmon. I peeled him off me at the landing and went inside to change.

I needed to think.

"Warning," a jovial voice called from my bedroom.

"I am Adrian Davis and I am in your room. Please don't hurt me."

I walked in and glared. "Thanks for the warning." Too drained to care, I stripped my fish shirt off and wiped my face with it. I grabbed a cotton sundress from my closet, pulled it on over my head and shimmied out of my shorts underneath.

Adrian was speechless for probably the first time in his entire life.

"I'm having a day." I flopped onto my bed face-first.

He stepped between me and the door. "I thought your guy was supposed to be protecting you. Where is he now?"

I groaned without lifting my head. "Sebastian followed me home. He's probably still sitting in his car outside."

"I saw him. What do we do next?" He shuffled, restless on his feet.

"Try not to die."

"Come on, Patience. What next? What are we missing?"

I'd asked myself the same question so many times it'd lost meaning. Where was my intuition when I needed it? Cowering, or on its way to Mexico if it had any sense, unlike me. "I don't know." Defeat dripped from my pores. "I don't know what the murder weapon was, or if it matters. I liked Mrs. McGee for Brady's death. Now I'm looking at Perkins. I guess I'll go talk to him again." I slapped the pillow and kicked my feet, which hung off the bed.

"Roll over."

I did and Adrian stepped closer. He had on an old football shirt with his college logo, gray basketball pants and sandals. I smiled. He looked like the perfect mix of cuddly and confident. "Don't worry. I'm keeping watch over you and so is Sebastian. You're going to be safe, but we need to find out who's doing this before someone else gets hurt."

"Or killed." My parents came to mind. Mrs. Tucker. Claire. Maple Shuster. I cared about everyone on the island. Adrian was right. I needed to pull it together. This wasn't just about him anymore. Someone dangerous walked among us. Who knew what might happen next.

A tear welled in my eye and coursed over one cheek. I sniffled and wiped it away. Adrian leaned over the bed, pressing massive hands into the blanket on either side of me. His expression softened and his lips parted. I was almost too lost in those stormy gray eyes to notice the massive black shadow stretching up behind him.

Crap.

Sebastian landed a giant hand on Adrian's shoulder and both men froze. Muscles clenched. Jaws went on lockdown. I stuttered incoherently.

"Hands up." Sebastian ordered, reaching his free hand behind his back for what I hoped were handcuffs and not a sidearm.

"Sebastian, this is Adrian." I squirmed into a seated position, hoping to diffuse the testosterone bomb exploding before me.

"I know who he is. I did my homework." In the fraction of a second Sebastian looked at me, Adrian rammed an elbow into his gut and the fight was on. Adrian tried in vain to get past Sebastian and into the hallway, but Sebastian blocked his every turn. My tiny room was already full of a bed and a dresser—there was no room for brawling giants.

"Stop!" I dodged Adrian as he landed where I'd been moments before. If I'd had a water bed, the impact would've shot me onto the ceiling. "Stop!" Adrian lurched into tackle stance and charged Sebastian like a bull. Together they dented my wall, ricocheted off the door frame and tumbled into the hall. "Stop!"

Adrian held his own, considering what I knew about Sebastian. Maybe all the college football improved his reflexes.

I plucked my laptop out of harm's way and looked at the pair exchanging punches and bone-crushing thumps against the floor. The sink caught my eyes—a dousing of water might cool them off—but I hated to soak my floor. Plus, I'd be the one who'd have to clean it up.

"I'm naked!" I screamed.

It worked. Adrian's head jerked around.

Sebastian cuffed him.

FOURTEEN

"You HAVE THE right to remain silent." Sebastian glared at the back of Adrian's head.

"Looks like you found yourself a hero." Adrian frowned at me.

"You have the right to an attorney."

"Do *not* arrest him." My voice cracked. Both men stared at me. A smile ticked up on one side of Adrian's face. Sebastian worked his jaw. I tried my best to look fierce. When he didn't budge, I let my eyes go wide and dropped my shoulders. "Please?"

I hated to be *that girl,* but desperation did bad things to me. He had to at least hear me out before he made a decision.

Sebastian threw his arms in the air and turned his back on me. He didn't take the cuffs off Adrian, whose face stretched into a full-on victory smile.

"I can explain." I stepped toward Sebastian with trepidation. What I asked of him was wrong. I asked him to break the law for me, when he'd sworn to uphold it. Adrian was on the lam. He belonged in jail until the court decided otherwise. His fate wasn't mine to decide. I stopped within an arm's reach of Sebastian and glared at Adrian. His smile vanished. Stormy gray eyes watched me as though his life depended on it. Maybe it did.

Sebastian looked over his shoulder in my direction, emotion swimming in the depths of his bottomless browns. He lifted his scowl in defeat and waved me to the couch. He stayed with Adrian. Both waited for an explanation. Eyes locked on me.

I cleared my throat. "Sebastian, this is Adrian Davis. Adrian, Sebastian."

Sebastian crossed his arms over his chest, looking somehow bigger than before.

"Adrian didn't kill Brady," I said.

Sebastian's gaze narrowed and slid to look him over. "All right."

"All right?" Adrian's face lit up.

Sebastian's lips turned down as he looked at Adrian. "You're a marshmallow."

Adrian smiled, taking the remark in stride.

If the bad guy didn't kill me, dealing with these two might. I let out a long stage sigh. "Arresting him will only stop the investigation. I mean, they won't bother looking for anyone else once he's in custody. That serves no one. People are still dying. His mom is missing. Something huge is happening here."

"Mom's not missing."

"What?" Joy and frustration fought for first place in my heart. "No one's seen her since my car blew up and she called for help.

"I have." Adrian rolled his eyes. Obviously there was more to this story.

"You think the arrest would make him a scapegoat?" Sebastian shifted his weight, resting a shoulder against the wall beside Adrian. He stayed within an arm's reach at every moment. Not that Adrian planned to run but, of course, Sebastian couldn't know that. Plus, he seemed to like the sight of Adrian in cuffs.

"Yes. I think the fact he fought with Brady meant nothing to whoever killed him. I think the two events are unrelated. The real killer planned to kill Brady. At first I thought it was a crime of passion. Blunt force seems passionate. I guessed his wife or girlfriend had had enough and lost control. But after talking with the girlfriend, I understood that she's scared. So was Mrs. McGee. In fact, I know they'll find she didn't kill herself. She was dead before she died."

The men exchanged a look.

"You know what I mean. Someone cold and calculating is out there—someone who took their time to kill Mrs. McGee then stage a suicide. Whatever this is about, anyone else involved with it will probably be next."

I hoped the next someone wasn't me.

"Don't go too far." Sebastian unlocked the cuffs and gave Adrian another stern examination.

Adrian rubbed his wrists. Conflict played over his expression. The set of his lips and crease between his eyes told me he didn't want to go. The hulk with the Glock said he did.

"Your mom's not missing?"

He shook his head.

"Where is she?" I'd gotten used to her following me, and I needed to thank her for calling an ambulance when my car blew up.

"Wherever she is, it's safer than following you around."

I breathed easier. I didn't get her killed after all. Sebastian ran a hand over his mouth, probably suppressing a laugh.

"If you need me, I'll be downstairs." Adrian kept his eyes locked on mine and headed to my bedroom.

"Where are you going?" I called. Sebastian and I watched him disappear around the corner.

"Why'd you let him in?" Sebastian turned to me, looking betrayed.

"I didn't. He uses the window."

"I nailed the window shut. Are you sure he doesn't have a key?" He didn't wait for an answer. He turned for my room.

I followed.

"See." He pulled the curtain aside and waved a hand over it. "Nails."

Sure enough, silver nail heads shined in the wooden frame. I gave it a few tugs to be sure he did it right. Nothing budged. "So, where'd he go?"

Sebastian unholstered his gun and checked the closet. I looked under the bed.

"What the hell?" Sebastian turned down the hall to look in the bathroom.

"I've been saying that a lot since I got here."

He stood, feet shoulder-width apart, in my bathroom doorway, hands on hips, frown on lips. "He didn't just vanish."

"He kind of did."

"I need some fresh air. Come on."

"Where're we going?"

"How about the national park? I could use the quiet, and I don't want anyone listening to us while we try to figure out what's happening."

I hated the park. The ponies lived there. I stuffed Mace into my pocket and checked behind all the doors before I left. Sebastian triple-checked the window and then the door when he pulled it shut.

"Your place gives me the creeps."

"Get in line."

Inside the Range Rover, I tried to ignore the purple golf cart sitting where my Prius belonged. The Prius was supposed to save the environment, not become part of it. What if I'd been in it? Would he have still blown it up? Was the bombing a warning like the break-in at my place? Why would someone so dangerous not kill me and be done with it?

I shivered.

Sailing over the marsh bridge to the national park, Sebastian laid a huge hand over mine and squeezed once before placing it back on the wheel. "We'll figure this out." He handed his pass to the park gatekeeper and rolled under the candy-cane-striped gate. He'd bought an annual pass to the national park. I hoped that meant he planned to be back after his week off was over.

Trees towered overhead, creating beautiful multicolored patterns on the road. We stopped near the lighthouse trail and climbed out.

"How much do you trust this guy?" Sebastian walked beside me, easily matching his pace with mine.

"To not be a murderer?" I laughed. "I know he didn't do this."

"What's your history with the suspect?"

"Adrian."

"I'd rather call him the suspect."

"Adrian and I met in preschool. I've known him my entire life. We were close." I took sudden interest in the trees.

"Do you love him?"

Thanks to my eyes being focused elsewhere, my toe snagged on a partially buried root. I pitched forward, calculating the damage before I hit ground. I never did. One broad arm snaked around my waist and tipped me back onto my feet. The hesitation between catch and release was so minute, it almost didn't register. I looked at Sebastian. His eyes were hidden behind his mirrored glasses.

"I did love him."

"What happened?"

I started to walk again. "He left. We graduated and he

went to Miami to play football. I eventually went to college on the mainland and got a job with the agency. You know the rest."

A ring sounded, and muttering something about stupidity, Sebastian pulled his phone to his ear. "I need a few more days." He walked back several paces, continuing his call. With his back to me, I grew nervous. Crunching leaves and snapping sticks worried me. Ponies. I turned in a small circle, one hand in my pocket. I hoped Sebastian wouldn't hesitate to shoot if necessary.

"I'm going to try to stay awhile longer. I need to run to the mainland during the day for my psych eval and debriefing, but I can be here with you at night." After hanging up, Sebastian swaggered back to me. "If that's okay with you."

"It's okay with me." Ponies forgotten, I stared straight ahead at what, lucky me, happened to be a view of his T-shirt, stuck to the planes and angles of his chiseled chest. I tilted my gaze up. His glasses had been removed. Dark and soft, his eyes held me in place.

"You didn't answer my question earlier. I asked if you love him. You said you did then. Do you now?" The deepness in his voice, slow and thick like honey, soothed me.

My skin tingled. Heat radiated off him, electrifying the space between us. He was so close. If I touched him now, raised onto my toes, I could finally know if I was right about those suggestive lips of his. Too bad he was asking about Adrian. Jumping naked into the seashore in January couldn't have done more damage to the moment.

"No." I headed up the hill toward the lighthouse, leaving my daydream behind. My knees wobbled with each step. Heat crept up my neck.

"Are you feeling okay?" Sebastian asked. His fingers touched my elbow.

"Fine." Weak. Woozy. Not fine at all, but far too stubborn to admit it. My tummy tilted with nausea. The day scorched around me despite the leafy filter of the forest.

"I don't like you aiding a criminal, and I don't like him. I think you need to stay away from Adrian for a while. I think you should be careful, too. You haven't seen him in a decade. A lot can change in that kind of time."

He had that right.

"I trust your judgment, boss. What I don't trust is him."

"I thought you agreed he didn't kill Brady."

When we reached the lighthouse, I climbed a few steps and took a seat, winded. The lighthouse sat on the highest point in the area, making it easily seen for miles and an exhausting walk from the road. A breeze tossed hair into my eyes. Spots danced at my periphery. It was hot. I hadn't eaten. I had stress. There wasn't enough air to breathe. Humidity had saturated everything beneath the leaf canopy above us. I tugged on my shirt to cool myself. The effort was wasted.

Sebastian looked as though he'd walked around the block instead of through the summer heat for nearly a mile uphill. He kept coming until the bottom step stopped him. He braced his hands against the rails on either side of my head and covered me in his shadow.

"I didn't say I thought he was guilty. I said I didn't like him." The look in his eyes sent my heart into a tailspin.

Reason eluded me. Words, too. A lump filled my throat. My tongue became too heavy for speech.

One massive hand released the railing and spooned under my jaw, tipping my face to his. For a moment, his fingers trembled. Reason filtered back, assuring me it wasn't the agent before me who trembled at my hand. "May I?" he whispered too close for me to think straight.

I closed my eyes and did the only thing I could in response to the situation at hand. I fainted.

SUNLIGHT TEASED MY lids open. Light and dark. Light and dark. A gentle rocking brought me back to reality, and I opened my eyes to the scruff of Sebastian's chin. Wrapping me in his embrace, he carried me off the mountain. Sure-footed steps barely registered, only the gentle sway of his gait. He smelled like musk and spice and man. I inhaled a deep lungful. If testosterone had a scent, I could name it now.

"Are you all right?" His voice vibrated in his chest.

I wanted to nuzzle against him. Thoughts inappropriate to our ridiculous and complicated relationship popped into mind like the whack-a-mole game at the local fair. Suppress one, another appears.

"Put me down," I blurted. "I'm fine. I can walk." I couldn't feel my legs, but I hated being carried. Okay. I hated that I *liked* being carried.

"No."

"What? No?"

"No." His pace didn't change. "You need water, food and to be out of the sun."

I struggled a minute.

His grip tightened. "Hold still."

"I'm fine."

"You're not. You wore your lunch today instead of eating it. You aren't sleeping. The stress you're under is too much. Plus, it's hot. This mess Adrian dragged you into is taking a toll. I hold him personally responsible for everything that's happened to you since you moved back here." We reached the car and he shifted my weight against his side and dug in his pocket with one hand. I considered letting go of his neck. Instead of opening the door, he set me on the hood and got a bottle of water from the cup holder. He opened it before handing it to me.

I took a few ginger sips.

"You're flushed. It's hot." He nodded to the bottle in my hand. "Are you finished?"

I gave it to him.

He dumped it over my head.

"Yow!"

Sebastian snapped the wetted tee away from my skin a few times. That cooled everything down.

I hoped it didn't show.

"Better?" His gleaming white smile captivated me again. A tiny drip of water worked its way over my nose and he swiped it away with his thumb.

Laughter bubbled in my chest and I smiled back. Who knew he was funny? Or so ornery?

"Patience?"

I shook water from my bangs to look at him.

His smile morphed into something darker, needier. Without another word, Sebastian slid one strong arm around my waist and pulled me to the edge of the hood. My knees moved on instinct to accommodate him. He cradled the back of my head in his palm and closed the narrow distance between us. His thumb caressed my cheek with a gentleness so contradictory to everything I knew about him, I sighed. Sebastian's lips moved over mine, and I melted deep into the kiss.

Before I was ready, he broke away. Our breaths mingled as he rested his forehead to mine. A groan rumbled deep and low in his chest.

"Now I need a bottle of water." A boyish gleam played over his features. I liked the look.

"I know where we can find a whole lot of water." Sounds of the surf whispered in the distance. I jumped off the hood and Sebastian ran around to the driver's side. Five minutes later we were splashing in the ocean beside a dozen children and nervous-looking parents.

I dunked under the water, feeling the pull of weight from my light cotton clothes. At least we'd tugged our shoes off before running into the surf like a couple of teens. Sebastian stripped his shirt overhead, too, leaving it with our shoes. I didn't have the same luxury.

"Who knew you were fun?" I teased.

"Back at you, boss."

"Touché." I licked my lips, still tingling from our kiss. "Race you."

Sebastian looked toward the buoy thirty yards away. Overconfidence changed his expression. Taunting him would've wasted time when my muscles twitched to swim. Swimming was all me. I turned and dove under the next wave rolling in.

I pulled myself up to the buoy, feeling young and vivacious. In the water, I was fast and powerful, sleek and… too slow. Sebastian looked as if he'd been waiting on me.

"How did you beat me?"

He pointed to a line of Indian ink up his side. I'd seen it the day he arrived but hadn't wanted to stare. From our position in the water, I could only make out the top. When I squinted, he pushed back in the water, floating before me, arms overhead. What looked like nothing more than barbed wire before registered as letters. *Seal Team 10.*

"Is there anything you can't do?"

"Nope."

"Must be nice."

"It is." He swept upright, dazzling me with a sincere smile, one he rarely gave. Out here he didn't need to blend in, save my life or watch his back. Out here, with just me, him and a buoy, things were different. "Race you back?"

I didn't want to go back. "Yeah."

He beat me again.

We sat in the sand until I was dry and pink from the sun, the kind of pink that turned a pretty bronze with cool air and aloe. Sebastian helped a kid dig a hole with a green bucket, and they watched it fill with water from below. The kid looked like he'd found a new best friend. When he came back to me, he was tired.

"I love those guys." Sebastian lifted a lazy finger toward a lone Sandpiper running away from the tide. The water receded; he ran back to look for food. A new wave slid in and the piper headed for dry land again.

"They're my favorites," I said.

His smile widened as he kept watch on the bird.

Sandpipers had fascinated me since childhood. The way their stick-thin legs carried their stout little bodies back and forth a million times without tiring. It was comical to watch and inspiring. They were the definition of fortitude. The waves kept coming. The little birds kept running.

"About the kiss," I said before I lost my nerve.

"You regret it already?"

"No." What? Maybe.

"You want to do it again?"

My heart beat in my throat at the offer. Did I look crazy? Of course I wanted to do it again. "No."

He chuckled. "Let me know when you do." He stood and reached to pull me up. "Let's get a shower, some dinner and go see Perkins. If he's still alive maybe we can get some information out of him. He's most likely to be the next victim, if he's not the killer. Either way, I'm on borrowed time, and I can't leave you alone while I go chase a crime family on the mainland. Let's wrap this up."

"A shower sounds amazing." Visiting Perkins, on the other hand, sounded like stupidity. At least I wasn't going alone.

"We'll stop at the Tasty Cream. I'll run in and get dinner. We can take it back to your apartment to save time."

I nodded. I didn't want to go in anywhere looking like a drowned and fried rat. "How did you end up in the Seals? Family legacy?"

Sebastian snorted. "No."

"Oh. Then why?" He'd been through so much when he could've been a frat kid, or a model.

"To piss off my old man. Turned out, I liked the military."

"Okay, but a Seal?" I saw *G.I Jane.* I knew that was a crazy endeavor.

He popped open the passenger door and I slid in. Sebastian gripped the roof over my head and dipped his head in an inch.

"I like a challenge."

He shut the door and I jumped.

"Did it work? Was your dad mad you joined the service?"

He folded in behind the wheel and wedged an elbow over my headrest to look behind him. Backing up, he raised his brows at me. "No."

"Clearly he's crazy then."

"Clearly. What do your parents think of your life?"

"They want me to read Tarot cards for them at their shop."

"Have they met you?" He drove out of the national park and back into town as if he'd lived there for years. In a week he'd gone from untouchable crush to friend. Who kissed me. There was something about island life that made all things better. Except for the killer.

I smiled at him as he pulled into the lot at the Tasty Cream. "I guess when it comes to me, they always have hope I'll see what they see."

"Me, too."

Sebastian opened the door and was gone.

FIFTEEN

I HELD MY breath the entire way to Perkins's house. When my chest burned from lack of oxygen, I took a sip of air and went back to silent panic mode. With each passing moment of silence, I was further convinced Perkins was the culprit. Now that the McGees were out of his way, the business was his to run as he pleased, without splitting profits and without interference of a fish-protecting Mrs. McGee.

I hoped he wasn't day drinking again. The cut of my sundress was intended for Sebastian, not a greasy murder suspect. The thin white fabric enhanced my tan, and in the right light, silhouetted my figure. So far the effort seemed lost. If Sebastian noticed, he didn't let on. Perkins would notice. He'd barely looked at my face last time I saw him, despite the fact I was splattered in paint. At least I'd brought backup this time. If the creep tried anything, he'd regret it.

"You're nervous." Sebastian looked my way often enough to make me fidget.

I pulled in a deep breath that shuddered on its way out of my chest. "He had a lot to gain from their deaths."

"Yeah."

The Range Rover slid into the drive behind Perkins's shiny black car. I jumped out and ran around to hide behind Sebastian, who wedged a pair of cuffs in his waistband. His lips twitched, never quite forming a smile. "After you."

Damn chivalry. I baby-stepped in front of him, wondering what to say when Perkins opened his door. Sebastian whistled behind me. I peeked over one shoulder. He stared straight ahead. Stupid glasses. I couldn't wait for summer to end so I could at least get a good look at his eyes. Who could guess what the man was thinking behind those glasses?

This assumed that we'd keep in touch after the summer. And we'd both still be alive.

I lifted a hand to knock on Perkins's door and froze. My fist hovered over the wood. Did I really have to visit a killer? Maybe I could go home and call, or shoot him an e-mail. Sebastian pounded the door knocker, and I jumped.

"You talk. I'll watch." Sebastian folded his hands behind his back and widened his stance. His gun was nestled in the small of his back. I'd watched him slide the holster on his belt right before the handcuffs. Weapons didn't make me more confident this conversation would end well.

"Hello, there." Perkins opened the door wide and took me in with red eyes. He licked his lips in approval.

Yuck. "Hi, Mr. Perkins. May we come in?"

The smile faded when his gaze made it over my head half a foot. "What's this about?"

"Did you kill Brady McGee and his wife?" I blurted. If he did, I didn't want to go inside.

He stumbled back a few paces and motioned us in. Not what I expected. A guilty man would've protested or slammed the door in my face. Sebastian stopped in the doorway, allowing me to take the lead and interview Perkins on my own. He widened his stance and crossed both arms over his massive chest. I sat on the couch while Perkins poured a drink. A tremor played over his hand, sloshing amber liquid inside his glass.

"Mr. Perkins, are you feeling all right?"

His head snapped up, as if he'd forgotten I was there. "You think I had something to do with their deaths?" He looked warily in Sebastian's direction.

"The last time I was here, you told me Brady fought with a woman the night he died. She told me you fought with him, too. About money. It seems to me you now have the business all to yourself."

"The last time you were here?"

"Yes." It hadn't been a full week yet. Was he buying time or did he truly not recognize me?

He tried to snap his fingers and failed. "I remember. You didn't look like that." He finished his drink and waggled his eyebrows.

Sebastian made a noise I hoped was throat clearing and not the growl it sounded like.

Perkins dragged his gaze back to my face. "What's he here for?"

I looked to Sebastian for help, but he maintained the blank expression behind his sunglasses. He looked like a mammoth blocking the door. The sight of him at the office used to both scare and thrill me. He came to work dressed all in black, like he was ready for surveillance or combat, usually with cargo pants. The pants kept me up nights wondering what he kept in his pockets. Sebastian made his superiors fumble for words. Intimidation was his specialty. After watching him dig a hole with a toddler, I expected to be less intimidated. A wave of goose bumps raised on my arms.

"We're trying to keep an innocent man out of jail," I said. "We know Adrian Davis didn't kill Brady McGee, and we think you know who did."

"I don't know anything, and if I did, I wouldn't tell the two of you." He pointed his glass at each of us.

"Well, I suppose that's what I'd have said if I was you, too."

He looked back at me.

"Until the real killer killed Mrs. McGee. Now, if I was you, I'd be wondering how long before I was reunited with my partner."

His Adam's apple dipped low and slow.

"We were taking payoffs." His gaze darted back and forth between Sebastian and me. "I don't know where they came from. A goon approached us a couple of years ago and told us he wanted to fish in our territory. We told him to forget about it."

Finally, this was something. At least he was talking. "Payoffs to fish." I shook my head. "It's a big ocean, Mr. Perkins. I don't buy it."

"I didn't, either. Brady laughed it off, too, but then the guy came back. With cash."

"Who was he?"

"A goon. A gofer. I don't know. It's not like we signed a contract. He didn't look like a fisherman."

"What'd he look like?"

Perkins shrugged with attitude. "Big clothes. Earrings. A punk. One with cash."

"How much cash?"

He walked to the desk and brought a bottle back with him. "Five grand."

"He paid you five thousand dollars to fish in your spot." Maybe I needed to take up fishing.

Perkins licked his lips, sucked on the bottle and wiped his mouth on his arm. "At first."

"I'm listening."

"Well, we had a good spot. We weren't catching enough in the new spot, and Brady's old lady was raising tons of hell about us trolling near her precious shoreline. We wanted our old spot back. It wasn't an easy choice. They paid us another grand every month to steer clear of them. Brady said it was wrapped in plastic and delivered to our box at the harbor. He'd open the bag and split it with me. That part of the deal was good, but this year we were losing that much in lack of fish by being shoved ashore so long. The good fishing is deeper, out where we'd been. You can't catch nothing but flip-flops up close like that. We figured that other boat didn't stay in our spot twenty-four-seven, so we started watching from a distance, waiting for him to clear out so we could sneak in." His knee bounced. A bead of sweat ran over his temple.

The anticipation killed me. "The goon saw you creeping back to your spot and got angry?"

Perkins shook his head. Desperation covered his features. Why was he taking so long to spit it out? I wanted to shake his shoulders.

"You went out to your spot," I guessed. "He came fishing and found you already there, breaking your deal, poaching his fish."

"They weren't fishing, they were—" A bout of coughing cut the sentence short.

Come on, man! I jumped to my feet and ran to the kitchen for a glass of water. Slapping open cupboard after cupboard, I yanked the first mug I saw off a shelf and shoved it under the tap. "I'm coming. Hold that thought."

I dashed back into the front room. Sebastian's lips pulled down at the corners. I had no idea what he made of all this.

"You could take your shades off. We are inside a house." My frustration level beat like a neon red *TILT* sign in my head.

"They're intimidating," Sebastian replied in a voice two octaves lower than normal.

"They are," Perkins wheezed in agreement.

I jammed the mug in his hand, pointed a finger and circled my wrist in the universal wrap-it-up signal. What happened with the other boat? If they weren't fishing, why did they pay for a spot on the water?

"Dumping."

"Ew." I turned to see Sebastian hide a smile under his fist.

"Not *dumping*." Perkins struggled to find his voice once more. "Dumping. They were lowering giant black barrels into the water. There must've been a dozen of them."

"What'd you do? Did they catch you watching them? Did you tell the sheriff?"

"No. Brady insisted we let it go. I said we could turn them in and get our spot back, but he wouldn't hear of it. I knew we could get triple our monthly paycheck if they knew we knew they weren't fishing. Brady said his wife would throw a shit fit. Said if she started up protests because boats were fishing too close to shore, what would she do if she knew we took payoffs so some guy could dump who knows what out there?"

"You wanted to tell anyway."

"Yeah, I wanted to tell."

That explained the opinion of the girlfriend. Perkins did want more money, but not from Brady. Still, Brady was the one standing in the way.

"Did you want to up your pay bad enough to kill your partner?"

"What?" Deep in thought, Perkins ran a palm over the top of his head. "No. I wouldn't kill Brady. I didn't." His knee bobbed into warp speed.

"You think the other boat knows you saw what they

were up to and now they're taking out those who could turn them in for dumping?"

He shrugged, jerking his shoulders up and down. "I don't know, man. I don't know what to think or what's going on. One minute we got a good thing going. The next minute people are dying."

I didn't think it was the time to mention my recent drive-by or car bomb. He looked about two breaths away from walking into traffic. My phone dinged and he rocketed off the couch.

"I think you better go. I gotta… I got things and stuff to do," he stuttered.

Sebastian turned and waited while I walked onto the porch. The door slammed shut on his heels. My mind whirled with the unexpected turn of events. He'd opened a whole new world of possibilities. No way did Perkins kill anyone. He was losing his mind in there.

I checked my phone. A text from my old office.

Safe on the highway and heading home, Sebastian lifted a fallen spaghetti strap onto my shoulder. His eyes remained on the road. "I think you should stay at Adrian's tonight."

My mouth fell open. "You want me to stay with Adrian?"

"Not with him. At his house. I assume he's not dumb enough to go back there, since the sheriff's looking for him. Whoever killed the McGees doesn't even have Adrian on their radar. You, however, definitely are on their radar. You'll be safe there. I'll stay in your room. If anyone tries to get to you, they'll get me."

A grin lifted half of his face like the Grinch, and I shivered. Danger oozed from his pores. If anyone came after me, I didn't want to be around.

With Adrian staying in the empty art studio downstairs from my apartment, I could make myself at home in his giant house. The big wraparound porch came to mind. Would Adrian mind if I made myself at home in his place? Probably not. He didn't seem to think we had any boundaries for some reason.

"Okay. I need to stop at home for some things first and get the golf cart."

"I'll drop you at his place."

"You can follow me, but I need the cart."

He raised a brow in challenge.

"I'm not a prisoner. I appreciate what you're doing, but I'm going to have some kind of wheels with me. It's non-negotiable. I'll park in the garage."

He grunted but pulled up at my apartment a few minutes later. I gathered my things while Sebastian checked every nook and cranny for signs of Adrian.

"What do you think he meant about being downstairs?"

I shrugged. The look on Sebastian's face said he didn't believe me. If those two engaged in another kerfuffle, I didn't want to be around. After I texted the new details to Claire, I returned two e-mails to the old office. No one could find anything there. My old boss had called and hung up. I didn't return the call. No, my counseling business hadn't taken off, but it would be a while before I started calling numbers from caller ID to ask what people wanted. If my old boss needed something, like to beg me to come back, he could leave a message. I had my hands full.

"Ready?" Sebastian looked comfortable on the couch. "You know, you don't have to go. You'd be safe here with me."

"You're the one who suggested I stay at Adrian's."

He shoved to his feet. "Yes, but I didn't expect you to leave without a fight. How about..." He cocked a hip out and tossed imaginary hair off his shoulder. "'No. You're my hero, Sebastian. I want to be with you because you make me feel safe and happy.'"

"I don't talk like that." I made a big arm circle between us. "Or stand like that or toss my hair."

He tugged my bag over one shoulder and walked out onto the stoop swinging his hips.

"You look ridiculous." Truth be told, seeing someone as serious as Sebastian pretend to be a woman made it extra funny.

He tucked my bags into the backseat of the cart, strode over to the Range Rover and climbed in.

I cranked the little engine and eased out onto Main Street. The Range Rover tailed me at eight miles per hour all the way to Adrian's. The sun had dropped low enough to offer some relief, but warm, humid breezes licked my skin as I drove. Not my favorite trade. It was like being inside a giant mouth. The only bonus of the evening was the mouthwatering aromas hanging in the wet, heated air. I passed the minutes trying to name them individually, starting with the obvious buttered scallops and fresh waffle cones then dissecting the muted scents of powdered sugar from the sharp tang of Italian sausage and onions. Before I tackled the kettle corn or elephant ear conundrum, I was at Adrian's.

Sebastian carried my things to the side door nearest the marsh, under cover of willows and cattails. Dark pillows of gnats floated above the wetland nearby. I stopped to ask how we'd get in, but Sebastian had already gone to work. He slid what looked like a black leather wallet from his pocket and removed a couple of big pins. A moment later, the kitchen door swung open.

"No alarm on a place like this? Stupid." Sebastian piled

my things onto a kitchen island the size of my living room and checked out the house.

"It's Chincoteague. Nothing happens here."

He cocked an eyebrow and walked away.

I hated to leave the kitchen. It was something off of HGTV. Forget the wraparound porch, I wanted to live in the kitchen. The refrigerator was bigger than my Prius, but empty. Figured. I guess it was too much to expect he cooked, too.

"I hate this guy." Sebastian's voice echoed through the house. I started down a long hallway toward the sound. On the way I passed an open fireplace in the middle of an enormous two-story great room, a wall of windows faced the marsh and a winding staircase. Then I found him.

The first-floor master bedroom made the rest of the house look mediocre. A king-sized bed draped in gray-and-black satin stood atop a two-step platform in the center of the room. A skylight in the cathedral ceiling overhead streamed in shades of pink from the setting sun.

"Look." Sebastian lifted a remote and a flat-screen television rose from a mahogany stand at the foot of the bed. A moment later the lights dimmed. Then a small corner fireplace flicked on. He tossed the remote onto the bed. "I can't imagine why you were so eager to stay here. Maybe I should stay with you. For protection."

"Ha."

"Fine. I'm going back to your place to try to get attacked so I can break this guy and put the case to rest. Plus, I need to contact the EPA about the dumping and the harbor to find out where Perkins's old spot was."

My head fell backward. "I should've asked him. Jeez. We were right there and I never thought to ask."

"I did. I figured he'd lie then tip off whoever he's got a deal going with."

"Tap his phone." We could run back there with one more question then wait to see who he called.

"Not without the proper paperwork. We don't have anything strong enough to get clearance on that kind of privacy invasion."

"Fine. Enjoy your vacation." Dumb rules.

I walked him to the door. He leaned forward and kissed the top of my head. Before pulling away, he breathed against my ear, "Call me if you need anything." A shiver dropped to my toes and my cheeks caught fire.

By the time my senses returned, Sebastian was long gone. My tummy growled. I considered a trip to the Tasty Cream, but decided I had temporary custody of a kitchen too fabulous to ignore. I grabbed my purse and headed to Frontier Foods, the island's only grocery.

Twenty minutes later, I had the makings of a feast with all the trimmings. I unloaded my arms onto the counter. The cashier's eyes widened when she saw me. Did she recognize me? I didn't recognize her. The family in front of me paid for a stack of fixings big enough for a great cookout, while I ran through a mental list of ways I might know the cashier. I came up empty.

My mind wouldn't stop working on more pressing issues. What kind of coldblooded killer bothered to whisper his threats to me? He'd had me alone. I was in his hands, yet he didn't kill me. The thought he knew me personally had taken up root in my brain. If we weren't connected somehow, I'd be dead. Wouldn't I? I'd run through a lengthy list of old teachers, coaches, friends of my parents, trying to label one a killer. I couldn't. Now I had new information to deal with. This threat-maker/killer moonlighted as an ocean contaminator and he had enough money to pay off Perkins and McGee. I didn't know anyone like that. Did I?

"Patience Price?" The lady behind the counter smiled. I was up. "Yes."

She burst into tears.

"Um." I looked around, nervous to discover no one in sight. No one. I patted her shoulder across the conveyor belt. "It's okay. Hey, don't cry. I don't have to buy all this junk." I had picked up way too many desserts. Stress eating.

She lifted a package onto the scanner. *Beep.* "It's my dog."

"I'm sorry?" I cocked an eyebrow.

Beep. She shoved the peppers and bruschetta into a paper sack. "He ran away when I was working in the garden last month. He never came back, and I think he might be lost in the national park."

My heart clenched. Did horses eat puppies? No. They could kick him, though. I bet they'd kick him for being on their turf. "I'm sure he's fine. No one's found him?"

"No." Sniff. Sniff. *Beep.* "I put signs up everywhere. What if a tourist took him home?"

Or he drowned in the ocean. "I'm sure he's fine. You need to stay strong for him."

Her eyes widened. "Yes." *Beep. Beep.* She slid the Oreos in beside the Nutter Butters. "I do need to be strong for him. I'm off tomorrow. I should pack his favorite treats and go door-to-door looking for him."

"I bet he'd appreciate that. No matter what happens, you'll know you did all you could."

She nodded in acceptance. We shook hands. "I'm Melissa."

"It's nice to meet you." I fished a pack of travel tissues from my purse.

"Have a nice night." She packed the eggs and bread on top and turned to leave her station.

"But…" I took the packages, wondering if I'd just made a friend or met a patient.

"It's on me." She smiled sweetly, wiping tears. "Thank you. Everyone around here's right about you. You're sweet. I hope people will stop shooting at you soon."

"Me, too." I raised my hand and started for the door. A wave of guilt crashed over me. I turned back for the counter and extended the cookie bag in her direction. "Did your puppy like cookies?"

"Y-y-yes." She burst into sobs and I wrapped an arm around her.

When I finally walked outside, it was dark. I approached the cart with trepidation, watching under it as I got closer. No bad guys in the backseat. I climbed in and my hand slid over something disgusting.

"Ah!" I jumped out, wiping my hands on my shorts, praying it wasn't blood. I dashed to the window of the store and examined my hand. Nothing. For a minute I wondered if a bird bombed me. I clicked my phone into flashlight mode and went back to the cart.

Eggs.

Someone had egged my cart while I was buying dinner. Every square inch of the seat was smeared in slick, clear slime and yellow goo. Cracked shells stuck to every surface. I turned the phone over to call Sebastian, and the light caught something else.

Someone had spray-painted *Whore* on the hood. *Home Wrecker* extended around the driver's side to the back bumper. I choked. *Home Wrecker?* Seriously? I snapped a few pictures and sent them to Sebastian. My life was ridiculous wrapped in impossible. Mary Franks had lost her mind. Apparently Hank hadn't come clean and admitted to seeing me for therapy. I couldn't tell her he was a patient. I took an oath. Confidentiality was paramount to counselors.

The minute my life wasn't in danger, I was registering those two with a family plan.

SIXTEEN

I woke to the sounds of an intruder. My unfamiliar surroundings disarmed me. Hurrying to hide, I tangled and slid in the masses of silk sheets. My legs were pinned, and the floor wasn't where it should be. I tumbled onto the floor, bouncing against the two steps below the bed. Ouch! Wide awake and sore, a shock of recollection brought my life back in focus.

Hooray! I knew where I was.

Boo! I still heard the intruder.

Scrambling to my feet, I ducked behind the door and listened, hoping to localize the sounds and form a plan. Running water set the backdrop. Sizzling punctuated the white noise of the sink, and scents of coffee and bacon danced down the hall. The intruder was making breakfast. I eased from my hideout and braved the hall.

Whistling drifted along with the scrumptious smells.

"Hello?" I wrapped my arms across my middle, hoping it was Sebastian and not a cooking killer.

"Remember when we used to play house?" Adrian flipped a pancake over his massive silver stovetop. "I always knew I'd make you breakfast one day. How'd you sleep?"

"What are you doing here?"

"I live here. What are you doing here?" He wiped his hands onto a towel on the counter and moved in my direction. The ridiculous dimple I'd kissed a thousand times made an appearance.

"Hiding. Sebastian thought I'd be safe here. He's sleeping in my bed, hoping the bad guy will go there to attack me."

Adrian frowned.

"Do you mind if I stay here?" I asked.

"Of course not. Sit. Eat." He returned to the counter, dished out bacon and pancakes for two and then poured coffee into twin mugs.

"Thanks." I sat down on a stool at the kitchen's island, wishing he hadn't mentioned us playing house. We set up house under my parents' home every day after school until fifth grade. I was the wife, and he was the husband. I made him sand pies and he kissed my cheeks the way we watched Dad kiss Mom every day. My gut twisted. I needed a subject change.

"We talked to Perkins."

"I heard." He pulled out a stool beside me and dug in. "Your roommate filled me in last night."

"Ah." Images of the fight I'd broken up between the two men flashed through my mind. I gulped the coffee. "How did that go?"

"You were wrong. He isn't any fun, but we came to an agreement."

"Which is what?" I couldn't imagine what they might agree on. Pistols at sunrise came to mind.

"We both want you safe. We both want to know what's going on with the dumping and why the McGees had to die over it. Once you figure that out, I'll turn myself in."

He looked more confident than I felt. No big deal. Have some pancakes, solve some murders.

"Your phone hasn't stopped dancing," he said.

My phone buzzed in a small circle on Vibrate. I couldn't believe I left it on the counter all night. I usually slept with it on the nightstand. Good thing I hadn't needed to call 911. I lifted it to check messages.

"You've got to be kidding me." What kind of people would keep calling their predecessor for help doing her old job? Rude didn't begin to cover it.

"So, what's the plan?" Adrian ran his empty plate under water. "Your guard dog didn't have a lot of answers."

"What makes you think I do?"

"You're always plotting something."

"Am not."

He stopped and turned to stare.

Fine. "Do you happen to know where Brady and Perkins used to fish until a couple of months ago?"

"Why? Are you planning to scuba dive and strap the toxic barrels to your back?"

"He told you about the barrels?" It didn't seem like Sebastian to share information with Adrian, especially when he didn't trust him. Or maybe he knew about the barrels because he was involved. I set my fork down and swallowed hard.

"I might've overheard him on the phone."

And he also might've been dumping them himself. Maybe that's what brought him back to the island.

I looked at my phone again, pretending to check the time. "Shoot. You'd better scram. Sebastian's meeting me here."

He looked at me, his expression wary. "McGee fished out by the Saturday-night spot." I blushed. I'd spent plenty of Saturday nights with Adrian at that spot, many of them skinny-dipping. "Thanks. I'll check it out."

He nodded. "I'll see you soon." He kissed the top of my head and let himself out the side door. "Don't trash the place. Here's a key. Don't leave the house unlocked anymore." He flicked a key dangling from a hook beside the door.

I'd had to leave the house unlocked when I went for groceries or I wouldn't have been able to get back in.

The minute he disappeared I ran to get dressed, then grabbed the oldest-looking towel I could find and slung it over one shoulder. I also texted Sebastian to let him know I was heading to my parents'. Once I dropped the cart off there, I wasn't driving it anymore. Ever.

On the way out, I locked up, checked the knob twice and wondered if Adrian would be back. Had he been here all night? How'd he know it was unlocked while I was at the grocery unless he walked in during that time? I unraveled a few feet of garden hose from the side of Adrian's house and turned the knob. Bracing myself for the strongest spray I could create, I hosed busted shells and egg from the cart. What appeared to be raccoon scat triggered my gag reflex. There was little to be done about the graffiti. I hung up the hose and rubbed the towel over the seat before climbing aboard. The golf cart purred to life and floated down the quiet streets.

Keeping my chin high on Main Street wasn't easy. Not in a purple golf cart with *WHORE* on the hood. Heads turned and cell phones appeared. Safe to assume half called to report my profanity mobile and the other half snapped pictures. I was sure to be tomorrow's front page news—again. Mom started a collection after the drive-by shooting. The car bomb made two articles for her scrapbook. Home Wrecker should make three. If counseling failed, I'd try my hand at local celebrity.

Mom stood on the sidewalk outside The Pony, chattering into her phone as she waited on me. When she saw me, she laughed. The cart stopped right in front of her, and she ran to give me a hug.

"Oh, honey. I came right outside as soon as I heard you were coming my way." She tugged me into the shop with her.

Dad slipped outside. He circled the cart slowly, rubbing his forehead. I held my breath, waiting. He waved and yelled, "Not a big deal. I can fix it."

For the first time, I wished I had some of his special water to calm me down. That was the most humiliating drive I'd ever made, even worse than leaving the FBI when they fired me. What if people in town thought Sebastian was my married boyfriend? Who knew what anyone would make of such an act of vandalism.

"It's bad karma." This was Mom's equivalent to "It's not your fault."

"I've done nothing to earn bad karma. I'm trying to help people." I sank into a nest of pillows by the children's book area of The Pony. Leafing through a stack of pony-themed board books, I felt almost like a child again.

The bell tinkled over the front door and I slunk lower into the pillows. Sebastian and Dad walked inside. My parents disappeared, and Sebastian joined me on the floor.

"Nice ride." I guessed the pictures I sent hadn't done it justice. The poor little cart was one of those things a person needed to see to fully appreciate. My parents disappeared. "Your ex stopped up to see you last night. I'm not sure he's convinced he's your *ex*."

"I heard."

Sebastian's face blanked. "When?"

"He made me breakfast."

His teeth ground together. The muscles in his jaw worked. His eye twitched.

"He didn't sleep over. He was in the kitchen when I woke up. I thought he was an intruder." Explaining myself bothered me even more than checking in with him. This situation wasn't working for me. The days when I made my own schedule with nary a thought of death seemed long past instead of just last week.

His shoulders relaxed. "I mean, if he did, that's fine."

Fine? That made me mad, too. I must've looked like I felt because he began to fumble.

"It's not fine. Or, fine to you, not to me." He cleared his throat, inhaled deeply and locked eyes with me. "You should be happy. I'm not here to tell you who to spend your time with. That sounds exhausting." His eyes looked wild, but somehow he concealed emotion like I concealed cellulite. "I came here to help you clear your ex of a crime, and then people started shooting at you. Now it isn't about him anymore, but he's still in the picture? Inconceivable." He shifted on the pillows, looking frustrated. "This is crazy. Right?"

I loved that he used the word *inconceivable*. It had been one of my favorite words since I watched *The Princess Bride* in kindergarten. "What do you mean? This isn't how it usually goes when you start seeing someone?"

His cheek lifted with the hint of a smile.

Crap. Did I say we were seeing each other? Were we seeing each other? We weren't. Were we?

"All fixed." Dad dusted his palms together, returning from outside.

I scurried to the door. "Oh. No." I shoved my way out into the sunlight, letting the door slap shut behind me. Dad had painted giant ovals and polka dots over the letters in a dark shade of hot pink.

"What do you think, Peepee? Pink's still your favorite color, right? Everyone likes polka dots."

"It looks like my sister's old lava lamp." Sebastian smiled at Dad.

"Yep." I marched back into the store, passing Dad and Sebastian. "Mom!"

Mom popped her head out from the back room.

"I'm going to ride home with Sebastian." I'd had enough of the golf cart.

I turned back toward the door. Sebastian and Dad stood side by side. They looked out at the harbor, arms folded over their chests, neither of them speaking. Next to Sebastian, Dad looked like a Care Bear. Dad trusted everyone. Sebastian trusted no one. Dad wore shirts to protest war and support PETA. Sebastian wore jackets to cover his Glock.

I never had to worry about my parents being too tough on a new guy before. They liked and approved of everyone, but Sebastian was the first true stranger I'd ever brought home to meet them. It was a little late to be nervous, considering we'd shacked up a week ago, but a horde of butterflies invaded my stomach anyway.

"You coming out, Peepee?" Dad pulled the door wide.

I'd stopped mid-push.

Sebastian furrowed his brow. "You all right?"

"Hot. I think. Tired." Crazy-sexy and apparently sixteen again. "Can I ride with you?" I waved toward the cart by way of explanation.

Sebastian tilted his head to the Range Rover and swung the passenger door open for me. I kissed Dad's cheek good-bye and climbed in. We went straight to Adrian's house. After he'd checked every room thoroughly, Sebastian turned to me. "I get the feeling Adrian has your place bugged. I don't know how he gets in or out, either. How about we stay here awhile? I'll make dinner and hang out with you until dark."

"I'll make dinner." While I worked in the grand kitchen, I cooked up a plan. As much as I enjoyed Sebastian's company and appreciated his protection, I had something I wanted to do alone.

"Can you believe this place?" Sebastian straddled a stool at the kitchen island. "How can he afford it? He doesn't seem to have a job."

"You don't need a job if you have a trust fund. Besides, he's had four years since he finished his MBA to rack up savings."

"No school loans?" Sebastian tapped his fingers against the marble island top.

"Nope." Unlike me. I had a ton of student loans. I'd insisted on paying my own way when my parents offered, and partial scholarships only go so far.

"Adrian's family's been on the island forever. I think his ancestors crashed here on a boat from Spain and stayed. They're like royalty here."

"He doesn't look Hispanic."

I shrugged. "I don't look Italian, but my mom's dad came over from Italy."

He nodded. "His mom owns the tanning salon?"

"She really likes a good tan."

"A tanning salon on an island doesn't seem like a big moneymaker." Sebastian snorted.

"The Davises are shellfish farmers. They have been for generations. Their stuff is sold in every grocery chain in the country."

"Shellfish." He released a little laugh and joined me at the stove. "What do you have going over here?" He stopped behind me. "This is grilled cheese."

"I'm not a great cook." I never had time to learn and frankly, my appetite waned by the day.

"I love grilled cheese." Sebastian's voice had a smile in it. He opened cupboards until he found two plates, and I dished up the sandwiches.

"No, you don't. I should've made something better."
My shoulders slumped. My heart wasn't into playing host-
ess. Life was too complicated and I was in a hurry.

He carried our plates to the island and we ate in companionable silence. Sebastian never wasted words. Quiet
people used to make me nervous. Lately I found a new
appreciation for being still.

"Are you sure you're comfortable here alone?" he
asked. He carried our empty dishes, washed them and
set them in the rack to dry.

"I'm fine. Really." I hoped he believed me. I hadn't
fully convinced myself yet.

Sebastian took another trip around the house, peeking
into doors and listening, as if someone could sneak inside
without him knowing.

"Yeah. I'm okay. Thank you for staying at my place,
and for looking after me. I know you have your own things
to deal with."

He returned to the kitchen and stepped into my personal space.

"I'm glad to be here." His eyes bore into mine.

My craning neck ached from looking up at him. My
mind went blank.

"I'll come back in the morning." He slipped his arms
around my waist and pulled me to his chest. I pressed
one cheek against his shirt and relaxed into the embrace.

"Stay inside. Don't open the door for strangers. Call
me if you need anything, if you hear or see something unusual, or just get nervous and want company. Anything.
Understand?"

I nodded against his shirt because I could only agree
to some of his requests. If I made eye contact during a
lie, even a partial one, I was toast.

He pressed his lips to my head and let himself out the

side door. I locked up behind him and watched his taillights disappear. The minute he was out of sight, I went
to change. I packed a gym bag I found in Adrian's closet
and tossed in some things I might need. Ready for reconnaissance, I headed to the garage. Just as I hoped, two
black-and-yellow oars hung on the wall. I pulled them
down and looked for the dingy. No dingy. He did, however, have a kayak.

I hated kayaking. The feeling of being pinned into a
little boat freaked me out. I walked down the hill outside
to the marsh. Probably he left his dingy tied to the dock in
the summer. A spiderweb wrapped around my face about
two steps into the trees outside his house.

Bleck. I spat it out and wiped my eyes free of the silk.
My head itched the rest of the way to the dock. No dingy.
Stupid Adrian and his dumb kayak fetish. I hiked back up
the hill to the garage and pulled the kayak off the wall.
For crying out loud. I'd never had to drag one, plus an
oar, down a hill. I left the second oar in the garage. By
the time I got the boat in the water, I was ready to call it
a night. I slid my cell into a Ziploc bag and left the rest of
my supplies on the dock. Nowhere to carry a gym bag in
a kayak. Dangling binoculars around my neck and checking for killers, I eased down into the seat.

I took the causeway around the marsh to the national
shoreline, past the beach and out to where Adrian told me
Perkins used to fish. I wasn't sure what I expected to find,
but I wanted to see the location someone paid thousands
to pollute. Maybe I'd see fish floating belly-up or wildlife
in need of rescue. I paddled faster toward the old Saturday-night spot. I knew the place well—a clearing in the
woods with room for private parties at the shoreline that
parents didn't know about. Many of my Saturday night

memories started there. A lot of broken promises haunted that hunk of sand, along with a few broken hearts.

When the clouds moved away, the moon was full. Its reflection rippled over the water's surface. I relaxed and inhaled. I snapped a picture for Claire with my phone, but it didn't turn out. Phone pictures never did scenery justice. I slid the phone back inside the bag and almost lost my oar.

In the darkness, a large ship motored past me and slowed. The wake bobbed me around like a human buoy. I tried the binoculars to see who it was. Thanks to the moonlight, I glimpsed shady images of people moving around on deck. Finally, luck was on my side. I had only intended to scope out the area and reminisce, but if this was the boat in question, I could get some answers. I placed the Ziploc bag in my lap and paddled slowly toward the boat, careful to keep my distance and stay in the ship's shadow.

The sleek white vessel looked closer to a yacht than a fishing boat. I imagined a private party on board with no idea that someone dumped who-knows-what in the same spot. I stretched my phone out in front of me to capture the boat name and numbers, just in case. I clicked, and my flash lit up the night.

SPLASH.

Whoa. The kayak jerked and bobbed beneath me. Someone had dropped a giant barrel right past my head into the water.

"What was that?" Men's voices swirled above me as footfalls pounded the deck overhead. I grabbed the oar and paddled for my life into the dark, away from the boat.

"There. Look there! Who's out there?" The voice seethed, gravelly and adamant. I kept my eyes on the moon's reflection on the water ahead of me.

"Get the light."

Crap. My arms burned from effort. I prayed their flashlight beam couldn't reach me. The ocean lit up. A giant spotlight trained on the back of my head cast a shadow of me onto the water ahead. Who were these people?

Bang! Bang! Bang! Split. Splat. Split. Splat.

Tiny splashes rained down around me. A shower of bullets hit the tail of Adrian's stupid yellow kayak, and I capsized.

"Eep!" I squealed and crashed face-first into the ominous darkness.

SEVENTEEN

I NEEDED AIR. I had lungs like a mermaid, but I wasn't one. Turning to my side as the surface broke over me, I inhaled and dove again, focusing my efforts on getting far away from the kayak, which they'd surely come looking for.

The shots ended, but the spotlight was going strong. Gaining on me. The light moved steady through the water. My kayak was either farther now than the boat, or it had already sunk. The fast-approaching boat scanned the shoreline. I mentally rolled my eyes. For once my horrible sense of direction came in handy. Someone drowning would head for shore. Unless they thought they were heading for shore while in fact they were headed out to sea. Like me.

Several minutes in, my limbs began to burn from effort and fear. Treading water in the dark ocean while a giant boat looked for me with a spotlight made the simple exercise excruciating. Not to mention, I had no idea how long I'd been stuck in the water, or how much longer I would be. The boat trolled back and forth, spotlight trained against the shallow waters and beach. Somewhere, at the bottom of the ocean, my cell phone sat protected in a Ziploc bag.

The boat changed direction once more and made a pass so close to me the waves sent out from it slapped me in the face. On instinct, I ducked beneath the water and swam in the opposite direction of the boat. Release stretched over my arms and legs at the opportunity to swim again.

Treading was tiresome. When I broke the surface gingerly after swimming about fifty yards, the boat was gone. Before I could spend too much time wondering how soon it might return, I dove again and swam for shore. My freestyle was quick, but beneath the surface, I was a bullet.

When my fingers dusted the soft sand, I knew I was close. Barely onto the mushy sandbar near the marsh, a light flooded overhead. Profanity I hadn't used since high school poured over my lips. All the while, my feet got busy carrying me away into the cattails and grasses ahead. Lucky for me the wind kicked up, hopefully disguising my flight through the reeds.

"Frick!" My left foot slid in muck, which felt suspiciously like manure. I slipped onto my knees. The warm squish encased my favorite old Chuck and sucked it off. I pulled my foot free to find it naked. Of all the ridiculous... The light slid over my head in the weeds. Shoe forgotten, my body flew forward in a full-out sprint until every new breath burned like knives in my sides and down my throat.

The forest at night had always looked ominous. Shadows rose and towered around me in every direction. Crickets chirped wildly and bullfrogs moaned near the marsh. My breath caught in my throat at every screech of an owl or scurry of night-creature feet. The shine of tiny eyes came and went in the distance. Raccoons? Possums? Deer? Thankfully all were too small to be ponies. I'd feared the forest at night for as long as I could remember. I'd never have believed it would one day be my sanctuary.

I rested against a large tree, concentrating on my breathing and taking bodily inventory. All the necessary appendages were accounted for. Next, I tried to acclimate myself. The full moon hid behind the canopy of trees overhead, making it impossible to get a good idea of where I came out of the water, or which way was town. Gnarled, drooping branches morphed before me into silhouettes of creepy arms. I reached for my phone, only to remember its new home at the bottom of the ocean.

Back on my feet, I began hobbling forward, hoping to get eyes on the biggest landmark I could think of, the old lighthouse. The lighthouse had a well-trodden trail to the main road out of the national forest. If I could get there, I knew how to get anywhere else.

In the distance, hoofbeats pounded the forest floor. Ponies. My heart jumped into my throat. I'd survived gunshots only to die at the hand of ponies. Owls screeched above me, adding urgency to my plight. Field mice scurried over the path ahead of me. An engine roared nearby, which, combined with the growing sound of the waves, let me know I was heading toward the national seashore and the road leading there from town. As much as I wanted away from the boat, the road would have people, park rangers at least.

"Patience!"

I stopped.

Silence.

Perhaps delirium was setting in. I began moving in search of the road back to town. My shoeless foot throbbed from my missteps on twigs hidden under leaves. Asphalt would feel like clouds underfoot compared to this.

"Patience!"

I froze, eyes closed to help me concentrate. No more stampeding horse sounds. No more engine noise. Murmuring hummed from the direction of the ocean. I opened my eyes and moved with caution toward the sound. Soon, red and blue lights floated overhead. Another engine approached. The sheriff?"

"Patience!"

"Sebastian?" He echoed my name, and I, his. The

exchange lasted only a few moments before a light bounced toward me.

"Patience!" A mixture of alarm and relief swirled in the word. He hit me like a brick wall, lifting me into his arms as though I weighed no more than the flashlight that he dropped and left on the ground.

"Here!" he called. "She's here!"

His embrace, wide and warm, formed a cocoon around me. He swept me into position like a parent used to carry a sleeping child.

Exhausted, I laid my cheek against his chest and lost my mind. Sobs racked my body. Frustration and anger threatened to set my hair on fire. I was not a damsel in distress.

Usually.

"Shh," he whispered against the crown of my head. The sound soothed me back to reality. I needed to get a grip.

How did he keep walking so easily? My sopping wet clothes and shoe had to add ten pounds to my weight. He didn't seem to notice.

"Patience!" Mom's voice pierced the darkness.

Blue and red lights appeared front and center as we emerged from the trees. The sheriff stood near an ambulance talking with several bystanders. A little circle of park rangers and miscellaneous strangers stood in the road near the emergency vehicles.

My mother nearly knocked me from Sebastian's arms. She checked me from head to toe, patting me like a blind person despite the full moon's light. "You're alive!" She crushed me to him, wrapping her arms around us both like a sandwich, successfully soaking the both of them with my wetness.

"Why wouldn't I be?" The thought came up short when

I noticed the kayak's pieces bobbing at the edge of the beach. My breath shuddered.

"I need to talk with the sheriff." I squeezed her hand in reassurance and kissed her cheek. "This will be over very soon." Shoulders back, I walked awkwardly to the sheriff's side and kicked off my last shoe for balance.

"Something you'd like to tell me, Miss Price?" His bushy gray brows rose.

"A boat dumped black barrels into the water about two miles out." I pointed in the direction where I'd been. "Someone's dumping where Brady McGee used to fish. Adrian didn't kill him. Something bigger is happening here. They shot at me and I swam to shore."

He didn't look as surprised as I expected, considering the revelation.

The deputy appeared at my side. His wide, eager eyes startled me. "How long ago was this? Did you see which way the boat went?"

How long ago had it been? I'd treaded water until I thought my limbs would give out. That was after they arrived, noticed and shot at me. How long had I been in the woods? Time had lost meaning when all I could think of was survival and then finding home. I swallowed emotion and turned the conversation away from the fact I didn't know how long the night had already been.

"I took a picture of it, but then they shot at me, and my phone sank. It was in a Ziploc bag." I didn't know why I wanted a pat on the back for thinking ahead about the bag. Fat lot of good it did.

The deputy questioned me about the boat while my parents, the sheriff and Sebastian watched. I'd seen the boat, photographed it, but couldn't remember anything specific. He radioed in my description anyway. "The Coast

Guard is on the lookout. You did good." He clapped me on the shoulder.

"How did you guys get here?" I turned back to the sheriff who'd crossed his arms over his chest.

"I called." Sebastian walked slowly in my direction. He was roughly the same height as Deputy Doofus, but infinitely broader. The men around us wore uniforms to announce their importance. Sebastian wore his announcement across his face. His square shoulders, narrowed eyes and clenching jaw made no room for error. Sebastian wasn't to be trifled with.

"You called the sheriff? Why?"

He held his empty hands out in my direction like an offering. "When your tracker failed, I knew something happened to your phone. Since I've never seen you without it, and with the week you've been having, I went ahead and called in the cavalry."

A low-flying helicopter complete with spotlight buzzed over us, blowing my hair into my eyes. The spotlight swept across the waters and into the night. The Coast Guard responded faster than I imagined possible. I said a silent prayer for their success and turned to Sebastian.

"My what failed?"

He stepped back.

"You put a tracker on me?" Fury sizzled under my icy wet skin. "Were you expecting me to be abducted?"

He tipped his head left then right, ear to shoulder. "I should've told you."

"You think?"

"You would've said no." As if this was a solid argument.

"I don't need to be tracked. I'm not a criminal." My voice rose. Mom came to my side. "What kind of tracker? Were you listening to me, too? Watching?" I shivered at the humiliating things he could've seen me do. I'd popped a stress zit the size of Wisconsin before I left Adrian's house. Did he see that?

The sheriff snuffled. I supposed he wished I was behind bars. I turned to him. "You think I'm a criminal? Someone who needs a tracker?" A week's worth of emotion bubbled up. I didn't care about the tracker as much as I didn't want to be shot at ever again. Ever. Never. Ever. Never.

"I think you've been at the center of every call I've gotten since you came home."

That wasn't true. I had nothing to do with Mrs. Mc-Gee's murder, and he beat me to her house. I bit my lip to keep from mentioning it.

"Got 'em!" The deputy strolled over, looking victorious. "Coast Guard boarded a boat fitting the description you gave. They found a spotlight and an arsenal on deck. They're taking them in for questioning and sending divers out within forty-eight hours to see what they left down there."

I fist-pumped the air before shoving my hands behind my back. The sheriff scowled. I suppose I had to fill out another report.

"Are we done here?" Sebastian spoke, drawing attention his way.

"Take her home." Dad wrapped a thermal blanket over my shoulders. "We'll come by with lunch tomorrow. Sleep in. Relax a little." He hugged me tight then took Mom by the hand and led her to the VW.

"You heard the man." Sebastian scooped me up again and headed for his Ranger.

"Why are you carrying me?"

"You're barefoot."

I didn't complain.

At my apartment, I took a shower and patted myself on the back. Case solved. Criminals caught. Moving on. Toweling the water out of my hair, I made my way to the kitchen for some tea.

"How does it feel to be a hero?" Sebastian stood at attention, evaluating me.

"You should know. I can't believe you came for me. Your stupid tracker stunt was kind of smart."

He nodded and moved to the living room. The couch looked more inviting with him seated on it. Sebastian patted the cushion beside him. "I'm glad you're safe. When I saw the kayak…" He shook his head and didn't finish the sentence.

"How'd you know I was in a kayak?"

"Your ex." He laughed. "He showed up right after I'd settled in. I told him what we found out and he guaranteed me you'd get involved. He hid his boat from you but left the kayak. He assured me you'd never go anywhere willingly in a kayak."

He'd hidden his boat? Adrian Davis was the single most annoying creature ever born.

"So, you made friends with the fugitive?" I asked.

"No." He smiled. "He's all right. Plus, we have something in common. We both think you need a babysitter."

I whacked him with Claire's pretty golden pillow. "No more putting trackers on me."

He shrugged.

No promises then.

"You weren't kidding about tourists." Sebastian sipped his coffee beside me on the stoop. Freud sat purring in his lap.

"Nope. This little island is a big deal every July…if you're in the market for a wild pony." I shivered. Yuck.

Cars lined every road in town, honking occasionally. I cringed with every honk. Honking didn't belong on Chincoteague. Rented bicycles dotted the corners and families streamed in and out of rental homes as far as the eye could see.

Arrooga! The bright blue-and-white VW bus pulled up in front of my place. The purple cart rolled up behind it. Dad waved from the driver's seat of the polka-dotted eyesore. Mom rounded the hood of the bus and jogged lithely up the steps toward me.

"We want you to take the bus until we get the cart re-painted, or until your Prius is replaced." She extended her hand, dangling the keys from a finger. "Everyone needs transportation." She smiled and the world grew brighter.

"Thanks." I locked eyes with her, concentrating on her generous offering and not on the fact I'd be driving a fifty-year-old love bus.

"Are you ready for Pony Week?" she asked Sebastian.

"I have to head back to work. Looks like I'll miss most of the fun. I would like to come by and check on Patience after work, if she'll have me." He looked uncertain.

"That would be lovely." Mom clapped. "You should come by tomorrow night for dinner. Do you like to grill?"

"Anything made on a grill sounds delicious." His smile widened.

I nodded. "Yes. Come back." My cheeks burned. Stupid blush. I cleared my throat. "I need to run by Adrian's and get my things. He should be home soon. I'm sure he's heard the true culprit has been apprehended."

My gaze traveled to the art studio below, wondering if he'd left yet for home. Sebastian followed my gaze and laughed before nodding in understanding. Adrian had literally hidden under his feet. I worried for a minute because I'd given away his hideout, but at least he wouldn't need it anymore.

"I'll walk over with you." Sebastian offered me his elbow.

"You kids have fun. Take the love bus if you want." Mom slid into the cart with Dad. He inched out into traffic, waving good-bye, then got stuck behind a string of minivans.

I turned a suspicious eye on Sebastian as we walked. "What? You aren't insisting we drive everywhere now? Is it the traffic?"

"It's the fact you're in one piece, unlike that kayak. You saved the day, caught the dumpers and saved an undetermined amount of sea life. Now I can relax again. You, on the other hand, have a pile of messages on the counter near the old landline jack. Here." He dug a BlackBerry from his pocket. "Carry this until you get the other replaced. Just in case."

"Thanks. A pile, huh?"

He nodded. "Enough to keep you busy awhile."

"And all is well just in time for you to go back to work."

"I don't know how I'm supposed to concentrate in Norfolk with you being shot at out here all day."

I aimed my elbow into his ribs. "They didn't shoot at me every day, and never for long. At least it's over and you can stop worrying."

Sebastian slowed his pace beside me. "That wasn't the end of your problems, Patience."

My feet pulled up short as we cut through a driveway onto Adrian's street. Sheriff Murray's car sat out front of Adrian's home. His deputy leaned against the handrail to the stairs, writing in his notebook. His face brightened when he looked my way.

"That was good work you did last night. It was nice to

have some good news this week. It's been a tough road lately for the island. Two deaths in a row." He shook his head. "We're real glad you thought to sneak up on them at night like that."

Sebastian elbowed me this time.

Deputy Fargas looked between us, fumbling for words. "I mean, it was dangerous and you should've let someone know what you were up to." He didn't suppress his smile. "But, hot damn, did one little kayak ruin their night."

"If you give up these rights…" Sheriff Murray appeared, dragging Adrian around the wraparound porch and onto the stairs with us. He raised an eyebrow as he passed me by. Adrian wore shiny silver handcuffs.

"What are you doing?" My hands balled into fists at my sides. A pain shot through my temple and one eye twitched.

One hand on Adrian's head, Sheriff Murray stuffed him into the backseat of the cruiser, finished his spiel and turned to me. "Do I understand correctly you were living here with a fugitive?"

"No. I was staying here as a house sitter." I uncurled my fingers and locked palms against my hips, daring him to push me. I had no idea what I'd do or say, but seeing Adrian in handcuffs did something to me. My insides twisted until I wanted to spring at someone. If the sheriff wanted a piece of me, I was good and ready.

"What'd you arrest him for now? Someone else commit a crime you want a scapegoat for?" The minute the words were out, I regretted them. I hadn't bucked authority like that, not in a decade. "The Coast Guard caught the dumpers. Why are you here?"

"The Coast Guard caught dumpers, not murderers, Miss Price. Do you have any evidence to connect a handful of ocean-contaminators with murder? Or do you think when one criminal goes to jail, another should be set free? No one has proven Mr. Davis innocent. He's under arrest. He'll need an attorney to get him off, not his girlfriend."

Sebastian stiffened at my side.

The deputy waved a chipper good-bye and slid into the sheriff's passenger seat. Adrian looked at us out the window like a kid being taken from his parents. It was the single most outrageous example of injustice ever. I wanted to stamp my foot and toss gravel at the cruiser. I had worked hard to clear Adrian's name. I was shot at and car bombed. How did I not see this coming? I couldn't tie the dumpers to the murders and neither could anyone else.

Strong arms pulled me to Sebastian's chest. My arms hung loosely at my sides.

Just when I thought the nightmare was over, Adrian was still going to jail for murder.

EIGHTEEN

I DIDN'T SLEEP. Sebastian kept me company late into the night, but my mind kept me up, running through scenarios where I might've done things differently. Even after I said good-night and moved to my room, I sat in bed looking out the window Adrian had climbed through so many times. The moon lit a path over my sheets. I stretched my fingers out to catch it and then I hugged my knees to my chest. How could I have prevented Adrian's arrest? No matter how many times I asked myself that question, I came up with nothing.

Blaming Adrian was easier. Why did he go home? Then guilt set in. Was he looking for me? Had he heard about my ordeal the night before? Did he come back to make me breakfast again? Was he worried about me? About his kayak?

I knew he didn't care about his kayak. My nose burned and my eyes ached to cry.

Adrian never cared about things. He loved people. The island. Me. Once upon a time anyway.

The moonlight softened as clouds passed overhead, still threatening the town with the storm that never came. Before I was ready, dim moonlight gave way to ashy hues and soon flickers of a new day replaced the night. I dozed off sometime after watching the sun rise. Basking in shards of amber-and-rose sunlight relaxed my shaky body into dreamland. How many times had Adrian and I stolen wine from my parents' cabinet and sat on the roof making plans?

In the space of a heartbeat, I stood at the back of a church, dressed in white and facing a long canopy of lilies, baby's breath and tulle. The wheezy old organ from the church on First Street blared out a tune, and I turned to find Dad at my side. It was hard to see through the gauzy material. I ran my fingertips over the veil. Daddy pulled me along, trampling rose petals and smiling proudly all the way, while I stumbled along, staring into curious faces.

Confusion seized my thoughts as we arrived at my final destination. The groom's back faced me, his head tilted away, speaking quietly to the preacher. Who wanted to marry me? I stumbled back over my long satin train. I was downsized. Unemployed. Small chested. I liked the last part, but men didn't share my enthusiasm. Probably because they never had to shop for a two-piece bathing suit.

"Dearly beloved," the preacher began. I gasped when my dad tried to hand me off to the groom. His face was concealed in shadows only a dream could produce. When I started to protest the assumption I wanted to be tethered to one man for the rest of my life, Sheriff Murray appeared in place of the preacher and looked down his pointy nose at me. The sight didn't derail my argument. I wanted assurance I didn't have to change my name or cook or clean. My groom didn't bother to look at me. What was his problem?

"Hey." I shook my bouquet in my groom's direction. "Look at me. We're getting married here."

Dad placed my hand in the groom's, and the man turned to me. Stained-glass windows surrounded us and their reflected color flickered over his stunning white tuxedo. I was about to become Mrs....

"Good morning, sunshine."

Sebastian knocked on my open door. My cheeks burned at the idea he might've heard my dream. He sauntered in, pausing at my bedside to make room for a tray. Sebastian wasn't the kind of man I imagined fixing breakfast.

"I wasn't sure what to make, so I prepared everything."

He wasn't joking. Mini-muffins, coffee, an apple, a banana, a bowl of dry cereal with a small cup of milk beside it. A bagel, butter, cream cheese and jelly.

"Good grief." I groaned, inhaling the wonderful aroma. "I can't eat all this." I pulled my pillow over my eyes in protest.

"Just eat what you want."

"I want to eat it all." I peeled back a corner of the pillow and peeked at the tray of my favorite breakfast foods. "I'm a stress eater who has stress."

Sebastian sighed. The mattress shifted under his weight, and I rolled toward him without meaning to. He set the tray on the bed beside my feet and leaned into me. One long finger trailed over my forehead, tucking a mess of wild bangs behind my ear and away from my face. He smiled, but the sentiment didn't reach his eyes. For a moment, he looked almost vulnerable. Something bothered him, too.

"I have to head back to Norfolk today. I'll be back tonight, but it might be late."

Of course. I couldn't keep him forever. "Is this about getting out of dinner with my parents?" When I smiled, his lips turned up with more sincerity. "Boy, you'll do anything to avoid those two."

"You're not kidding. It's awful being around such uptight, unaccepting posers."

We laughed together and my heart thumped. While I'd been toiling with the mystery at hand, he'd been getting to know me. I didn't let people do that, especially not men. My parents knew everyone on the island. Aside from Adrian, I'd never dated anyone from Chincoteague. After I left home, I never brought anyone back—not that there'd been anyone to bring home. Sebastian was the first outsider.

What did it mean to my parents that he came and stayed? I remembered my first impression of Sebastian. My parents had grounds to worry. I hoped dinner at their house would work out soon. They needed to get to know him.

"When will you be back?"

His deep brown eyes pinned me to the bed. "When would you like me back?"

I opened my mouth to speak, and air caught in my throat, thickening it. My words mattered more than ever. Whatever I said would give me away. I couldn't tell him what I wanted—for him to stay and protect me, like a little child.

I pulled my lips in over my teeth, angry at that thought. It wasn't too late for me to get to the bottom of things. I could redeem the mess I'd made.

He waited for an answer.

"According to Sheriff Murray, there's still a killer on the loose." I glanced away from his face, cursing my transparency. *Stay.* I sent out a mental plea, unable to voice the word aloud. *Stay with me.* My ears burned with a blush. Were my suspicions correct? Could he see through me? This time, I hoped he could.

"It wouldn't be prudent for me to stay away, then. If there's a killer on the loose, I should come back as soon as I can."

I nodded. He'd heard my plea.

When I walked him to the Range Rover after breakfast,

saying good-bye was awkward. Half the island watched from somewhere. Careful to keep an appropriate distance, I stepped aside when he climbed in behind the wheel. His lips pressed tight. Mirrored glasses covered his eyes.

"I'll be back soon, tonight sometime. Text me if you need anything. If I can't be here, I'll send someone."

"Okay."

"Don't walk alone. Take the love bus. Lock your doors. Be vigilant."

I forced a smile to show I accepted his advice. Darn skippy. Vigilant was my new middle name.

Unfortunately, the questions I still needed to ask were sure to get me extra-negative attention, and the killer remained at large. My protection was leaving. I'd be a sitting duck. The weight of it knocked the air from my lungs.

He'd let me go with him if I asked.

"Sebastian?"

He pulled his glasses away, revealing weary eyes. The set of his brow and clench of his jaw worried me. "Yeah?"

For what felt like an eternity, the words wrestled on my tongue. I had no idea what might come out of my mouth. "Be careful."

He snorted.

The minute his taillights disappeared, I took the stairs two at a time and double dead-bolted the door behind me. I flopped onto my couch and pulled Claire's pillow to my face. It smelled like Sebastian. The couch, the air, my world smelled of spice and musk and hair gel. Sitting tall, I took a long look around.

The boxes I'd stacked against the far wall were missing. Not taken by Sebastian, of course. Who would take my books and old movies? Not Adrian. Stories of the ghost who haunted my apartment popped in and out of my head. I stood and began to examine my place. The musty stink of the walls and carpeting had faded to nothing. I trailed my gaze over the room. A row of well-worn paperbacks lined the shelf above the window. My stack of Blu-Rays sat beside my portable DVD player on the television stand, right where nice audio-visual components I didn't own were meant to go.

I flung open kitchen cupboards. Everything was arranged neatly behind doors that no longer squeaked. Food practically spilled out of the refrigerator. Fruit, cheeses, milk, water, greens. I couldn't believe it. I went on to the next room. Linens filled the closet in my bathroom. I ran to the bedroom closet. Everything was hung or folded and meticulously organized. A black duffel sat near the inside wall beside rows of my shoes. I recognized it as Sebastian's.

Had he left these things on purpose or forgotten them?

I turned in a small circle, taking it all in. Sebastian had unpacked and decorated my apartment.

Huh.

The fact needed probing, but something else pushed forward in my mind. He'd left a stack of messages near the old landline for me. I dashed to the kitchen and found several slips of scratch paper.

Hank stopped by to apologize and ask if I needed more help with the boathouse. He was one brave guy, or completely bonkers. Bad things happened at the boathouse.

Melissa bought a dog and wanted me to meet him. I took a minute to think about that. Melissa was the grocery store clerk. She made a good decision. Lost dogs rarely returned. If he did, there was always room for one more. I hoped.

Sam Fines wanted to golf with me. Golf? I didn't golf. He must have something he wanted to talk about. Sam owned the pharmacy. I wondered what he needed help with. Hopefully he didn't have a pill addiction because that wasn't in my realm of experience.

The last slip had a funny face drawn on it. Mrs. Franks stopped by to apologize for vandalizing the golf cart. Then she asked Sebastian to warn me to stay away from her husband. Then she left her number so we could get together.

I rubbed my forehead. This wasn't the island practice I'd had in mind.

A floorboard creaked. A flash of red caught my eye. I placed the notes back on the counter and opened a cupboard door, removing one solid serving plate. With a white-knuckled grip, I whipped around, plate held high. Mrs. Davis screamed and made the sign of the cross over her chest.

"How did you get in here?" My arms shook over my head.

She bent forward, grabbing her knees and huffing for air.

"Where have you been?" I asked. Who disappears after a car bombing then breaks in? Jeez. I didn't know if I wanted to hug her or smack her.

"I was staying at Adrian's until you showed up. Then I had to sleep in the crappy art studio downstairs. You know what cold cement does to a woman my age?" She flipped upright, holding her back. "Get me some water."

I obeyed without thinking. Mrs. Davis sat on the couch and waited for me. "You didn't have to leave when I went to Adrian's house. I never got to thank you for calling me an ambulance. Why'd you hide after that?"

"I didn't know if I was spotted out there. The van pulled up, blocked the view of your car for a minute, then it drove right past me. From where I stood, I could see a blinking light on the ground under your car. Then you came running like the devil was chasing you. I called nine-one-one and took off. I didn't want to be a crime witness some maniac set his sights on getting rid of."

Oh. I couldn't blame her. "I wish I'd have known you were okay. It was scary when you disappeared like that."

SPLAT.

A *pop* sounded against my window. Only a foot over Mrs. Davis's head, a shadow appeared.

She dove for the floor, but I knew that sound. I flung open the door. Mrs. Franks wielded a carton of eggs in the road outside.

"Hey!" I threw my hands in the air and marched onto my stoop. "Stop it. What are you doing? You know how hard it is to get egg off of stuff? Especially after it bakes in this heat."

Her eyes stretched wide at the sight of me, and she shoved the carton behind her back. "Sorry."

I chewed my lips to keep from announcing her husband was a patient like her. I did not want to sleep with Hank Franks. I had enough problematic men in my life. One was in jail because of me. Another was thoroughly confused—also my fault. Plus, somewhere nearby a third man wanted to kill me.

"Can we get together next week?" she yelled up the steps.

"Call me."

I ducked back inside, locked the door and pulled the shades. Now that she was calmer, Mrs. Davis's drawn expression reeked of distaste. I'd let her down, and she wanted to make sure I knew it. Long red fingernails tapped the sides of her sweaty glass. Purple creases weighed beneath her eyes. Her extreme tan had faded to a normal healthy glow. Thick black eyeliner rimmed her lids into cat eyes. The look fit.

"Well?" she screeched when I didn't speak.

"What?" I couldn't very well explain the strange exchange with Mrs. Franks, if that's what she meant.

"Well, what are you going to do now? You're supposed to keep my boy out of prison, not sign his arrest warrant. What good were all those days of hiding out, freezing cold nights and going hungry, if he winds up doing life for a crime he didn't commit anyway?" Her eyes glistened. I hadn't thought of how Adrian got his hands on food or stayed warm. Adrian was a survivor. I assumed he had his meals somewhere people didn't know he was wanted for murder, maybe on the mainland. But how could he get money? They probably watched his bank accounts. He had friends everywhere, I'd assumed...

Sadness flattened me to the wall, and a weight settled on my chest. I'd failed big-time. At everything. I'd wasted an entire week with Sebastian, and I wasn't any closer to finding Brady's killer than the day he arrived. I'd failed Adrian. Now he was in jail and I was alone. The killer only had to make a move and I was toast. With any luck, Sebastian left a weapon I knew how to use in his black duffel. The odds weren't great. The only weapon I'd wielded lately was a laptop. His government-issued handgun was secure in the holster when he headed home. What was in his duffel?

"Well?" She smacked her glass onto the coffee table and glared. "I asked one thing of you. One." Her voice cracked. A tear fell. "I don't understand. They arrested someone. I saw the lights and commotion. They had the guy. You found him." Emotion spilled from her tough shell, setting me back. I'd seen her laugh. I'd seen her yell and command. I'd never seen her cry.

"Sheriff Murray says the men they caught are guilty of contaminating the national seashore, but it doesn't make them killers. He says there's no connection between the men he arrested and Brady McGee. Adrian was still the last one to argue with him before he died."

But I knew that wasn't true. Those dumpers were connected to Brady. He'd also argued with his girlfriend and possibly Perkins, too. Maybe he'd had a fight with his wife the night he died. The truth was, I didn't have all the facts. Anything could've happened that night.

My head fell into my palms and my knees buckled. I sat on the couch beside Mrs. Davis and tried to see past the frustration. What had I missed?

Perkins. I needed to question Perkins again. He'd given us just enough information to get us off his trail. Smart. Maybe he wasn't drunk or distraught. Maybe he was a cunning fox and I'd been duped. He probably packed up and fled the state the minute we left his house. My head throbbed.

I raised my eyes to meet hers. "I told you I'm not an investigator. I'm a counselor. Nothing more. I can't fix this."

She held a tissue out between us. The movement of her head was so small, I almost missed it. "No." She righted herself, wiping her cat eyes with the pads of her thumbs and tugging the hem of her shirt down when she stood. "You can. If you want to. You always get what you go after. Don't forget who you're talking to. I didn't meet you yesterday, you know."

I didn't get everything I wanted. She knew that better than anyone.

She headed for my bedroom and I followed her dumbly. Myriad rebuttals and complaints clogged my throat, not the least of which was *get the hell out of my room*. She surprised me when she pulled the closet door wide and stepped inside. Shoving aside half my wall, she took a set of dusty steps down to the art studio without looking back. I covered my mouth with my fingertips. Adrian

Davis was a genius. I knew he made up that ghost story. I secured the woodwork behind her and closed my closet. On second thought, I dragged Sebastian's bag out, shut the closet again and shoved my dresser in front of it. Dissatisfied, I left my room, locked the door and went to sleep in the living room, hoping Sebastian was right and no one would break into a room overlooking the street. Thankfully the stream of tourists made mine a busy street, at least until the pony swim ended. I had a week.

My mind whirled and hummed. Perkins had sent us on a goose chase, I was convinced. No man who loved money turned in his payday the way he did unless he had something much larger to cover up. Like two murders. A shiver sent goose bumps over my flesh. I needed to question Perkins again.

I sent Sebastian a quick text. Are you busy? If he really could read my mind, he'd know what my text really meant was "Are you too busy to cover me on my third excursion to question a killer?"

I counted to ten twice while staring at my phone. No response from Sebastian.

I yanked Claire's pillow back over my eyes. If Perkins knew someone was on to him, he could flee with all the money he gained from his business venture. He'd get away with murder while Adrian sat in jail. I peeked at my phone from beneath the pillow.

"Answer me, Sebastian," I told the phone. "This can't wait."

Nothing happened.

Stupid. Stupid. Stupid phone. I groaned and righted myself. He'd respond soon. Sebastian wouldn't ignore my text. If he didn't text or call before I left the island,

I'd try to reach him again before I knocked on Perkins's door. Maybe he could meet me there.

What else could I do? Perkins had the answers I wanted.

NINETEEN

It was time to check out what Sebastian had left for me in his bag.

I unlocked my bedroom door and peeked inside. The dresser still stood guard against the closet. I dragged Sebastian's duffel onto the bed and unzipped it, hoping to find more than spare boots and underpants.

"Good grief." He left me the mother lode of equipment. Night-vision goggles, a stun gun, a burner phone, Mace, handcuffs and a knife I nearly cut my finger off with while removing it from the sheath. Wow. I set that back in the bag. I thumbed through the clothes in the bottom. He had a spare change of all-black essentials from socks to his undershirt. Beneath those was exactly what I needed. I hefted an enormous flashlight in one hand, feeling the weight against my palm. Now this was a weapon I could use. I stowed the weighty Maglite inside my favorite hobo.

The drive to Perkins's house passed in a blur. I lost my nerve after turning onto his street and parked a couple blocks away against the curb, hoping a quick pep talk was all I needed. Facing him alone stole my breath, and for a moment I considered turning back. I needed backup.

My thumbs danced over the screen of the "spare" phone Sebastian had "borrowed" from his office.

"Special Agent Sebastian Clark is unavailable." He wasn't at his desk. With all the hoopla going on, I kind of hoped he was safely in his office filing reports or getting his story straight. If he needed to get his story straight. I wouldn't know. He didn't talk to me.

I huffed my way off that bunny trail and disconnected without leaving a message. I tried him again. This time I dialed the phone he carried with him.

"This is Sebastian Clark—"

"Sebastian." I looked heavenward and blurted out my predicament over his voice. "I'm so glad I caught you. Listen, I'm on the mainland and I need to talk with Perkins again, but I can't stop thinking he's the killer and I don't want him to kill me. Can you meet me on his street and maybe we can talk to him again together?"

Beep.

I pulled the phone around and stared at the screen. I was so far gone I didn't notice it was a recording? And now I'd left a desperate message on his voice mail. My heart pounded with embarrassment and worry for my mental health. This whole nightmare had gone too far. I shoved the keys into my pocket and jumped out of the love bus before I turned tail for home. Determination to complete my mission shoved me forward. I marched along the sidewalk, running through a few possible conversation tracks. Perkins seemed to think women were stupid, so I decided to work that angle.

I took a deep breath, knocked on the door and waited. A dog barked once in the distance. No answer. No car in the drive. Maybe he'd skipped town. I peeked through a window. His coffee table was overturned and a couple bottles of booze lay busted on the floor. Uh-oh. Either Perkins had a temper or I was wrong about him. If he wasn't the killer, it made sense that Perkins would be next. He knew about the payoffs and the dumping. I went around to the back door, peeking in windows, terrified of what I might find. A privacy fence separated his yard from the neighbors.

Something thumped inside as I edged along the side of his house. I stopped short. The back door stood open several inches. What if Perkins was inside with a suicide note like Mrs. McGee? A flicker of determination hit, stronger this time than before. I dialed 911 and hovered my thumb over the screen ready to call an ambulance.

I pulled the door wide and waited. Silence. Wishing I had a crystal to rub or some sage to burn, I stepped across the threshold and listened.

"Hello? Perkins? Everything okay?"

The sound started above me and grew in the span of a few heartbeats. I recognized it at once, then as if to confirm, I tripped over a water dish labeled "Killer." Toenails over hardwood scrambled down the stairs into the foyer. Oh, my sweet stars. I dashed toward the back door, planning to dive out headfirst when I realized I'd pulled it shut behind me on the way in. A mammoth black Doberman slid around the corner, blocking my path. Frozen, I eased my backside onto the countertop. He edged toward me, growling low and fierce.

I searched the marble behind me and spotted a package of pepperoni rolls. I grabbed the package and jerked to my feet on the countertop. "Good doggy. Nice Killer." I braced one palm flat against the cupboard. He sat. A tongue the size of my head licked his chops, as I slid my hand into the bag and ripped a hunk of one roll off with my trembling thumb and first finger.

I threw the chunk of one roll as far from me as possible. It landed in front of the back door. Terrible plan. The front door was in sight. I had a straight line from the kitchen, through the hall and outside to freedom, but Killer was back watching me. The growling had stopped, but his lips hitched in warning. The expression said, "No sudden moves and hand over the food." I grabbed a full roll this time and tossed it against the window. He went for it and so did I.

I launched myself from the counter and barreled down the hallway to the front door. Flipping the dead bolt with one swift movement, I watched in horror as Perkins's shiny black car pulled into the drive before me. Killer closed in on my heels with a quick *woof!* No going forward. No going back. I swore loudly when the car door slammed outside.

Killer barked again, and I threw the whole bag of rolls at him, hitting him square in the face. He caught the bag and shook it hard in his iron jaws. Ice slid over me at the idea I might be the next snack for Killer to gnaw on. I took the stairs two at a time as the front door swung open.

Perkins immediately laid into Killer for stealing food from the counter. A loud yip sounded, and I dashed into the first open doorway, heading straight to the window. Perkins screamed and yelled like a lunatic over the pepperoni rolls. He had definite stress, a probable drinking problem and could use a little anger management. I should've left him my card during one of our visits.

I climbed onto the roof without hesitation. The drop below was at least ten feet. I eased the window shut and climbed up instead, hoping to find another piece of roof angled lower to the ground.

On the next patch of roof there were two options. I could climb off onto the front-porch roof and down to safety or attempt to shimmy around the chimney onto the roof covering the porch where I broke in. Option two won by a long shot until the tirade downstairs ended with Killer being thrown out into the backyard.

Forget the Maglite. I needed to carry Prozac if this was my new life.

Careful not to be seen by anyone driving by, or Killer in the backyard, I pressed myself to the hot shingled roof. The sun beat down on me, drying my mouth and forming a throb behind my eyes. I had my phone but didn't want to call anyone. Killer would hear my voice, bark and give me away, or maybe get another beating. Perkins was a mess. I could text, but whom? Who could I tell that I'd broken into the home of a man I believed was a killer, then, worried said man had been attacked by the real killer, was chased by his dog, Killer, and was currently hiding on his roof? No one.

Really, what could anyone do?

My parents were understanding enough to take it in stride and burn sage over me later, but I had their car. Sebastian was dealing with his own life-or-death problems and not available anyway or he would've responded to my insane voice mail. Plus, he was supposed to uphold laws, not cover for me when I broke some. Claire was at work and hours away from me without the freedom to come and go that Sebastian had. I rolled onto my tummy, and waited for a stroke of brilliance that didn't come.

I woke to the sound of a ringing phone and reached for my pocket. It wasn't me. Groggy from so many sleepless nights, I moaned and nearly rolled off the roof. Eep! My feet scrambled for purchase, knocking a few loose shingles into the gutter. Killer barked and I flinched. Every inch of my skin screamed from sunburn. The front of me baked against the hot shingles while my back took the brunt of the sun, which had settled low in the horizon.

I checked my phone for the time. Almost seven. I'd slept for four hours in the hot summer sun without sunblock. My cheeks hurt. One was pocked and speckled with tiny gravel from the shingle it had melded to all day. The other was probably the proud owner of a second-degree burn.

"Because I had to do something," Perkins snarled nearby. He'd wandered into the room below me. "What would you have had me do, huh?…Well, that's what I did… That's your problem. I'm out." He screamed a slew of f-words intermingled with "I'm out" a dozen more times, then began breaking things inside his house again.

Out? What did that mean? I strained to hear more, but based on the amount of damage occurring inside, I guessed he'd ended the call. The number of possible scenarios plucked my curiosity to insanity level. I should've found a way to tap his line.

A door slammed, then another, and an engine roared to life. I dared a peek over the porch eave. His car swung out of his driveway, and the tires barked as he tore down the street. My mind screamed at my limbs to work. I had to get away before he got back. My skin felt tight enough to split open as I eased my foot onto the ledge near the chimney. I hugged the stone chimney-face as if I wanted to marry it and didn't look down. On the other side of the chimney was the covered porch, a short drop to the ground and a two-minute sprint to the love bus. My phone rang in my pocket, and I froze midair, straddling the chimney. I had no hands to answer the call. As it continued to ring I worried neighbors would find me there, clinging to the house.

Grrrrruff! Grrrrruff! A familiar snarl sounded from the ground beneath me. I mashed my eyes shut. My luck sucked eggs. I inched back to where I came from. His barking grew louder and more consistent until neighbors began to scream at him to shut up. I crushed my face back against the shingles, hoping not to be noticed. As if a bright red woman could be camouflaged against the stark black roof. Killer clawed and crooned at the siding beneath me for an eternity. Night fell before I dared move again.

When the streetlights flickered on, I slid over the eave onto the front porch roof. The street was quiet. One leg at a time, I swung down, placing each foot gingerly on the porch railing beneath me. I jumped to the grass and swallowed a scream as my sunburn flared at the stretch of skin. I didn't look back as I ran for the bus, cursing myself for parking so far away.

I dove onto the driver's seat and checked my phone. Headlights swept along the side of the love bus, and I ducked on instinct. Perkins's car crawled past. The look on his face was grim. He parked in his drive and an enormous SUV pulled in behind him. I swung the love bus away from the curb and into a U-turn without looking back.

Claire had sent several texts. I called and spilled the entire story to her before she could say hello. Delirium hit when I crossed the bridge back to the island. I finished the story laughing and crying interchangeably. Claire, for the most part, was silent.

"Does Sebastian know what you were up to?"

"I don't know. I left him a voice mail before I knocked on the door, but he never called back."

She groaned. "Today he had to drive to Williamsburg and give a deposition. He tried everything to get out of it, but they insisted. I don't know if he's getting back tonight or not. Either way, you need to stay put."

"Oh." Relief ran over me. I wasn't ready to tell Sebastian all I'd told Claire. He had his own life to worry about. If I could find Brady's killer without him, that would be better. Maybe afterward I could help Sebastian with his situation.

I parked outside Fine's Pharmacy, hoping they were

still open. Lucky me. They were. As I walked in, Sam Fines stood at the counter, smiling.

"When will you be back?" I asked Claire.

She huffed. "I planned on coming out today but you never answered your phone. Now I'm not sure. What are you doing tomorrow?"

"Hello, Patience." Sam waved.

"Let me call you later." I disconnected and smiled at Sam with the unroasted half of my mouth.

"That is some sunburn you have there. What happened? You look like one of those sports fans who paints half their face red."

"What's the fastest way to heal it?"

"Cool compresses, aloe, maybe something topical to cut the sting." He searched the white racks behind the counter. "Try this. If blisters form or red lines run through it, call your doctor. You could have sun poisoning."

"Okay." What I meant was *no way*. I no longer had health insurance.

"With a burn like that you're likely dehydrated. Expect some headaches, dizziness and nausea. Possibly diarrhea."

"Thanks." I shuffled into the aisle and collected Tylenol, Pepto and a gallon of water. Sam met me in the aisle with a bag.

"When this settles down—" he motioned to my skin "—are we on for golf?" He enunciated the last word.

"Yes." I wanted to do a dramatic, stage-wink back at him but refrained. "Golf sounds nice."

"Then consider this on the house." He placed everything except the gallon jug inside the bag and lifted a hand to pat my shoulder. He cringed and dropped it back to his side. "Remember, call the doctor if the symptoms are too strong tomorrow."

"Yep."

I shoved my way out into the night and threw up on the sidewalk.

My parents brought over every remedy they could think of when news of my sunburn reached them. Sebastian got in late and knocked on the bathroom door. I sat in the tub, steeping my body in a tepid bath of tea leaves and other mystical whatnot. I dried with care and slid into a cotton nightgown.

Sebastian filled me with Tylenol and kept my water glass full while conducting an inquisition of my every move and narrowing his eyes with my every answer. He didn't love the voice mail I'd left him.

"Don't confront anyone alone again. No one. If I'm busy, I'll haul you with me first, then we'll do your thing together. You are not to go alone."

I wanted to jump and scream about being a grown-ass woman, but half my face hurt too much for screaming and half my body hurt too much for jumping. Who was I kidding? I was a mess and had no one to blame but me.

"Affirmative?" A vein in his neck pulsed blue beneath his skin.

"Affirmative."

TWENTY

THERE WASN'T ENOUGH coffee or aloe in the world to help me with my guilt over Adrian and my paranoia over what Perkins was up to, or to soothe my screaming sunburn. I tugged on my favorite cutoffs and one of Sebastian's T-shirts. The faded blue cotton covered my shorts completely. I tucked in the front and stuffed my feet into sandals. I had a feeling it was a ponytail and dark glasses kind of day.

Sebastian's laptop sat on the kitchen counter with a scrolling screen saver. *"I'll be back late. Don't wait up."* A handful of ellipses followed. I waited. The follow-up to his note made me smile. *"Don't do anything impetuous until I get back."*

Looking at the screen-saver warning, a number of impetuous options sprang to mind, but Sebastian meant "don't get hurt." I had no intention. Until my sunburn healed, nothing would convince me to go anywhere near the boathouse or Perkins. I pulled my bedroom door shut and locked it before leaving. Then I locked and double-checked my front door. I had plenty to think over, but without coffee I couldn't even apply mascara.

Making coffee required more energy than I had in reserve, so I went to see Mrs. Tucker at the Tasty Cream. Freud followed me across the street.

"Wait here."

When I opened the door to the ice cream parlor, I shuddered at the cold blow of the air-conditioning over my burn. Mrs. Tucker took one look at me and stopped wiping the countertop. She didn't look surprised, only a little sad. Probably someone had reported my condition already. After all, I'd been out of the house for at least three minutes.

"Oh, honey." Her bottom lip pressed forward.

"Coffee." I slid onto a red vinyl-topped stool at the counter. "Ouchie."

She tipped her head over one shoulder. "Sam wasn't joking. He came for breakfast this morning and said he saw you last night." She retrieved a cup from under the counter. A few minutes later an aroma so heavenly I wanted to cry swam up my nose.

"Cappuccino."

Mmm. I lifted the cup to my mouth, careful to keep it on the unburned half of my lips as much as possible. Each sip brought the world more into focus. By the time I finished my second refill, the hamster wheel in my head had churned out a dozen possibilities about Perkins.

"You want to talk about it?" Mrs. Tucker smiled. Her kind face used to comfort me in times of trouble. This time I needed more than the assurance of unconditional friendship.

"I think I need to talk to Adrian first. I owe him an apology."

"Honey, no one blames you. Least of all him." She held up a finger, signaling me to wait.

"Well, well, well." A brassy voice screeched through my peaceful moment.

I took a deep breath and turned to greet my high school nemesis. "Karen Holsten. How delightful to see you." I tried to smile but failed.

She waved her enormous diamond in my face, wiggling

her fingers. "That's Karen Holsten-Thompson now. In case you haven't heard, I'm soon to be the mayor's wife."

"Good luck to your husband."

Mrs. Tucker returned with a foam bowl of milk and a to-go tray. A lidded cup and small white bag sat on the tray. "For Freud and your friend." She looked between Karen and me. Worry changed her friendly features. "The one you're going to talk to."

"Oh." Befuddled by Karen's ability to look better than she did ten years ago, it took me a minute to catch on. "Oh! Thank you." I walked past Karen without a goodbye. I had no idea what to say to her. "Have a nice day," I called out, speaking mostly to Mrs. Tucker.

A pair of heels clicked over the floor behind me. I kept going.

"Is that little to-go order for the man who's been staying with you?" Scandal coated the words. Her face was so eager when I turned to look at her, I wanted to laugh. Who could blame her? She had agreed to marry Beau Thompson and cuddle his portly physique for the rest of her life. I got to live with Sebastian, who, for all she knew, I got to cuddle every night. Everyone with eyes could see his physique was far from portly.

"Congratulations on the engagement."

She looked me over. "What happened to your face? Did someone forget her sunscreen?" She pressed out her bottom lip and locked her fingers around the curves of her tiny waist. "That sunburn will add ten years to your face and increase your likelihood of skin cancer."

My blush flamed hotter than my sunburn. "Best of luck with the campaign." My voice hitched.

Mention of the campaign seemed to snap her out of attack mode. Karen smacked her lips. "Oh, we don't need any luck. Our only competition is in jail for murder. I'd say Beau and I can take an extended vacation if we want and come home on Election Day to accept the position."

"Wow. That's a lot of 'we.' Are you running in tandem for mayor?" The joke flopped.

Her face pinked up like a strawberry milk shake. The color stood out against the pale yellow of her suit. "Of course not. Beau will be mayor. I'll be First Lady." Her chin lifted high.

I snorted and left while her highness still glowed like my sunburn. Freud followed me back to the apartment and I left the milk for him on the sidewalk near the steps. Walking up to the top, only to come right back down, sounded too much like exercise. I planned to save my energy for stop number two on my morning visits.

The little pink tile roof came into view a few blocks later. Time to face Adrian. I cringed at the sight of Sheriff Murray's cruiser parked at the curb. Climbing the steps to the front door, I hoped he was in his office blowing a gasket at someone else for a change. He wasn't.

"Come to fill out those reports?" He leaned over the receptionist. She looked busy marking up a map of vendor placement for the upcoming auction.

"I hoped I could see Adrian." I tried to make one of those puppy dog faces that get television women what they want.

"Is there something in your eye?" He stared back while I continued to rearrange my features to something sympathetic. When I didn't speak, he turned back to the receptionist. "The ones near the marsh need to maintain a standard ten-foot clearance."

She nodded.

Then his eyes were back on me. "What's in the bag?"

I blinked and looked at the bag, which I'd forgotten I

was still carrying. I'd never asked what might be inside. "A file for cutting cell bars."

His eye twitched. Whether from watching my face contort so long or simply from his proximity to me, I couldn't be sure. "Ha." The word, devoid of humor, confirmed the latter of my theories as true. Then he stuck his hand out, palm up.

I surrendered the bag, and he dug in forearm deep. As it turned out, the bag contents included one large cruller drenched in gooey icing. He held it to the light, poked at it, squeezed it then placed it back in the bag.

"Gross."

He sucked on his poking finger. "What's in the cup?"

"Jeez. Are you for real?"

His fingers opened and closed in the universal sign of "gimmee." Unwilling to let him drink Adrian's coffee, too, I removed the lid and tilted the cup slightly toward him. Steam lifted and spiraled into the air.

"Where's your sidekick?"

I smiled and fought the urge to text and tell Sebastian that Sheriff Murray called him my sidekick. The receptionist smirked and turned her face away. I wasn't sure what she found amusing, but my smile stretched wider in response.

"I'll give you ten minutes." He walked away.

The receptionist shooed me after him. I left the cruller on her desk. She pushed it into the trash with a quiet laugh. I suspected she and I might make great friends, but I needed to come back when the sheriff wasn't around.

I followed the sheriff as he wound through a maze of cubicles and short hallways to the single holding cell inside the station. I'd been given the official tour after an incident senior year involving condom balloons and whipped cream. Sheriff Murray, a deputy then, had brought me in as the only suspect, but he never found any evidence against me beyond the fact that I taunted him on a regular and ongoing basis. If I'd known then he'd become sheriff one day and that I'd still live here, I might've rethought things.

"Patience!" Adrian ran to the bars and smiled. "I hoped you'd come. I know you're blaming yourself. Please don't. This isn't what you think. When I heard you found a thread to pull in this case, I knew the whole thing against me would unravel. I called my attorney and then Sheriff Murray."

"You turned yourself in?" I almost dropped his coffee.

"I shouldn't have run to begin with."

Sheriff Murray stepped away and watched us.

I tried to ignore him. "Mrs. Tucker sent you coffee." I handed it through the bars to him and then turned to Sheriff Murray. "Can I at least go in and sit with him?"

He grunted.

"He fingered your cruller," I informed Adrian.

"What?" Adrian's nose wrinkled in confusion.

"Fine." Sheriff Murray stepped forward and opened the door to let me pass. Then he pointed to a security camera in the corner of the room. "You have seven minutes left."

The metal door banged shut, and he disappeared down the hallway.

I hugged Adrian tight to my chest. "That was really honorable of you to admit you were wrong for running. I'm glad you called the sheriff."

"It's not like he could apprehend me."

"Right. Either you're really good at hiding, or he's really bad at finding." On an island as small as ours, I couldn't figure how Adrian had kept from being arrested. Unless the sheriff had a heart under all that attitude and didn't want to bring him in. I doubted that was the case.

Adrian and I sat on a bench against the wall, and he wound one heavy arm over my shoulders. I shifted against his chest and exhaled long and deep. The room was depressing. No wonder his arm felt like lead across my shoulders. Gray concrete floors. Gray bars and walls inside the cell. Gray drywall outside the cell. Adrian sipped his coffee in silence. Time ticked by. The faint scent of fish threatened my composure. All the gray confinement reminded too much of the moments I spent under a pillowcase. Knowing the person Adrian rescued me from was still out there coiled my tummy.

"I found your secret passage." I lifted away from his arm and smiled. Hank could probably patch up the opening after he fixed the rat door at the boathouse, although I hated the thought of letting anyone in on our secret.

I rolled my eyes. Adrian was the one who started the silly rumor about my building being haunted. He'd convinced our entire senior class and eventually the island got behind the story.

"When you used to work at the art studio downstairs, did your boss tell you about the passageway?" I asked.

"No. I found it on my own. I don't think anyone knew it was there."

"Who knew one day you'd be on the lam for murder? I guess your secret escape hatch comes in handy for a man in your position." I bumped my shoulder into his.

"I didn't kill Brady."

"I know."

"My attorney will get things straightened out."

I looked into his pale gray eyes. His hurt and apprehension couldn't be masked from me. We'd been too close once. Being deceived by him would be impossible, like being lied to by part of your own soul.

"I promise to bring you something from the Tasty

Cream as often as possible. Maybe that will help during the wait for this to sort itself out. You'll have something delicious to look forward to." I squeezed my hand on his leg.

"Let's go, Price." Sheriff Murray's voice boomed down the corridor. Keys rattled in his hand. Time was up. I kissed Adrian on the cheek and left before I gave the sheriff any reason to forbid my return.

Sheriff Murray eyed me. "What's your problem? You look like you sucked a lemon."

"It smells like fish in here."

He crossed his arms over his chest, unimpressed. The whole island smelled like fish to some degree.

"It smells like the pillowcase yanked over my head." Tears welled in my eyes, surprising me. I cleared my throat and bit the inside of my cheek to get my emotions in check. "Your jail reminds me of the stinky pillowcase that psychopath used on me." I spat the words, suddenly livid.

Find him! My heart screamed. But with Adrian in custody, I had no doubt the "investigation" was over. I swiped a tear from my cheek and blew a puff of air into my bangs before storming off.

"Hey," Adrian called after me. I turned back to see a glint of mischief in his eye. "Buy some sunscreen, would you?" He winked, and I left him behind in the saddest place I'd ever been.

Outside in the sun, free of the gray inside Adrian's cell, hope floated up. I went straight to see my parents at The Purple Pony. I wanted to help Adrian. During the walk, thoughts swirled and mingled and mutated as I tried to figure out what I was missing. Some key piece of information either eluded me, or I had it and hadn't realized how important it was yet.

Adrian seemed so small and helpless inside the holding

cell. He trusted the system. Admirable. I wanted to trust the system, but the sheriff had never proved to be much of a sleuth in the past. I doubted that had changed since I graduated high school. With no crimes to investigate, he couldn't have had much practice.

When I opened the door to The Pony, Dad greeted me like Dino from the Flintstones. His arms wrapped me tight. He arched his back and lifted me from the floor. I sucked air, stifling a scream.

"Put her down. She hardly comes to see us as it is." Mom came to pat my back.

"Ah!"

They both stepped back and stared, wide-eyed, at my face. In unison they circled me. A whispered chorus of "Ooohs" and "Ahhs" followed until they arrived back in front of me.

"It's worse than we thought." Mom looked at Dad. "The bath didn't do a thing."

Dad disappeared and returned with his special water. I accepted.

"You want to talk?"

"No. I need to think."

"You want to go fishing?" Dad looked expectant. "Fishing always gives me clarity."

Mom frowned. "We could knit? On the deck at home? Your father could watch the shop. Oh! Let me read your cards."

"No. I don't know what I want to do. Swim maybe. Swimming used to do wonders for my drama."

They exchanged a look.

"What? I'm still a strong swimmer."

"You should stay out of the sun for a few days." Mom looked victoriously at Dad. Fishing, known to Mom as marine life capture-and-kill, was an in-the-sun activity.

"I'll wait for evening." Suddenly I was exhausted and wanted a nap.

"Is Sebastian coming back again tonight?" Dad looked worried.

"Yeah. Late."

"You two want to meet us for mai tais on the deck?"

For some unknown reason, drinks on the deck with my parents and Sebastian sounded marvelous. "Is ten too late?"

"Ten's great." Dad beamed. "I'll grill something."

"Deal." I texted Sebastian as I left The Pony, feeling infinitely happier than I had thirty minutes earlier. But a nap still sounded wonderful.

I WOKE TO A gorgeous stream of pinks and golds coming through my window. Sunset. I was rested and still had enough time to go for a swim before Sebastian came back. I craved the sensation of ocean water on my skin, bobbing in the surf, free from captivity. The timing was perfect. A setting sun wouldn't hurt my healing burns. Thanks to the love bus, I made it to the beach in time to see throngs of tourists head home for dinner. I had the whole place to myself. Life was giving me a break for a change. I climbed into the back of the bus like old times and stripped out of my shorts and Sebastian's T-shirt. I adjusted the suit I'd slid on underneath and looked for a bottle of water. Staying hydrated proved to be more difficult than I expected.

I opened a red Igloo cooler and found a flattened, folded one-man inflatable boat. Fate and I didn't get along, but omens I believed in. Sitting at the beach alone with a one-man boat seemed like the universe trying to tell me something. I hooked up the air pump before I could talk myself out of things. Maybe swimming alone wasn't the best idea. Maybe a boat ride would help me get my head together.

The phone startled me. For whatever reason, the ringer was stuck in ear-bleed mode since I turned it off silence, and the mega-loud *ding-ding* announced a text. Sebastian would be late. He'd meet me at eleven. I texted him back to let him know I was at the beach. Before the boat was fully inflated, he'd already changed his story. He'd be on the island in two hours, but he'd have to finish some reports at my place. I shrugged and shoved the phone in my shorts then slid them back on.

By the time I'd maneuvered the boat into the surf and paddled out beyond the waves, all I could think about was whether or not the Coast Guard had been back with divers to investigate. Hopefully they were on top of things. I struggled to get the little boat turned around and headed back to the scene of the crime. Not far from my destination, my heart sped. When I came near the place where Adrian's kayak went down, I couldn't go any farther. Panic filled my throat. I headed for shore instead.

I dragged the vessel onto the sandy shore where I'd attended so many parties, and sat in the soft white sand, scooping and releasing the grains by the handful. Being at the scene of the crime gave me a panic attack. I should've expected as much. The sun shifted lower on the horizon until only a sliver of silver remained against a backdrop of shadows. Hues of deep purple and gray gave my nostalgic spot a creepy edge. Tiny sand dunes formed under my hands as I worked through everything I knew.

What was Perkins up to? I remembered him talking to someone on the phone. What did he want out of?

I leaned back on my elbows, debating how soon to start paddling home, when a huge yacht passed in view. The lights were off and the motor quiet. It slowed and blinked out of sight against the dark horizon. I squinted into the night, stepping carefully into the grasses at the water's edge. As I crouched against a weedy bank, my teeth chattered with nerves. Though it wasn't the same boat, the memories were fresh. Definitely anxiety.

After ten days at home, I was the one who needed a therapist.

A splash in the distance put my muscles on lockdown. Every inch of me tensed to flee, but curiosity pressed through the veil of fear. I inched through the dense grass, needing to know what was happening, careful of every step, mindful of every breath. When I got as close as I dared on the shore, I pulled my phone out to tell Sebastian I was running late. I planned to stay until the boat left. No way I'd ever enter the water on the inflatable boat with another suspicious vessel around.

The groaning turned to chain clinking and then another splash. I choked on my tongue. The black barrels dumped by the first boat were being carried up by the new boat. In my experience, Coast Guard boats didn't perform covert ops. Also, their boats had lights. I sent another text to Sebastian. Bad guys wouldn't clean their own dump site.

My guess? This had never been a dump site.

I thrilled at the revelation. The missing link. The Coast Guard would find nothing when they searched later because this boat wanted what was left behind. Ha! I performed a tiny victory dance alone in the dark weeds. I sent another quick text. Trafficking. Brady and Perkins were traffickers. My fingers couldn't text the new theory fast enough.

Onboard, shadows moved around the barrel. The unmistakable silhouette of automatic rifles appeared in the moonlight. I gasped. The men on deck removed the barrel lid. Prying the top took several hands. Anticipation paralyzed me. How much drugs could fill a barrel that size? A million dollars' worth? How big had Brady and Perkins's cuts been?

The men maneuvered the lid away from the barrel and reached inside. They removed long barreled Rambo guns and passed them to one another. Guns. Not drugs. A weight settled over my chest, flattening my lungs into my back. Satisfied, they reloaded the barrel and rolled it against the wall. They lowered the pulley into the water again.

Ding-ding! The return text came as loud as a freight train against the silent, eerie night.

Four words from Sebastian. Get Out Of There.

Voices carried from the boat, loud and fast. Chattering. Swearing. Oh, no.

Ding-ding!

Damn it!

Now!

A spotlight swept over the grass, landing on me. I uttered another four-letter word and ran. Dashing through the forest was impossible. The area was deeply wooded. Branches flicked out to catch my skin as I passed. The rev of a small-craft motor broke through the night. They were coming for me. I darted and jumped around what I could see. My sunburn flamed with the assault of the thickets and trees. This time I knew where I'd entered the forest and which direction to find the access road.

Ding-ding!

The motor stopped. The boat was on shore. They'd be in the forest in seconds, with lights and guns. My stomach dropped to my toes, but adrenaline propelled me on. I needed to tell Sebastian what was happening but couldn't afford the time it would take to send the text.

Shots rang out behind me, and I threw my back against

an enormous tree trunk. Breath seared my throat with every gasp.

"Did you get her?" A loud, gravelly voice boomed.

"Aw."

The response confused me. How long did I have before they came to take me away? Perhaps they'd kill me and leave me in the forest. I blinked back tears, brokenhearted for my parents to lose me this way. Parents shouldn't outlive their children. How many hours had I spent consoling moms after losing a child to a government assignment? Too many.

"I thought it was a person," the second voice said more softly.

Every sound in the forest disappeared until only one, save their voices, remained. A sound I'd grown up hearing in the same forest. The gentle snuffling of a pony. *Bang!* One last shot, and then there was no more snuffling.

Footfalls and crackling branches marked the pair's trip away from me. The roar of their small boat's engine vanished into the night. My heart stopped beating. The *whoosh* of blood beat inside my head.

Ding-ding!

Good grief. I wiped silent tears and fumbled to check the phone. A dozen panic-infused texts from Sebastian. A tiny sob slid over my lips. My legs wobbled. Too terrified to stand, I told him where to find me. I didn't want to be seen in the woods.

I surely didn't want to see the pony.

TWENTY-ONE

TIME TICKED BY. I held my breath again and again, afraid I'd be heard, afraid to be found, afraid someone still stood nearby. Tears escaped for the stupid pony. I hated the ponies, but they'd never seemed vulnerable before. Now, one had suffered a fate meant for me. Did I owe it something? Mom would go berserk when she heard about the pony. My karma was probably wrecked for life.

Hoofbeats in the distance. I hoped they weren't headed my way. What would they do when they found their fallen brother? Did ponies grieve? My mind circled through endless thoughts at random. I tried every suggestion I gave patients struggling with anxiety. I sang jingles in my head and replayed favorite memories: Adrian building sand castles. My parents walking hand in hand. Claire's crazy closet. Sebastian's kiss.

My eyes stung, and their lids grew heavy. Distant shadows morphed and changed. The trees and night creatures made it impossible to relax for the briefest moment. I leaned against the tree, and an owl screeched overhead, causing me to jump and scrape my burned back against the rough bark. My muscles ached from the tension. Mice dashed over leaves on the ground.

Thunder cracked, and a flash of lightning ran sideways across the sky overhead. Clouds darkened the forest around me one moment, only to be lit the next with a burst of light. The process reminded me of a heavenly strobe light. I pulled my knees to my chest as drops of rain made their way through the canopy overhead. Despite the day's heat, the drops were cold, stinging my burn. Shivers racked my body. Nerves and rain took over.

With every flash of lightning, I counted, waiting for the thunder. The storm moved closer until I could only reach three before the sky lit over me. The hair on my arms stood at attention. Gooseflesh covered my body. Little by little the drops covered me, falling faster, closer. Soon it became impossible to listen for killers in the forest. The steady pitter-patter of raindrops and cracking thunder masked everything, including my thoughts.

One distant shadow bothered me more than the others. While it remained silent, it seemed to draw near. With every flash of lightning, the shadow moved forward. Taller than the others, there was a distinct humanlike quality to it. I stretched my hands to the ground beside me, gripping a fallen branch, and keeping it close to my chest. If I was still enough, and the shadow was a man, he might not see me in time to shoot me before I brained him. A weak plan, but my only plan.

Maybe I could drag him over to the pony afterward. My throat tightened. What kind of person shot a pony? Rational thought returned, forcing my focus onto the shadow.

Oh. The kind of man who thought they were shooting me. My mind kept rejecting the direct process of this information. The idea registered and bounced off, replaced by a more abstract and general idea. A protective mechanism. I'd diagnosed the behavior in others, never expecting to ever find myself in the same condition.

The shadow drew nearer, creeping over the trees and earth. My fingers burned from their grip on my feeble weapon.

Crack! Boom! Lightning and thunder arrived in the

JULIE ANNE LINDSEY 265

same beat, shaking the earth around me. A man in a hunter's crouch moved in at rapid speed. In a flash, I was on my feet swinging for a home run.

"I've got her," he spoke into the air.

I glanced around, expecting to see his cohorts, then swung the limb with every ounce of bravery I could muster. My arms braced for the hit, expecting backlash, and hoping for an opportunity to escape.

The moment didn't go as planned. My hit was thwarted. The branch was wrenched from my grip. My body crushed against the man. His warm hands burned my icy wet skin. Tears erupted at the firm but familiar touch. I recognized the quiet shush of breath over my hair. Sebastian. I gripped him back and he loosened his hold. He wore a big pair of night-vision goggles. Standard issue. I recognized them, and I approved. This meant he could see the coast was clear.

We walked briskly back to the service road, rain pouring over us. The energy surging through me, replacing defeat and driving me forward, came as a surprise. A few minutes before, I'd been frozen in fear. Sebastian's presence melted through the ice and fueled me. I filled him in on everything I'd seen, recounting every detail. He belted me in the passenger seat of his Range Rover, locked the door and sighed. He called the sheriff and the park ranger while I let my parents know we wouldn't be over for drinks after all. Mom sounded near hysterics. It must be hard to be my mom this week.

"Didn't you get my message this morning?" Sebastian tossed his phone in the cup holder and turned out of the park. No paramedics and flashing lights. This time he'd come alone.

"You didn't call in the cavalry?"

"I didn't know who I could trust. I stayed on with Mark

Eaton until I reached your cell. I had no idea what would happen if we found the cell and you were gone. Did you see the screen saver? I thought you'd look at my laptop. I should've texted you."

He didn't know who he could trust. Mark was tech support, not an agent. What had he learned today while he was at work?

"You weren't supposed to get into trouble." He exited the national park and shot me a pointed glare.

"I didn't mean to." I swallowed another urge to bawl. I didn't need to be scolded by him. I needed him to tell me things were going to be all right.

His jaw worked as he looked my way.

I turned my face to the window. "I went out on the water to think."

The Range Rover pulled by the sidewalk outside the police station. Sheriff Murray and his deputy climbed into the cruiser. With his window down, Sebastian nodded in their direction and waited. Raindrops bounced off the window frames, landing on my soaked body.

"We need to talk." Sebastian wedged an elbow over the armrest between us. The rain had slowed to less than a drizzle. Enormous claps of thunder rocked the world around us. The sheen of water on the road glistened under the streetlights.

I wiped my face with the back of my hands and jumped at the sight of Sheriff Murray outside my window instead of Sebastian's. He looked mad enough to spit. His expression shook loose the words building in my head. Sebastian powered down my window from the driver's-side control panel.

"I think Perkins killed Brady." I cleared my throat, hoping to sound brave and well-informed. "Perkins was

Brady's partner, and they were getting paid to look away while those guys the Coast Guard arrested dumped barrels of guns into the ocean. I saw another boat retrieve them tonight. I was wrong. They weren't contaminating the water. They're using the shelf where Brady fished to make an easy exchange of weapons."

Sheriff Murray's face paled visibly under the cone of the streetlight. Sebastian laid a hand on mine. The act might've looked like comfort to someone else. I felt instinctively it was his way of warning me not to go on. He'd said he didn't know who he could trust.

The sheriff took note of our touch and his eyes narrowed on mine. Blood returned to his face, pinking him up like a tamale. "Perkins is dead. Murdered on the mainland." His palms clamped down on the edge of my door frame. He leaned his torso in toward me. "Don't make any plans to leave town, Miss Price."

"What? Why?" Did he honestly believe I'd somehow overpowered Perkins? Why would I even try? My body trembled, and my teeth chattered.

"Did you go to see Perkins? Keep asking questions? You think the officials need your help figuring this out?" He shook his head in disgust. "You government types are all the same."

"I was human resources." My mouth went dry.

How did he know I went to see Perkins? I looked at Sebastian for guidance. He moved his head a fraction of an inch to the side. All expression fell from his face. If he'd been in the passenger seat, he might have dragged the poor sheriff in through the window.

"No." Really, how much damage could one more lie do? My karma was already toast.

"So, I suppose the blue-and-white love bus neighbors

saw parked a block from his house at the approximate time of his death belonged to someone else?"

"I—" I looked at Sebastian. He squeezed my hand again.

The sheriff shot eye daggers at both of us and then returned to his cruiser. When he pulled the driver's door open, the interior light blinked on, revealing the deputy riding shotgun. They crept away, pulling past us at two miles per hour, never looking away from the Range Rover, though I doubted they could see much inside, considering the hour.

"Breathe." Sebastian squeezed my hand then shifted into Drive.

I let out a long breath and pulled in a fresh one. Dizziness swept over me. "I—I thought Perkins was the killer. He was a maniac last time I was at his place. He yelled at his dog, screamed at someone on the phone and thrashed around inside his house like a madman that day."

"You've stumbled into an ongoing investigation." He raised an eyebrow and smiled.

My mouth dropped open. "How are you smiling about this?"

"Irony. I enjoy the irony." He passed my apartment and angled up to the curb outside the boathouse.

"Irony. Like visiting the place I keep getting shot at?"

"Yep." He rounded the front of the Range Rover and helped me out onto the grass. My legs wobbled a moment before finding strength enough to hold me. "I think it's safe to say they won't be here tonight."

"Because no one in their right mind would expect me to come back here."

"Precisely."

I wasn't sure I loved his logic. "Why not my apartment?" Though I could guess the reasoning there.

"I'm afraid it's bugged, or at the very least someone's watching it, and we need to talk."

Swinging the front door open took me aback. The inside looked amazing, not at all like I'd left it. Sebastian shut the door and moved to hit a light switch in a room away from the street. Soft light illuminated the area. My office.

"Your dad, Hank and some others have been here every morning. I ran into Maple Shuster at the grocery and she told me everything. They wanted to surprise you."

I ran my hand over a row of mahogany file cabinets. A credenza on the far wall held all my books and a picture of my dad and me at high school graduation. I blinked out a tear. The drawers were filled with office supplies. Freshly sharpened pencils tied with a ribbon sat inside a mug on the new desk.

"You went to Crate and Barrel." I sniffed. "You shouldn't have."

He pulled me to his chest. "I didn't. Claire ordered it all and sent it to The Pony."

"I love her so much."

"Well, this town certainly loves you. Everyone wants to thank you for your help, but no one wants to admit you counsel them." He chuckled. "I love this place."

"Thinking of moving?"

"I don't think I could keep up the commute on a regular basis." He pulled me back and rolled out my perfect ergonomic chair. A tiny bowl on the floor had the word *Freud* painted on the side.

"Freud?"

"I thought he could stay here. He's a pretty good mouser."

"Perfect."

I took a seat in my new chair and Sebastian positioned

himself on the desk in front of me. He wadded some tissues from the box beside him and handed them over.

"Thanks. I promise to repay everyone when the insurance comes in. This was way more than a couple of conversations are worth. I would've talked to all those people for free." I dabbed my face with the tissues. What a night.

"We know. That's part of your draw. And don't hold your breath for any insurance money. Where bombs and guns are involved, there's always an investigation."

"After I complete the police report." Of course.

He gave me a half smile. "What am I going to do with you?"

Kiss me? I sent out telepathically.

He looked away. "Tell me everything about your visit to Perkins's house."

I started at the beginning, being more thorough than ever, in case Sebastian heard something in the details I'd missed. When I finished the story about Killer and the rolls and my sunburn, I recounted the dark boat and pony killing. Sebastian kept his expression dry, but heat flashed in his eyes at some of my facts. His fingers curled tighter around the desk's edge when I was in danger. He looked as if he wanted to travel through time and flatten someone.

If only he could.

"So, I was sure Perkins killed Brady to collect all the money. Then I saw the barrels and realized how much money he stood to gain. I assumed traffickers wouldn't be stingy with the monthly stipend. I guess I was wrong."

"Maybe. But his death doesn't prove him innocent of Brady's murder. It only shows someone wanted him gone, too."

"You said this is an ongoing investigation? The FBI knew about the trafficking?"

He nodded. His eyes shifted around the room. "Someone on the inside is supporting this. I need to find out who that is. There's a chance you've been spared so far because they know me, not you. I've been asking around and following threads at the department since you found the barrels offshore. Gun trafficking is big business. This afternoon I got word of an internal investigation with a file fitting what you saw off the coast. We need to be careful until this is sorted out. Know that I'm on it all the time. I won't allow you to continue living in fear or danger."

I'd confessed my worries late one night to Sebastian—what if someone I knew and loved was involved in the mess? At the time, I'd worried it might be Adrian.

"They wouldn't have spared me tonight."

A curt nod showed we were in agreement, and he didn't want to dissect the idea any more than I did.

"I'm going to go back to work tomorrow as if I don't suspect anything. I'll plant seeds and drop ideas to see if anyone bites." Sebastian looked glum.

I imagined believing the agency he served so dutifully might be crooked would take a toll on a patriot like him. Personally, I believed most people had a price tag. Not to be negative about humanity, but everyone had something they found hard to pass up. Money for food, a surgery, aging parent, sick child, debt, gambling. Everyone had a moment of weakness at some point. The sad thing about working with murderers was the finality. There was no backing out. When I was weak, it involved cheesecake. An extra slice of cheesecake I could undo with a little effort. Getting in bed with gunrunners, not so much.

"The sheriff looked pretty mad."

Sebastian nodded. "Well, from his position, it looks like you swept into town pulling a truckload of trouble along with you. Until the day you came back, there hadn't been a crime larger than jaywalking or truancy in three years."

"I should do something nice for him."

That earned me a loud and hearty laugh. "I think we'd better get back to your apartment. You need to get some sleep."

"What about you? You saved me. Again. Can I do something nice for you?" We moved into the front room, and I said a silent good-bye to the most delightful office I'd ever owned. I planned a trip back as soon as possible to add personal touches and write thank-yous to everyone who loved me enough to brave car bombings and drive-bys to do this for me.

"I like to spoon."

"What?" I giggled, trying to remember what I'd said last. "Shut up." I shoved him through the front door and followed him to the Range Rover, wondering if what he said was true and imagining how much I'd enjoy it if it was.

"Looks like the storm's passed." The engine purred to life.

I hoped he was right. And not just the rain.

TWENTY-TWO

A CHILL CREPT over my back, alerting me to a new day. I slept easily with Sebastian. The first night back in my bedroom had a great memory attached now. He lay fully dressed, one arm protectively over my side all night. Turned out, he did like to spoon. A smile crept over my face. I slid from bed, checked the closet for creepers and locked up on my way out of the room. Sundress in hand, I knew what I needed to do. I spent a minute in the bathroom getting presentable and felt more confident than I had in some time. Onward to face the day.

The quiet island had transformed into the annual tourist trap. Cars lined the streets, bumper to bumper. The briny air teemed with kettle corn and cotton candy. After days of preparation, the big finale was only twelve hours away. Cowboys from all over would show off their rodeo chops all afternoon at the fairgrounds. Vendors selling inflatable ponies, cowboy gear and food served on paper plates stood at the ready.

Something about the growing crowd made me smile. The familiar scene, complete with honking horns and screaming babies, erased years from my mind. My worries dissipated and blew away with the wind. I'd eaten my weight in corn dogs and funnel cakes at this event over the years. Sebastian would love the quirky island tradition. I couldn't wait to introduce him to it.

Coffee in hand, I bounced down the front steps and headed straight for the police station. I had reports to complete. Claims to file. The sheriff rolled his eyes when I walked in and excused himself to his office. A first time for anything. I guessed, considering the day, he had bigger things to grouch about than the sight of me.

"Good morning." I focused my attention on the receptionist. "I need to fill out a police report."

She stifled a grin and handed me a file folder. Inside, I found several reports, all completed to the point of my commentary. She'd filled in my name and contact information, the location of the crime and who was called. All I needed to do was write down my account. She and I would be great friends.

"Thanks. You didn't have to do this."

"I wanted to. My job was pretty boring before you arrived." She gasped as if she'd inadvertently insulted me. "I mean, no one blames you for these things. They aren't your fault. I just…" She covered her mouth. "It's been interesting." The words were muffled behind her fingers.

I stretched my hand to her. "We haven't officially been introduced. I'm Patience Price. It's nice to meet you."

"Frankie Dimmer."

"Are you going to the pony auction today?" I still hadn't decided if I planned to attend the auction portion of the events. Watching cowboys herd up wild ponies and force them across the marsh to be auctioned made me sad. As much as I avoided the ponies, I didn't like the idea of herding them. Anyway, I wanted to see my parents and then sit in my new office awhile before Sebastian came back. He promised to take me to the fireworks after drinks with my parents. I had all day to spend as I chose. The day ahead was certain to make up for the day before.

"How long have you and the FBI guy been dating?" Frankie's cheeks turned rosy against her milk-white skin.

The dash of freckles on her cheeks became instantly more pronounced. "You don't have to answer that."

Girl talk. I missed girl talk. "We aren't dating. We met at the FBI and he's helping me sort things out here."

She shook her head at me. Long platinum locks fell over her shoulder. "I see the way he looks at you, and it's not like a coworker."

"Ha!" I covered my eyes with one hand. "What? No. He's intense. That's all." I went back to the reports on my lap. "I'll introduce you sometime. He's an incredible guy."

I forced my concentration to focus on details that eluded me. Unfortunately, Frankie threw off my groove, and too much time had passed for me to remember everything other than the night before. I peeked at Frankie. Obviously Sebastian wasn't as smitten as I was, but could he like me enough to give people that impression? No. I was too intuitive to miss something so huge. Wasn't I? I did have plenty on my mind these days. Our kiss took over my thoughts, and my fingers moved to touch my lips. The tips of my fingers tingled with the memory. Frankie smiled. It was my turn to blush.

"I think this is everything." I handed her the file. "Can I see Adrian before I go?"

"Sure. I'll walk you back."

To my surprise, Sheriff Murray didn't come in yelling that I had only ten minutes to visit. Adrian roused when he saw us. Frankie smiled and shut the door behind her on the way out. I appreciated the privacy, but I had no idea what to say to Adrian.

"Coffee?" I slid the cup between his bars.

"Thanks."

"Don't thank me yet, it's not from Mrs. Tucker. When do you get out? Have you talked to your attorney?" I expected him to be released on bail until the trial. The fact he remained incarcerated broke my heart.

"Tomorrow, I think. Turns out the entire island is involved in something. Offices everywhere are closed."

"Yeah, what is everyone up to?"

His eyes drooped. "You know this is the first pony auction I've missed in my life. And I'm right here."

"Really?" I hadn't been back more than a handful of days since I left for college. I chose holidays and avoided pony week as best I could.

He chuckled darkly. "Yeah. I love this island, traditions and all. Some of my best memories are wrapped around the auction."

I blushed. "Are they being nice to you here?"

"Frankie's nice. She brings me things and keeps me company when the sheriff's out. Lucky for me that's more and more with all the chaos going on out there. Your parents come by, too. Your dad plays cards with me."

A tear pricked my eye. I summoned my inner calm. Adrian needed me to be positive, not emotional. I hated seeing him behind bars.

"I think this will be over soon. Turns out, Brady's partner is dead now, too. The two of them were involved in gun smuggling. Can you believe it? Just when you think it can't get more bizarre. I'm certain the investigation will show they were murdered at the hands of the same man. Not you. You'll be free in no time." I feigned bravery.

He probably saw through me, but he smiled. "Thanks."

Stupid tears sprung up again, blurring my vision. "Besides, you need to get back on the campaign trail. I don't want to have to move again."

That earned me a smile.

"I can't live here if Beau Thompson is mayor," I told

him. "Do you know Karen Holsten called herself the First Lady of Chincoteague?"

We laughed together like old times, at Karen's expense. It was true. Things would be all right. All the facts were out. Sebastian knew firsthand the traffickers were under investigation. Now he knew the drop site and the droppers were in custody. I could assure Adrian from experience, when cases got to this point with the bureau, they wrapped up quickly.

"I'm not sure how this town will feel about an ex-con as mayor." The twinkle in his eye said he was being cute. The set of his jaw told me it was a legitimate concern.

"Nope. This island loves you. You're a shoo-in." The faint fishy smell crawled into my brain. I couldn't fight it any longer. I wondered if Adrian could smell it anymore, after being here so long. Probably I was oversensitive. I glanced at my watch. "I hate to go so soon, but I had an incident last night and I need to stop over at The Pony. My parents are probably ready to pack me up and send me back to the mainland where nothing remotely dangerous ever happened to me."

"Go." He waved me off, propping his feet dramatically on the bench beside him and sipping coffee. "You know where to find me if you need anything."

"Sure. I'll let you know."

"Tell 007 to step up his game, would you?"

"Get out and tell him yourself." I blew Adrian a kiss and called for Frankie to let me out. Frankie walked me back to the front and waved good-bye before facing the small crowd, fielding a throng of tourist complaints. The scent of stale coffee was a relief after being in the cell with Adrian. Sheriff Murray's office was dark and his cruiser was gone. His day was sure to be busier than mine.

I didn't have to go far to find my parents. They'd set up

a booth on the corner of Main Street and First. Half their merchandise was displayed on racks around their table. Mom looked the part of a circus mystic, and Dad talked fishing with a couple of men on the sidewalk.

"I hear you had an interesting night." Mom looked at me through huge white sunglasses, her eyes hidden behind the blackened lenses. "Do I need to send you away to boarding school or something?"

"I have no intention of getting into trouble ever again." I crossed my heart and flashed two fingers. "Girl Scout's honor."

"That's the Boy Scout sign." Dad slipped back into his fishing talk without missing an unnecessary beat. Nothing got past him.

I shifted my fingers into an "okay" sign and smiled.

"You said the same thing the last time I saw you," Mom said. "You want to tell me what happened last night? The scuttlebutt around town is pretty bad."

"You shouldn't listen to scuttlebutt."

We stood facing each other for an infinite length of time. How could two people who looked so much alike be so different? I envied her carefree life. The woman stopped to watch butterflies, for crying out loud. She found joy everywhere. It drove me nuts.

"Sebastian took me to the boathouse."

"Hey! Did you like it?" Dad interrupted his talk again to wait for an answer. "It looks great, right? Hank and I have some ideas for remodeling the dock portion. It's a boathouse. You don't want to lose the dock. We can seal it up and make it real nice."

"Claire did the shopping. She knew what you liked." Mom smiled a little.

"Thank you." I leaned down to hug her in her lawn chair. "I love it."

Her lips pulled to the side. "Are you taking Sebastian to the festivities tonight?"

"That's the plan. He's going to try to get back here in time for dinner. He'll have paperwork, but I promised to help him as much as I can. We're hoping to meet you two for drinks since we had to cancel on you last night. Maybe we can watch the fireworks together after the auction?"

"Sounds lovely. I bet he'll enjoy the cowboys, too."

"Maybe. As soon as he gets back, I'll ask if he wants to go watch them. I'm going over to the boathouse now…I mean, to my new office." My smile was huge. It took effort not to run to get there faster.

"See you tonight." Mom patted my hand. Dad pulled me into a hug on my way past, leaving the scent of licorice in my nose. I kissed his cheek and moved against the crowd down Main Street.

Considering everything, I felt good. Though the sight of the pony paraphernalia everywhere reminded me of the tragedy in the forest. I was careful not to look at the pony last night, but my mind had created its own images. The unquenchable curiosity in me wondered how Perkins went out. Had it been at the hand of the man in the black SUV following him home when I left? Was it violent? What happened to Killer? If I'd called the police, would it have saved him?

If Perkins wasn't at the bottom of this, who was? His death didn't mean he was innocent of Brady's murder. I got that, but it seemed more likely one killer was eliminating the evidence than a number of killers coexisted in one crime circle, each with their own motivation.

I opened the door to my office, admiring the easy swing of the door. Thank you, Hank. I walked into the tiny kitchen area and plugged in a new red Keurig. Claire must've shopped for this. Adrian was enjoying my coffee.

Time to make more. The cupboard brimmed with granola, dried fruit and oatmeal—Mom had done the grocery shopping. A pint-sized refrigerator held bottles of water. A creamer carousel sat beside the coffeemaker. I imagined long nights, completing files at my new desk, enjoying a cup of tea and a pinch of granola. The stove was clean but clearly a hundred years old. I hoped I'd never have a reason to use a stove at the office.

I struggled to remember the boathouse from my childhood. I had no recollection of it. I wondered if anyone in the community had photographs from earlier years I could frame and add to newer ones on my waiting-room walls. My waiting room. A zing of anticipation shot through me. No one would willingly sit there in front of the giant glass windows. Too risky. Some neighbor might pass by, see them and think their life wasn't perfect. The subtle scent of vanilla drifted through the room. Would it be enough to put people at ease? The fragrance must've been Claire's idea. Every detail was perfect. Vanilla was calming. Mom would've opted for burning incense.

Ding! An e-mail from the insurance company lit my borrowed phone. They'd received the reports from Frankie and had begun processing my claims. Excellent.

I stretched out in my desk chair and ran fingertips across the giant calendar in front of me. I wanted to savor the moment, but a tiny flick in my brain intruded on my peace. Like the lightning in the forest, an idea illuminated and vanished before I had a full understanding of what was before me.

The man who shot the horse never hesitated. He thought it was a person and pulled the trigger without making certain who he might kill. The dumpers shot my kayak, and if I'd been drowned, they wouldn't care. No one came to check. Someone wanted Perkins, Mrs.

McGee and Brady dead. They died. All these facts were a direct contrast to the other thing. Someone bombed my empty car, shot up the boathouse from afar and broke into my apartment to warn me. Sebastian worried the killer might know him. I worried the killer might know me. Why else would I still be alive?

And then, like a massive set of dominoes connecting one at a time, the flicker came faster and faster until I saw what I'd been missing.

The sheriff's anger at my intrusion. His irritation with Sebastian at my side. The way he didn't explode at the idea of dumpers polluting our stretch of national seashore. How his face paled in the streetlight when I told him about the guns.

He knew.

I dialed Sebastian before the idea finished working itself out. No answer. The call went straight to voice mail. I began to text it all.

Sherriff Murray is in the perfect position to allow the trafficking. He runs the island. He could make a ton of money by looking the other way. No harm. No foul.

He knew me, and even if he didn't like me, he might have been reluctant to hurt me. He was close enough to stop by and threaten me, then make his protective rounds. The fishy-scented pillowcase probably came from the cell where Adrian sat. Argh. Of course. I hopped to my feet, not sure where to go first. I'd announced to the sheriff his jail smelled like my abductor. Last night Sebastian and I stopped to tell him about the guns. Why did I have such a big mouth?

His car was gone from the station when I left there an hour before. He could be anywhere.

My heart raced in my chest. How soon could Sebastian get here and bring Sheriff Murray in? Adrian could be free in time for the fireworks. We'd be safe. I tapped my nails against the desktop and checked my phone. Nothing. I looked to be sure all the texts had gone.

The phone showed no signal. "Oh, come on!" I stood and waved my phone overhead. I'd just gotten the message from the insurance company. Did I have trouble getting reception in the office before? Surely I'd remember. I walked from room to room, thinking of the silly commercial for better reception. What on earth? I couldn't work at an office where I had faulty reception. I refused to get a landline. Maybe a new cell plan...

I grabbed my bag and headed for the front door. If I had to text from the lawn, I would. My hands began to sweat as the ideas became more cemented in my mind. Sheriff Murray was in on it the whole time. He knew exactly what happened and he'd covered for it. He'd killed...and he threatened me. I teetered between the thrill of figuring it out and the terror that Sheriff Murray could be so dangerous. Everyone in town believed he protected them. He was a killer.

Eye on the failed texts, I swung open the front door. Sheriff Murray stood looking back at me. "Ah!" I grabbed my chest. Behind him the streets were empty. Everyone had moved to the marsh side of the island for all the fun. His expression worried me. The crease between his brows looked almost apologetic, which confused me.

"Sheriff Murray, hi!" I pulled my phone behind my back.

"I'm afraid we need to talk, Patience." Not Miss Price? Uh-oh. Things were worse than I thought.

"Oh, well." I stepped to my left. He mirrored my move. "I—am—meeting my parents—and Sebastian. I'm late."

He stepped forward, forcing me back. "I spoke to your parents on my way over here. They said they're meeting you tonight for drinks. Late tonight. Hours from now. After Sebastian gets back from the mainland." He tsked his tongue. "It's not nice to lie."

"You should know." I fumbled my fingers over the keyboard of my phone, hoping a text might send. Enough gibberish should alert Sebastian to my trouble, assuming the text went and also that I didn't accidently navigate away from his number.

He tilted his head over one shoulder and lifted his hand into the air, waving a small black device. "Cell blocker. Radio Shack."

"You planned this?" A shiver ran over me. Had I underestimated him all this time?

"I planned to retire early and leave this hellhole."

Despite the ominous circumstances, it irritated me to hear him speak ill of my home, my people. "Rude." I stepped back another inch as he moved forward, invading my personal space. He underestimated me, too. I remembered one thing clearly about the phone in my hand, one I purchased for the agents.

Sheriff Murray's breath reeked of coffee. My stomach churned. The cologne and coffee stirred memories of the night in my apartment. "You broke into my apartment."

"And warned you. But you didn't listen. You should consider yourself lucky. The others didn't get a warning."

Others. Oh, for the love of creation! "You killed them all?" I'd assumed he was a lackey, handling things on the island as peacefully as possible, while the true bad guys went on being psychotic elsewhere.

"Everyone wanted a cut. It was my idea. My arrangement. Then Brady started complaining about Perkins wanting more money. Their relationship was falling apart. Brady's ridiculous wife was spearheading protests about the fishermen coming too far inshore. She pressed him about doing the right thing and going back out where he belonged. I risked him giving in to her or telling her too much or reneging on our agreement. I had a lot to lose, Patience."

"So you killed him?"

He nodded. "You couldn't leave it alone for some reason. None of this had anything to do with you, but you kept on pushing. Then you came to the station to visit your boyfriend. You knew the pillowcase came from the jail, and I thought you put it together right then, but you didn't say a thing. Lucky for me, you're slow on the uptake. Now the entire island's busy by the marsh and my alibi is airtight. I'm out doing my rounds right now."

"Are you going to kill me?"

"I didn't want to kill you. Please don't misunderstand. I never liked you, but I do like your parents. They're so innocent and humble with their old cars and homemade clothes. It's sweet, really."

My calves bumped against a waiting-room chair, and I sat. I forgot the place had been outfitted. I hoped to reach the wall and turn the light out to buy me some time. Sheriff Murray pulled something from his belt and waved it between us. A little flicker of light jumped from left to right on the stun gun.

Crap.

A jolt ripped through my chest and the world went dark.

TWENTY-THREE

SNAPS AND POPS drew me back to the world. My hands burned. I couldn't swallow. Tendrils of smoke billowed from beneath the storeroom door. Sheriff Murray sat texting a few feet away. I tried to speak and recognized the reason my throat was so dry. He'd literally stuffed a sock in me, or some other disgusting cottony article.

"Oh." He looked disappointed. "I'd hoped you'd sleep through it. I don't want to shoot you. Too messy. Very amateur." His phone rang, and he took the call.

Unbelievable. I remembered my phone, but my hands were empty. And tied. I couldn't move them more than a couple of inches behind my back. I probably dropped the phone when he zapped me with the stun gun. Jerk.

Smoke caught my eye. Did he know the place was on fire?

"Everything's quiet on this end. I'm headed out to the harbor, then down to the dock. I'll meet you at the counter. What do you have going on over there?"

I rocked in my chair, which was unreasonably comfortable and impossible to tip. I worked my wrists, hoping to loosen the binds. At least they weren't cuffs. As long as he didn't shoot me, I had a chance. Maybe even then. The idea of letting him get away with everything he'd done and seeing him go back to posing as the friendly, law-abiding sheriff was too much.

"Alrighty. Meet you over there in fifteen. See you then." He disconnected with a smirk. "Mrs. Tucker wants to treat me to some ice cream for my part in making this annual event so successful. She's such a nice lady."

I thrust my head in the direction of the smoke. Someone needed to call the fire department. The place cleaned up nice, but it had to be a little outdated on the fire safety measures. For example, no smoke detectors. Little gray curls rolled along the floor and drifted up, filling the ceiling over our heads with a cloud of toxins. He dipped his head, resting his forearms on his elbows, staying clear of the smoke.

He ran his tongue over his teeth. "You've got a fire. It's small now, but it'll take off in a bit. I blew out the flame in your stove and cranked the gas. For good measure, I tossed a couple of bags of fireworks in here. You'd be shocked at the number of accidents caused by careless fireworks owners every year."

I tried to shove my mouth clear of whatever he stuffed in it, but it wouldn't budge. My mouth had dried around it like paste on paper. I scrunched low in my seat, suppressing a gag when the smoke caused a cough that couldn't escape. I hated him for ruining all my family and friends had done for me. Taking my dream. Making me feel helpless. I'd never see a patient seated in my new waiting room, recently renovated with love.

"Well..." He dragged the word into three syllables and slapped his thighs. "I'm going to get going. I can't leave Mrs. Tucker waiting, and I'd never miss a chance for her ice cream." He stretched tall. Arching his back, he pressed his palms into his lower lumbar and sighed. A heavy cough choked through him. He laughed and coughed all the way to the door, pulling his shirt over his mouth and nose. "It's not as clever as condoms and whipped cream, but you'll still go out with a bang." Chuckling, he pulled the front door shut behind him.

Yelling for help was impossible. Desperation threatened to crush my hope. Unable to loosen my binds or tip the chair, I struggled onto my feet, straddling the seat. Coughing through the smoke at a higher altitude, I wriggled my shoulders and climbed onto the chair. One side of my binds caught against the fabric behind me. I pulled in another panic-filled gasp of smoky air and vomit arrived over my tongue, wetting the fabric, loosening it from my lips and gums. When yanking against the chair didn't serve to free my wrists, I fell from exhaustion and lack of oxygen.

As I crashed against the floor, a screaming pain ripped through one shoulder. My left arm hung limp at my side. Smoke filled the room to meet me on the floor.

Whizzzz! The distinct zip of a bottle rocket soared somewhere close by in the darkening room. How long before the fireworks and gas set the building ablaze around me? Soon the smoke would be second to the fire. I struggled onto my knees and crawled toward the door, staying low, moving slow but steady toward much-needed air.

Zzzzzip! Whizzz! Zing! Pop! Pop! Pop!

Of all the ways to die! I'd go out with a bang, he said. My heart leapt in my chest as the words grew roots. I motored over the floor, lifted to my feet, turned around and tried the door. Locked. "Ahh!" I screeched into my barfy sock. How could I contend with the stupid lock when my fingers were still behind me and one lifeless arm screamed with every movement and jostle? I concentrated on my good hand, pinching the tiny knob on the handle and turning.

Zzzzzip! Whizzz! Zing! Pop! Pop! Pop!

I ducked. Fireworks exploded from the storeroom, showering the waiting area in colored sparks. Tiny fires began on the new carpet and upholstery. Flames licked up the curtains to the ceiling above. The doorknob turned. I stood clear, keeping an eye on the display of fireworks a few feet away and stumbled out onto the tiny lawn.

The grass smelled better than anything I'd ever smelled in my life. I inhaled deep and rammed my face against the earth, using the ground to wrench the material free of my mouth. Tears burned over my eyes. Surely someone saw the fireworks. Through the open door, I watched my dream go literally up in smoke.

Zzzzzip! Whizzz! Zing! Pop! Pop! Pop!
BOOM!

The windows burst loose without warning. Glass rained down on me as I buried my face in the grass for protection, my arms held captive at my back. In the distance, a siren hummed low and steady. Help was on the way. I did it. I'd made it. My chest heaved with adrenaline. I was safe.

BOOM!

My ears rang and the ground shook. Daring a peek over one shoulder, the roof erupted like a volcano behind me. Shards of wood blew over my head and into the street. Clumps of furniture and shingles crashed into the lawn around me. Embers and debris landed on my horrendous sunburn and injured shoulder. So help me, if I had my way, I'd be sure our town's beloved sheriff was stoned in the town square.

Pow! A lesser racket blew some printer paper and a desk drawer onto the sidewalk. The roaring in my ears blocked quieter sounds. For the first time in days, I no longer heard the bleating tugboats or singing birds.

Firemen jogged up the sidewalk past me. A paramedic crouched at my side. He pressed something cold against my back. Shiny black shoes arrived at my face. Murmured voices spoke over me. Sheriff Murray's face came into view. I screamed at the burst of pain through my shoulder when the paramedic rolled me onto my back.

The look on the sheriff's face frightened me. His chest rose and fell at a runner's pace. My body was rolled again and my wrists released. "Ah!" I gasped and vomited a river onto the sheriff's perfect shoes. Paramedics moved me away from him and onto a gurney, rolling toward the ambulance. My arm was placed carefully at my side. People streamed down the street toward us, snapping pictures and taking videos on their cell phones. My phone! I'd had the evidence I needed but dropped it. The odds of its survival weren't good.

A paramedic climbed inside with me and began to set my arm and clean my wounds. Everything hurt. I cried out, but I still couldn't hear through the steady roar in my ears. The words he spoke were lost. His lips stopped moving after a while, replaced with a nod and careful smile.

The world shook and I cried out. He placed a hand on my arm and motioned to the open doors at my feet. Thunder? The storm had returned. Maybe the drops would help the firemen staunch the fire. I nodded, feeling weary. An IV port was set into my good hand. To my dismay, he gripped my other arm tightly. Moving it slowly, he watched my expression. In full understanding, he secured his grip on my arm and pulled it straight toward him, away from my body.

"Yeeow!" I screamed. Then there was release. The excruciating pain with every breath subsided. My arm was back where it belonged and the paramedic placed it in a sling before he pointed to the IV. I hoped he meant there was something in there for pain. I closed my eyes and pretended the rain beyond the doors would wash away the day.

Before I fell under the spell of whatever was in the

IV bag, I reached for him with my good hand. "Sher-riff Murray." The vibration in my throat felt strange and raw. "Did this."

He frowned and looked beyond the doors. I followed his gaze. Sheriff Murray spoke. Sounds filtered in bit by bit, like trying to comprehend the words of my swim in-structor when my head was underwater. The paramedic climbed out.

"No!"

Sheriff Murray climbed in. He shook his head and closed the doors behind him. He had nothing to lose now by killing me. If he didn't, I'd tell all, and he'd spend his life in jail. If he got rid of me, and managed to get off the hook, he'd escape with all the money he'd taken for fa-cilitating the gun trafficking. I figured he'd kill me and take his chances with the court system.

Garbled words flowed over his lips. A creepy serenity relaxed his brow. He removed a syringe from the red bag on the floor beside us. He shrugged and leaned over me, burbling incoherent words at me and tilting his head side to side. Then he squeezed the syringe, accidentally shoot-ing liquid from its tip onto my face. I tossed my head and fought to keep my eyes open. Whatever the paramedic had added to my IV was pulling me under.

Sheriff Murray scowled, raising the weapon as if he might jam it into my heart. He pressed his mouth to my ear. His hot breath sickened me.

I rammed my forehead into him as hard as I could.

He grabbed his head and yelled a slew of jumbled pro-fanity.

Scowling, he leaned toward me once more, and I bashed him again. The pain medication was handy after all. I could cream him with my forehead all day. I didn't feel a thing.

His hands shot out this time. Wising up, he kept his distance and wrapped his stinky fingers around my throat. They smelled like matches from lighting the fireworks and natural gas from my stove. I kicked and thrashed, making it as difficult as possible for him to hold on to me, but the fight in me gave out. He was too strong. I was too tired. And the medication. My lids blinked, heavy and numb.

When things grew darkest, all at once light shone over us anew and the sheriff flew away. Voices barked and yelped close by. My ears worked hard to make sense of the sounds as the roaring died down in my head. I tried to swallow and gagged. I turned my head in case I threw up again.

Lifting my head, I blinked back exhaustion. Sebastian stood outside the open ambulance doors, screwing Sheriff Murray's arms up behind him. He slammed cuffs over the sheriff's wrists and shoved him forward. The man struggled uselessly under Sebastian's iron grip.

So, that was where Sheriff Murray had flown off to.

Dressed all in black, sidearm in place, and a Bluetooth lodged in one ear, Sebastian looked every inch of his title. No one escaped Special Agent Sebastian Clark. With another rough push, the sheriff fell into the waiting hands of his deputy. A pair of men in FBI jackets escorted them out of sight.

Someone climbed into the front of the ambulance. It rattled to life and the door shut. Sebastian turned immediately toward me and mounted the step to my side. Slamming the doors shut behind him, he barked something low and deep. The ambulance rolled away, and Sebastian turned his deep brown eyes on me. The set of his jaw said he was in a dark place emotionally. Ferocity oozed from him, zinging across the space between us.

The vein in his neck kept time with the clench of his jaw. He stared into my eyes and squeezed my hands all the way to the hospital.

I OPENED WEARY eyes to the sound of more explosions and the assaulting scent of alcohol and bleach. The bright light coming at me arrived by way of fluorescent bulbs, not fire as I feared. A steady chorus of *whoosh, whoosh, beep,* settled my heart rate. Beyond the window, fireworks sailed into the night and ignited the sky. Chills ran over my skin. I concentrated on the song playing on the machines at my head. *Whoosh, whoosh, beep.* I could hear it.

"You are one tough therapist." Sebastian stood from the chair in the corner, placed a tattered magazine on the stand beside him and sauntered to my side. "I still think you should consider working as an agent. The position as my sidekick is still available."

I crinkled my nose. For the first time in my life, words escaped me. Memories filtered back like a movie seen years ago. Brilliant colors continued to explode beyond the window, casting tiny, blinking rainbows over the white marble floor.

"Sheriff." I coughed until my eyes blurred. My throat felt like fire.

He handed me a tiny plastic cup of ice chips. "You got him."

I sucked on a chip and mulled that over. Unless he counted being choked into oblivion as me getting him, I disagreed. I shook my head, afraid to talk again too soon. Sebastian evaluated me.

"Would you rather have something hot? Tea? Your parents left a thermos. They're in the cafeteria right now."

I leaned forward and whimpered as my shoulder refused to hold my weight. Sebastian set a cup of tea on the rolling tray in front of me and handed me the bed controls. Inch by inch I crunched upright. Being a mute sucked eggs. I had a million things to tell him and ten times as many questions. I sipped the tea and immediately breathed easier. Dad's sassafras tea. I detected a touch of whiskey, which was perfect.

I tried again. "Sheriff." The word would have to be enough to get him going. I didn't want to risk another coughing jag.

"He's in jail and no longer the sheriff. Thanks to your quick thinking, I not only got those texts but found the phone in his cruiser's glove box along with his taped confession." He smiled and poured some tea for himself. "Three counts of murder. Attempted murder. Arson. Gun trafficking. Who knows what else will be piled on. He won't be out anytime soon. Like I said, all thanks to you. Good thinking to use the phone's recorder."

My face heated with pleasure.

"Now, you didn't answer me about the sidekick opening."

"No." I smiled. "Adrian?"

He sipped the tea and frowned. "Is that whiskey?"

When I nodded, he took my cup away, shooting a meaningful eye at my IV. Hmph.

"Boathouse?" I croaked.

"Sticks. They'll have to rebuild, I think." Anger flashed over his beautiful eyes. His lips pressed into a thin white line. "Murray's lucky to be behind bars right now after what he did to you. He's safer where I can't reach him."

From the look on Sebastian's face, I didn't doubt that.

I adjusted the awkward sling my aching arm was stuffed into. My beautiful office was gone. Everyone worked so hard and made it perfect. I'd never be able to afford insurance again in Virginia. After three claims in two weeks, who'd be dumb enough to insure me?

"Don't worry about that now. Rest."

My mind craved information. I needed a pen and paper. Before I could stifle the yawn, it stretched my face.

Sebastian smiled as if to say he told me so. "I'm going to stay with you until you're fully recovered." It was a statement, not a question. As an afterthought, he threw in, "I hope that's all right." His deep brown eyes smoldered. Emotion played beneath the words.

"I'm safe now," I managed, pressing a hand to my throat. "You don't have to."

He raised his palms to me. "Just until I can find a place."

My expression must've said what I was thinking. "A place?"

"My place in Norfolk's not safe. The department's working on a new assignment for me. Meanwhile, I'll adjust to the commute from a town half of the state's never heard of."

"Hey." I clamped a hand over my neck, ending my protest. People had heard of Chincoteague.

"Until you get a new sheriff, Deputy Fargas is in charge. I'm a little concerned."

I nodded. Yep, he should stay. I didn't bother hiding the crazy smile edging across my face. Sebastian was staying. Frankie the receptionist's interpretation of how he looked at me came to mind. Could there be truth in her observation?

Sebastian brushed bangs off my forehead, and my heart thrummed manically in my chest. He leaned over the bed's railing, bringing his eyes in alignment with mine. "Everything I want to protect is right here."

Featherlight lips dusted my forehead. His warm, spicy scent beat the heck out of the bleach and antiseptic of the hospital.

"Get some rest. I'll be right over there when you wake up." He motioned to the chair, but I clamped a hand over his.

"Thank you." I mouthed the words, unable to voice the emotion building in my heart.

He lifted my hand and kissed my fingers before retreating to the window across the room.

I had every intention of waiting to see my mom and dad return from the cafeteria, but exhaustion, meds and Dad's secret ingredient pulled me under. I took the image of Sebastian's strong frame leaning against the hospital window with me.

Whoosh, whoosh, beep.

"I CAN'T BELIEVE this is your life." Claire smoothed sunscreen over her arms, leaving the warm scent of coconut caught in the air between us. "I have to go back to Norfolk tomorrow, don a suit and sit in meetings. You get to work here." She lifted her giant red sunglasses to give me a pointed glare.

A warm breeze kicked up, tossing sand and curling the corner of our blanket. She moved our tiny cooler to hold the blanket in place without missing a beat. "You live on an island, get to work on the beach…"

"I don't always work on the beach. Only when I meet with moms." I nodded toward the crowd of kids burying someone neck-deep at the edge of the water. "They can talk privately and their kids get to play."

"Mm-mm-mm." She settled onto her back. "I could get used to this, is all I'm saying."

"It took some adjusting."

"Concierge counseling. So, what happens in the winter?"

"I don't know yet. The whole idea of counseling on the go irritated the snot out of me before. Having the boathouse blown back to the mainland helped motivate me to be more flexible. Hopefully the insurance case will settle soon and I'll find another spot for my office."

"How about the empty studio under your apartment? No one's breaking down doors to rent that place. Think of how easy your commute will be."

I tugged on the sling holding my shoulder in place. The skin inside the material itched and burned. "I always forget to put lotion on my arm before the sling."

"How much longer do you have to wear that thing?"

"A week. The surgery was a breeze. Wearing this thing stinks." Considering how things almost turned out, I counted myself lucky to get off with only a sling.

"So what do you think about the art studio for your office? It has the secret entrance and everything."

"I love the idea. In fact, I bet I could get it as cheap as I get my apartment." The more the idea settled in, the more I wanted to call my landlord immediately to secure it.

"Let's do it! I can reorder everything from Crate and Barrel. I have the receipt in my e-mail." She pulled out her phone and began to work. Like everything else about Claire, her phone sparkled in the sunlight. Tiny crystals in various colors covered every inch of the protective cover.

I checked my watch. I had another half hour before my next appointment. Plenty of time to get a little sun while it lasted. Fall would come to steal it soon enough. I laid my head on the rolled towel behind me and let the sun heat my skin through. With eyes closed, I listened to all my favorite sounds—children laughing, the waves crashing, Claire humming. In that moment, it was hard to remember why I ever left.

"Hey, Peepee."

I cracked open one eye. Adrian smiled down at me.

Now I remembered.

"Enjoying the sun?" he asked.

"I was."

"I liked you better when I was in jail."

"Ditto." Despite my best effort, my lips turned up. "What's with the suit? This is the beach. Are you lost again?"

He flopped onto his bottom in the sand beside my blanket. "I wore a suit to meet with my Realtor."

"Moving?"

"No." He chuckled. "I need office space. As it turns out, you were right. The islanders don't care that I was wrongly accused, and they petitioned me to run against Beau Thompson in the mayoral election." He winked, looking pleased with himself to no end.

"Great. Mayor Davis." I let the words sit on my tongue. "It does have a certain ring to it." I studied him.

As he looked back with stormy gray eyes, his infuriating dimple caved in, pulling a couple days' worth of stubble with it.

Captivated, I leaned in a fraction of an inch. Not enough for him to notice, I hoped. He smelled like soap and mint and…Adrian. Familiar. Obnoxious. I pulled back. "So, where's the new office? I'll be sure to steer clear."

"Oh, I don't think you have a chance in that endeavor."

"Great." Claire startled me. I'd forgotten she was there. "The empty studio isn't listed on the Realtor site. We should just head over there and talk to him. They probably don't keep the site current."

"It's current. I have plans for the space, actually. I rented it for my campaign office." Adrian stretched a hand over me toward Claire to introduce himself. "Adrian."

"Claire." She looked between us. "How does it feel to be a free man?"

"Exquisite. I can thank my girl here for it, too."

A perfectly sculpted eyebrow rose from behind Claire's glasses. "So I hear."

"In fact, I hoped to invite her to dinner." His eyes locked on mine.

"Is that the going rate for saving your heinie these days?" My heart thumped at the invitation. Old habits and all that. I had no intention of accepting.

I didn't think.

"Actually, when I'm mayor, I was hoping to make you first lady, but let's start with dinner."

"Uh-oh." Claire looked across the sand.

"Wow. This guy has impeccable timing." Adrian stood to shake Sebastian's hand as he arrived in black board shorts and Ray-Bans. "Mr. Bond," Adrian taunted.

"Hello, Fugitive." Sebastian accepted Adrian's hand.

"That's soon to be Mayor Fugitive," I pointed out.

"Oh, yeah? Congratulations." Sebastian's expression was flat and guarded. I could only imagine what was going on inside Adrian's head.

Sebastian had rented a room at the bed-and-breakfast on my street while I recovered in the hospital. Half his stuff was in a storage unit near the marsh. Widow Moore gave him a rate he couldn't pass up when he'd promised her several months of occupancy while he looked for something permanent. I told him to check for peepholes in the shower.

"Adrian rented the art studio downstairs for his campaign office. Right when I planned to rent it for my new office," I tattled.

"I don't think you need an office. I think this is your office." Sebastian tipped his chin skyward.

"Patience?" Melinda Crown approached me with a warm smile. A gaggle of children at her feet, she stopped in her tracks to look at my friends.

"Hi, Melinda. You know Adrian. This is my friend Claire." They exchanged hellos.

Claire stood and brushed sand from her legs. "This is Sebastian Clark, the next special agent to be schooled in my volleyball smackdown."

Sebastian shook her hand. Sun glistened off his perfect bronze skin. His washboard stomach put ideas in my head. I pulled my eyes up to meet his.

When he noticed, he knelt beside me and whispered in my ear. "After your appointment, I'd like to buy you dinner."

My toes curled into the sand.

Every sound on the beach stopped for a moment. Then he was gone. Righted. Clapping Adrian on the back and looking at Claire.

"You ready?"

"To teach you how it's done? Darn skippy." Claire pulled a volleyball from her beach bag and smiled at me. "See you in a few."

Adrian watched the pair walk away. "I don't like that guy."

"Shocker."

"See you around." He winked, and a posse of butterflies took off in my stomach. I needed a pill for that.

He slipped out of his suit jacket and threw it over one shoulder before making his way back through the sand.

Melinda had set up her umbrella and beach chairs

around a number of towels and buckets. Her children splashed in the water ten feet away.

"How's summer break going?" I asked.

She handed me a juice box and melded into her chair. "I can't wait for school to start. Does that make me an awful mother?"

"That—" I watched the children push and shove in the surf "—sounds very human."

Relaxing into an easy pattern of conversation and encouragement, I embraced my new identity: Patience Price, Counselor at Large.

* * * * *